# Comes a Chopper

## Bryan Cassiday

Bryan Cassiday

ISBN 978-1496162045
Bryan Cassiday
Los Angeles

Printed in the United States of America
First Edition:  June 2014

# BOOKS BY BRYAN CASSIDAY

Poxland
Kill Ratio
Sanctuary in Steel
Zombie Necropolis
Zombie Maelstrom
Helter Skelter
The Anaconda Complex
The Kill Option
Blood Moon: Thrillers and Tales of Terror
Fete of Death

Bryan Cassiday

Oranges and lemons,
Say the bells of St. Clement's.

You owe me five farthings,
Say the bells of St. Martin's.

When will you pay me?
Say the bells of Old Bailey.

When I grow rich,
Say the bells of Shoreditch.

When will that be?
Say the bells of Stepney.

I do not know.
Says the great bell of Bow.

Here comes a candle to light you to bed.
And here comes a chopper to chop off your head!

—Old English nursery rhyme

4

## Table of Contents

# Condemned

It was an unfriendly town Bronson found out as soon as he got there.

After taking one look at him, the townsfolk shied away from him and took a powder. They weren't big on strangers. Small towns could be like that, he decided with a sigh. They would close ranks as soon as a stranger set foot in them.

It wasn't like he wanted to be here. He had come here to find his brother Sam and tell him that their mother had died. Bronson didn't look forward to doing it, but it had to be done. San Remo was Sam's last known address. Bronson had been unable to contact him either by phone, e-mail, or snail mail. That left a face-to-face meeting as the one remaining option.

It had been over ten years since Bronson had had any contact with Sam. Bronson wouldn't even swear to it that Sam still lived here. San Remo was the last address Sam had given him.

Bronson hailed a thirtysomething man with a wind-scoured face that looked like crumpled sandpaper. The guy's face looked inordinately dry, like it was leached of all fluid. He was dressed in jeans and suede boots and was walking with bandy legs on the sidewalk toward Bronson, his inch-high heels clacking on the sun-warmed cement.

"Hello," said Bronson. "Do you know where I can find Sam Bronson?"

The man cut his squinty eyes toward Bronson then strode off toward his pickup parked on the side of the street.

A knee-high tumbleweed blew down the macadam past the man. He didn't give it a second look. He climbed into his pickup, slammed the door behind him, and peeled off down the street, his pickup fishtailing on bawling tires.

Par for the course, decided Bronson, sniffing burnt rubber as he watched the trucker speed off, typical of the kind of reaction he was getting from everybody in town.

Tricked out in a suit and wearing a green surgical mask over his face, the next man that walked by Bronson ignored him when Bronson hailed him. The suit's only response was to quicken his gait away from Bronson.

Talk about weird towns, decided Bronson and kept walking. It was like nobody wanted their face to be seen. They either turned away when he looked at them or ran away or wore a mask.

Bronson walked with a slight limp courtesy of a car accident this side of six years ago, which reminded him his feet were aching. He had been pounding the pavement around town for hours after he had disembarked from the bus and cast around asking local residents where his brother lived. Now he could do with a rest.

He glanced toward a window of an apartment house up ahead and picked up on the curtain swinging shut as a shadowy figure shied away from the window. Somebody had been sizing him up from the apartment, it seemed.

Bronson wondered if he should just say to hell with it and hightail it out of town. He hadn't wanted to come here in the first place. He was a bearer of bad tidings for his brother. Not much of an incentive to be here. Maybe Sam was better off not knowing about their mother's death. Maybe he should spare Sam's feelings and not tell him.

Bronson could beat it out of here on the next bus. It was giving him the willies just standing in this town. He felt hungry. He hadn't eaten all day. He decided to grab a bite to eat.

Shading his eyes from the California sun he could make out a Tex-Mex joint at the corner ahead. He struck out for it.

A couple of cars cruised by him on the street. Maybe he was imagining it but he sensed the passengers were scoping him out. He couldn't be sure. But why else would the cars be going so slowly, almost as if they were dogging him? The blinding sun was reflecting off their car windows, its glare blocking his view of the vehicles' interiors.

As he craned his neck toward the vehicles, they rocketed away.

Ducking into the poky Tex-Mex joint he caught sight of a woman eying him across the street. As he caught her glance, she kept looking at him. That was refreshing, he decided, after all these other residents he had encountered who kept averting their eyes and rushing away whenever he looked at them.

He bellied up to the counter, pored over the menu on the wall behind the blank-faced twentyish cashier, and ordered a tamale with a Coke.

"Do you know a guy named Sam Bronson?" said Bronson.

Pulling a face the cashier shook his head. "Never heard of him."

Bronson withdrew his wallet from his trouser pocket. He flipped through the wallet and selected a photograph. He handed the photo to the cashier.

"Recognize him?" said Bronson.

The cashier glanced without interest at the photo of Sam Bronson. "No."

"You barely looked at it."

The cashier scratched the tip of his nose.

Bronson saw that he was getting nowhere with his questioning. He paid for his order, took it, and grabbed a seat at a small round table near the plate-glass picture window that overlooked the street. The deal table didn't have a tablecloth. He gazed out the window. It had streaks of grime on the pane but no flyspecks. He would have suspected flies in such a dingy joint.

The woman from across the street was walking toward the restaurant, he could see. Wearing a pin-striped outfit, she must have been pushing forty and had shoulder-length chestnut hair. He wondered if her pin-striped jacket came equipped with shoulder pads. Her shoulders looked squared off and a tad on the broad side.

8

He offered her a tentative smile as she entered the restaurant. It wasn't like he felt friendly in this town, what with the treatment the residents had been doling out to him. But he was still trying to get one of them to talk. This woman had made eye contact with him when she had entered, which was more than anybody else here had done. Maybe she would be more cooperative than the other residents had been when he had asked them about Sam.

"Hello," she said to him, walking up to his table.

Nobody else here had said hello to him. It was refreshing to hear somebody say hello.

"Hi," he said.

"My name's Caitlin Poindexter. I'm looking for Sam Bronson. Do you know where I can find him?"

Bronson did a double take. "That's funny. I'm looking for him, too."

"Don't you live around here?" said Caitlin, puzzled.

"No. I'm from out of town."

Caitlin shrugged. "So am I."

Wonderful, decided Bronson. The first person who had acted halfway decent toward him wasn't even a citizen of this forsaken town. He should have known she was a stranger like himself. But one thing puzzled him.

"Why are you looking for Sam Bronson?" he said.

She searched his face, trying to decide whether to tell him.

"I happen to be his brother Dan," Bronson went on.

It was her turn to do a double take. "Then you must know where he is."

"This town's the last address he ever gave me. That's all I know. I'm looking for him because I have news for him." Bronson eased a bit of his tamale into his mouth with a plastic fork. "Like I said, I don't live around here," he said between bites.

Caitlin weighed his answer for a moment then came to a decision. "I guess I can tell you why I want him, since you're his brother. I'm an insurance investigator. His wife filed a claim on him."

Bronson stopped chewing his tamale. "What kind of claim?"

"She's trying to collect on his life insurance policy."

"You mean he's dead?"

"According to her."

"This is the first I've heard of it."

"Are you saying he's not?"

"All I'm saying is it's news to me."

Now he had two deaths in his family to deal with, decided Bronson, but still not convinced Sam really was dead.

"I'm trying to establish proof of her claim. That's why I'm here in San Remo. She hasn't shown us a death certificate."

"I wouldn't recommend San Remo as a tourist spot. I get the impression strangers aren't welcome here."

"You too, huh?"

What in the world was going on? wondered Bronson.

"I'm being rude." He gestured to a chair on the opposite side of his table. "Have a seat."

Nodding, she sat down across from him and leaned toward him. "Do you know his address?"

Bronson shook his head no. "I only know he lives in this town. It's not very big. I figured I could track him down once I got here. But everybody's so close-mouthed . . ."

"You're telling me."

"Doesn't his wife know where he lives? I didn't even know he was married. That shows you how much we kept in touch."

"They're estranged. She doesn't know his exact address. She said she last heard from him from San Remo. He gets his mail by general delivery at the local post office."

"What makes her think he's dead?"

"She can't find him, so she filed a life insurance claim."

Bronson took a long pull on his Coke. "Kind of premature, don't you think?"

"I think she wanted to save money on hiring a PI by filing a claim on Sam's policy and forcing my employer the insurance company to track down her husband for her. She knew we wouldn't pay off on her claim unless we could establish proof of his death."

"Does she have any reason to think he's dead other than that she can't find him?"

"If she does, she didn't tell it to us. Which brings us to you."

"How do you figure that?" said Bronson, taken aback.

"Why did you come here to meet with Sam?"

Bronson looked glum. "Our mother died last week. I came here to tell him about it."

"Sorry to hear that."

Bronson shrugged. "Maybe it was for the best."

"How can you say that?"

"She had Parkinson's disease for the last several years. She broke both her hips this year and was confined to a wheelchair. Then she choked to death last Tuesday."

"Death is never for the best." She paused and fingered her bangs. "Were you and Sam close?"

"No. I haven't seen him in ten years. We never had much in common. Women seemed to like him, though. I could never figure out why."

Caitlin smiled sympathetically. "Yeah. The guys go for my sister, too. But not for me. She got the beauty, and I got the brains in the family."

Feeling like he was wallowing in a melancholy that he wouldn't be able to extricate himself from if he kept dwelling on his mother's death, Bronson changed the subject.

"Doesn't it strike you as strange that we're both here looking for Sam at the same time?"

Caitlin nodded. "The thought crossed my mind."

"In a town where nobody likes strangers."

"What do you make of that?"

Bronson couldn't get his head around it.

"Don't you find it odd that your own brother wouldn't give you his street address?" said Caitlin.

"And didn't give it to his wife either. Yeah. Getting his mail by general delivery? What's that all about?"

"Sounds like he didn't want anybody to find him."

"Why not?"

"Does he have something to hide?"

"Beats me."

"His wife says he's some kind of accountant who goes around inspecting company books to make sure nobody's cooking them. Is that right?"

"Probably. He always had a head for numbers. He took accounting courses, I know that. I don't know exactly what his job was, but it had something to do with accounting. What his wife said about his job sounds right."

"Do you think his death had something to do with his job?"

Bronson jacked up his caterpillar eyebrows. "I didn't even know he was dead."

"Do you think she's lying about Sam's death?" said Caitlin, fixing Bronson with a penetrating stare.

"People will do anything for money."

A man weighing close to three hundred pounds barged into the restaurant. He had a thick mustache that jutted out above his upper lip like the bristles on a wire brush. He had a cast to one eye and a no-nonsense expression that was taking in Bronson and Caitlin. At his hip he sported a handgun in a leather holster. He wore a butternut sheriff's uniform.

"I'm Sheriff Lapman," he said, sashaying toward Bronson, one hand on the top of his closed holster. "I've been getting an earful of complaints about two strangers asking a passel of questions around town."

"Hello, Sheriff," said Bronson. "Maybe you can help us."

"What's your name, sir, and your business here in San Remo?"

Bronson gave his name. "Maybe you can help me, Sheriff. I'm looking for my brother Sam Bronson."

"Never heard of him. And if you don't mind, sir, I'm the one asking the questions."

Bronson said nothing.

"Why are you disturbing the fine folks of San Remo?" said Lapman.

"I just told you, I'm trying to find my brother."

"What makes you think he's here?"

"He told me he lives here."

"And I just told you, I never heard of him," said Lapman with an edge to his voice. He drew a deep breath, which swelled his barrel chest.

"Have you had any deaths here recently? We have reason to believe he may have died here."

"How should I know? I don't keep track of everybody that dies."

"Have you had any murders here recently?"

"What's that got to do with anything?"

"I can't understand why I can't find my brother. Maybe he was murdered."

"That'a a real leap," scoffed Lapman. "Just because you can't find him here you figure he upped and got himself offed."

"His wife says he's dead."

Lapman ignored Bronson's answer and turned to Caitlin. "Are you with him, Ms. . . . ?"

"Poindexter," said Caitlin. "No. I'm an insurance investigator and I'm also trying to find Sam Bronson."

"Do either of you plan on moving here?"

"Not gonna happen," said Bronson.

"Fine. Then I'm asking you both to kindly leave town."

"What for? We haven't done anything illegal."

"If you had done something illegal, I'd throw you in the joint. If you leave town, I won't have to."

Bronson bristled. "Why are you telling us to leave town?"

"You're upsetting my citizens with your loitering, and you're a disruptive influence on my town. How many other reasons do you need?"

"I'm just trying to find my brother," Bronson said heatedly, bolting to his feet, jostling the table and all but knocking it over.

"Nobody knows him, so he must not live here. And watch your tone with me," said Lapman, wagging his meaty forefinger in Bronson's face. "You got an hour to leave town."

Bronson didn't take kindly to Lapman's finger in his face.

Lapman lumbered out of the restaurant, breathing heavily with the effort.

"He can't throw us out of town," said Caitlin, watching Lapman barge down the sidewalk away from the restaurant.

Trying to cool off Bronson sat down.

"You better do as he says, you two," said the cashier, wiping the counter with a towel. "You're not the only ones he's told to scram."

"What happened to the others?" asked Caitlin.

"Nobody ever saw them again."

Still hot under the collar, Bronson peered through the window at the retreating sheriff. Darkness was falling. Bronson didn't look forward to spending the night here, but he was damned if he'd let himself be cowed out of town by a tin-pot bully of a sheriff. He came here to find Sam, and that was what he was going to do. He was on annual leave from his job at the warehouse for the next couple of days. Geno could handle Bronson's job as forklift operator while Bronson was away, and Bronson could extend his stay here without any problem—except for Lapman.

And what about this Poindexter woman? wondered Bronson, eyeballing her as she sat across from him. He didn't believe in coincidences. What were the chances they'd both be in town at the same time looking for Sam?

"When are you gonna come clean with me?" he said.

"What are you talking about?" said Poindexter.

"We just happen to meet in the same town while we're both looking for Sam? Gimme a break."

Caitlin paused a beat. "All right. I'll confess."

"Let's hear it."

"I've been following you since you got on the bus and headed here."

"I didn't see anybody else get off the bus when I did."

"I got off at the edge of town then doubled back and picked up your trail."

"Why are you tailing me?"

"That part of what I told you is the truth. I'm looking for Sam. I thought you as his brother would know where he is, so I followed you."

"What about that rigmarole about his wife trying to collect on his insurance policy?"

Caitlin held up her hands as if beckoning him to inspect them. "All true."

Bronson considered her answer. He believed her, if for no other reason than he couldn't think up a more probable explanation.

"If Sam really is dead," he said, "there may be a way we can check."

"I'm all ears."

"We check with the local doctor and see if he's filed a death certificate for Sam."

"There's likely more than one doctor in town, though. Could take a while."

"It's gonna take longer than an hour. That's for sure," said Bronson, getting to his feet. "Unless we get lucky."

Caitlin whipped her smartphone out of her purse and fell to tapping numbers and sliding her fingers across the device's glass face.

"Who are you calling?" said Bronson.

"Nobody. I'm using the Internet to find the doctors in town. I got 4G. Lucky this is a small town." Reading the smartphone's screen she screwed up her face. "There are still quite a few doctors—and which kind do we want? You got surgeons, GPs, gerontologists, and the list goes on."

"We're going about this the wrong way. Let's check with the city morgue. The coroner will have a record of deaths."

"The problem is he works for Lapman and might not want to cooperate with us," said Caitlin, looking up from her smartphone.

"We'll visit him at his home address, not at work, so the sheriff won't know about it."

"The coroner should have left work and gone home at this hour."

She consulted the Internet for the name of San Remo's coroner and his address.

It turned out his apartment was inside of two miles away. Bronson and Caitlin walked it. Whenever they encountered pedestrians, the pedestrians ducked away and hustled past them as if afraid lest Bronson and Caitlin might try to strike up a conversation.

"This cold-shoulder treatment's getting old," said Bronson, watching a white-haired man in his seventies avert his head and bustle past him.

"I'm never coming back to this place after I leave it," said Caitlin.

Its siren keening and its light bar flashing, a squad car careered down the street behind them, approaching them, burning rubber with its shrieking tires.

Bronson didn't know if the cops were chasing him or not. He wasn't taking any chances. He snagged Caitlin's arm and ushered her into a recessed, darkened doorway.

The patrol car shot past them.

"You think they're coming after us?" said Caitlin, watching it recede into the distance.

"No sense in taking any chances after meeting up with Lapman," said Bronson, relieved that the squad car hadn't stopped.

He and Caitlin continued walking to the coroner's apartment.

"Here it is," said Caitlin, nodding at a three-story flesh-colored stucco apartment house on their right. "He's on the third floor. Herbert Wisnisky."

A eucalyptus tree that sprouted out of the sidewalk was buckling the cement in front of the building's entrance. Bronson and Caitlin had to tread carefully on the contorted sidewalk to avoid tripping. They climbed a short flight of cement steps and entered the lobby. A row of bronze mailboxes lined one of its walls.

Bronson and Caitlin traversed the lobby to the elevator, rode up to the third floor, found Wisnisky's apartment, and rapped on the door.

A fiftysomething jug-eared, stoop-shouldered man with thick black-framed spectacles and a receding hairline answered the door. He had horizontal slashes for lips.

"Yeah?" he said, holding the door half open like he might slam it in their faces at any moment.

"Are you Herbert Wisnisky, the coroner?" asked Bronson.

"Who wants to know?" said Wisnisky, waving the door back and forth fixing to shut it.

"I'm Dan Bronson. I'm looking for my brother Sam. Do you remember burying him recently?"

"You're not one of them?"

"One of who?"

Wisnisky stopped swinging the door back and forth and opened it. "Come on in."

"Who are you talking about?" asked Bronson, following Wisnisky into the apartment.

Pulling up the rear Caitlin closed the door behind them.

"Gangbangers," answered Wisnisky. "The Zetas drug cartel from Mexico controls this town. They ship narcotics through here to the rest of California, Nevada, and points east."

"Is that why everybody in town's afraid of us?" said Bronson. "They think we're gangbangers?"

"Why doesn't the sheriff do something about it?" said Caitlin.

Wisnisky scoffed. "He's bought and paid for. The drug dealers have bribed him to keep his mouth shut and run anybody out of town who makes trouble for them."

"That explains the ultimatum he gave us earlier," Bronson told Caitlin.

"What about the mayor?" said Caitlin. "Why doesn't he do something?"

"Surprise, surprise," said Wisnisky. "He's on the take, too. All of the local politicians are." He added dryly, "How about them apples?"

"How can you stand living in this town? It's got poison running through its veins."

"I got a family to support. Bills to pay."

As if on cue, a woman's voice came from another room. "Herbert? What do they want?"

Bronson could discern a figure's shadow gliding about in the nearby linoleum-tiled room.

"My wife Mary," Wisnisky told Caitlin. "Nothing, dear," he called out. "We're almost finished."

"I need your help in the kitchen," said Mary. "The sink's stopped up."

"Just another minute."

"How do you keep it bottled up inside you?" said Caitlin. "Knowing the entire town's corrupt."

"You gotta watch what you say in this town. It could get you killed."

"What about my brother Sam Bronson?" said Bronson. "Do you recall signing a death certificate for him recently? He looked sort of like me, but was shorter."

Wisnisky eyed Bronson then squinted in thought. "No. I don't recall the name. We had a John Doe last week. That's about it. How far do you want me to go back on the calendar for death certificates?"

"This John Doe. What'd he look like?"

"Hard to tell."

Bronson shook his head in bafflement. "I'm not following you."

"His face was beat to a pulp. I'd say the gangbangers got to him."

"What'd he die of?"

"Unnatural causes."

"Could you be more specific?"

"Blunt trauma to the head is what killed him, but he had fractured bones all over his body."

"You think he was tortured?"

Wisnisky nodded. "Unless a steamroller ran him over."

"Why would they beat him to death?"

"Who knows? Maybe he was working for them and double-crossed them."

"You saying my brother's a gangbanger?" said Bronson through his teeth, taking a menacing step toward Wisnisky.

"If you don't want to know, don't ask."

"That could explain why he didn't want anybody to find him," said Caitlin.

Shutting his eyes Bronson clasped his brow. "It's hard for me to believe my own brother was a gangbanger."

"You said yourself, people will do anything for money," said Caitlin.

Wisnisky fetched a sigh. "It's the way of the world."

Caitlin turned on him. "Why don't you call the feds and have Lapman busted for taking graft?"

"If I rock the boat, I'll lose my job, or worse—my life."

"Where's the John Doe buried?" asked Bronson.

"They haven't buried him yet. He's over at the Green Shade Mortuary."

"Let's head over there," Bronson told Caitlin.

The two of them angled toward the door.

"If you tell anybody what I've said, I'll deny everything," said Wisnisky. "I don't want to end up like that John Doe."

"That's unfortunate," said Caitlin. "This town needs to be cleansed of the scum running it."

"Easy for you to say. You don't live here. There's one other thing."

"What?"

"Now that I think about it, there was another death last week."

"What was his name?"

"It wasn't Sam Bronson. It was Tommy the grocer that lives around the corner." Wisnisky cleared his throat. "*Used* to live around the corner, I mean. I knew him."

"Did he die of a beating, too?" said Bronson.

"Actually, he died of the bubonic plague. Which is another reason the townsfolk are upset."

"Plague?" said Bronson, not believing his ears.

Wisnisky nodded. "The black death. It wiped out three-quarters of the population in Europe in the Middle Ages."

19

"Then notify the CDC in Atlanta," said Caitlin, alarmed. "Deaths by plague need to be reported to the federal authorities."

"Lapman told me not to. He doesn't want the feds descending on our town like a swarm of locusts. We're trying to kill all the rats in town to put a stop to the spread of the disease."

"You still need to report it to the feds."

"The townsfolk know about it. They're taking precautionary measures."

"That explains the surgical mask I saw a guy wearing," said Bronson.

"Yeah."

"But that's not enough," said Caitlin in an outburst of indignation. "You need to notify the CDC so they can monitor the situation here. The plague could spread to another state."

"We're doing all we can."

"It's not enough. You sound like *you* at least have a conscience. Not like your sheriff."

"My hands are tied," said Wisnisky.

"I'm gonna tell the feds everything as soon as I blow this town."

"I wouldn't do that if I was you."

"This town's evil to the core. It's got to be cleaned out root and branch."

Bronson opened the door. He and Caitlin stalked into the hallway.

"Are you coming with us?" said Bronson.

"That wouldn't be good for my health," said Wisnisky and shut the door.

"The sooner I get out of this town the better," huffed Caitlin.

"We can't leave yet," said Bronson. "We have to check out the mortuary and see if Sam's there."

Except they weren't going anywhere.

Sheriff Lapman and two of his deputies were cocking down the hall toward Bronson and Caitlin, taking up the entire width of the hall.

Bronson cursed.

"How did you know we were here?" said Caitlin.

"Mrs. Wisnisky phoned us, said a man and a woman were harassing her husband," said Lapman, plowing to a halt in front of Caitlin and Bronson. "It wasn't difficult to peg you two as the culprits. Hold your hands behind your backs."

"What! Are you busting us?" said Bronson, fit to be tied.

"I'm not asking you to marry me."

"My brother's been murdered. You should be investigating his murder."

One of the deputies stepped backward, and another man stepped forward out of the shadows. Bronson recognized him with a start. It was Sam. Three days' worth of stubble on his cheeks, he had a rakish half smile pasted on his lips. Maybe it was that to-hell-with-the-world smile that attracted the women, decided Bronson.

"Who did you say was murdered?" said Sam.

"Sam. What's going on?" said Bronson, flummoxed.

"Why did you come here, Dan?"

"I was looking for you," said Bronson.

"I didn't want to be found."

"The coroner said your face was smashed to a pulp."

Sam snickered. "That wasn't me. That was a snitch. Why do you want me?"

"I came here to tell you Mom died."

"You weren't supposed to find me."

"Did you hear what I said?"

"I heard. What do you want me to do about it?"

"I thought you might be interested," said Bronson, annoyed at Sam's reaction, or more precisely, the lack of one.

Sam's face became grim. "You weren't supposed to find me, Dan. Who's this woman you're with?"

"I'm an insurance investigator," said Caitlin. "Your wife hired me to prove you're dead so she can collect on your policy."

"Figures."

"What are you?" said Bronson. "A CPA for the drug cartel. Is that why you don't want to be found?"

"You aren't gonna tell anyone about it, Dan. If you had just stayed out of my life like I wanted you to, none of this would be happening to you."

"What's gonna happen to me?"

Sam stepped back into the shadows behind the deputies.

Lapman advanced toward Bronson, a pair of handcuffs dangling from his hands. "Me. I'm gonna happen to you. You're coming with me."

"Why? We haven't done anything illegal."

"Nope. You haven't."

"Then what's the charge?"

"There's no charge."

"Then how can you bust us?" said Bronson, flabbergasted, face working.

"I'm doing my job as sheriff."

"Not the way I hear it," said Caitlin.

Lapman ignored her. "I'm quarantining the both of you. You got the plague. You'll be staying with us a long, long time. Welcome to San Remo."

## Lizard Man

Taggert's next-door neighbor Buckholtz was at it again.
Doors were slamming. Objects were crashing against the walls
and floor. Voices were raised. Buckholtz and his girlfriend were
having another smash-down drag-out fight.

Taggert couldn't sleep with the ruckus. Why did they make
apartment walls so thin? he wondered as he lay in bed. He had yet
to live in an apartment where you couldn't hear the neighbors
through the walls, ceilings, and floors, depending on where your
neighbors lived.

A particularly loud crack sounded in Buckholtz's room. It
was a wonder nobody called the cops, decided Taggert. But then
again what would the cops do about it? Buckholtz was in the
privacy of his own home. But that didn't give him the right to
batter his girlfriend—if that was what he was doing. Taggert
didn't know what Buckholtz and his girlfriend were doing. All he
knew for sure was that they were making a whale of a racket.
Maybe they were just throwing things around the room.

Taggert tossed and turned in his bed. They were flat-out rude,
that was what they were, he decided. They had no respect for their
neighbors. He had a good mind to go over there and give them
what for.

But he didn't want to get involved in a domestic dispute. He
had read somewhere that even cops didn't want to go anywhere
near domestic disputes. In any case, Buckholtz was a big bruiser,

23

pushing six three, and must have weighed close to three hundred pounds. His meaty arms were covered with tattoos, which he liked to flaunt along with his hairy chest by wearing a wife-beater most of the time.

To hell with it, decided Taggert. He squeezed his pillow around his head to blot out the cacophony.

He tossed and turned in bed for the rest of the night, sleeping in fits and starts.

He dreamed he sent someone over to Buckholtz's place. The character Taggert dreamed up was a brawny six-five guy with a peroxide Mohawk who had particolored tattoos surrounding his squat neck, giving him a reptilian aspect. Lizard Man had no trouble throttling Buckholtz, who was sound asleep in a drunken stupor.

The next morning when Taggert woke up he was exhausted. He couldn't even get out of bed. Probably because he didn't get much sleep last night thanks to the thug Buckholtz and his drama-queen girlfriend. Taggert's head throbbed as he lay in bed watching a new day's sunlight filtering through his window's vertical blinds. At least Buckholtz's apartment was quiet, Taggert decided listening to a bird chirping outside his window.

Taggert wanted to lie in bed all day.

Which wasn't going to happen.

Somebody knocked on his door. The rapping exacerbated Taggert's headache. He cursed under his breath.

Taggert hauled himself out of bed and stumbled to his feet, clutching his pounding head with one hand. He staggered to the front door and opened it.

The LA morning sun glared in his eyes. Taggert squinted. A rangy twentysomething guy all of six-feet tall was standing on Taggert's concrete stoop eying him.

It was Collins.

"You look like roadkill," said Collins with a grimace.

"I love you, too," said Taggert.

"I didn't come here to give you flowers. Open the door and let me in. I can't talk out here."

"Why not?"

Taggert had no desire to talk with this killer headache eating him alive. He especially didn't want to talk to Collins, figuring he knew what Collins was here for.

"This is private," said Collins. "Let me in."

"Can't it wait?"

"I'm not gonna say this again," said Collins. "We need to talk. Sledge is pissed."

Taggert didn't have much choice. He opened the door and let Collins in.

"What's this about?" said Taggert, closing the door behind Collins, still squinting on account of his headache.

"You know what it's about. Sledge wants his money. He wants all of it now, including the vig."

"He said I had till next week."

"Something's come up. He wants it this afternoon."

"I don't have it now."

"Then you better get it."

This was what he got for playing the ponies, decided Taggert. He followed the bangtails around California. Wherever they went he went—from Santa Anita, to Hollywood Park, to Pomona, to Del Mar. He wouldn't be going to Hollywood Park anymore, of course, since they had just closed it down last winter. Losing Hollywood Park was like losing an old friend—even if Holly Park had been going to seed lately.

This was what he got for being a professional gambler, he decided. Ten large in debt to Sledge, plus three more for vigorish. Taggert saw life as a lottery: if you wanted to win, you had to gamble. Even if you just wanted to stay alive, you had to gamble, for that matter.

He never bet on other sports, only on horses. He had been going to the track since he was a kid. His father used to take him there every Saturday afternoon when the horses were running until he died from lung cancer when Taggert was fourteen. Horse racing must be in the Taggert blood, decided Taggert. Except his

Bryan Cassiday

father had been a plumber, not a professional gambler. For him horses were entertainment, nothing more.

"Hello? Hello? Don't bug out on me, Taggert," said Collins.

"Where am I gonna get it?" said Taggert, brought back to reality by Collins's demanding voice.

"That's your problem."

"How can I get anything today? I can barely walk."

"If you like your knees, you better get it. Walking will be much more difficult without them."

Involuntarily, Taggert cut his eyes down toward his knees.

"I got a Louisville Slugger in the trunk of my car outside," Collins went on. "I haven't swung that bat in quite a while. To tell you the truth, I might be a little rusty. There's no telling what I would hit if I took a swing today, being that I'm out of practice. I might hit your thigh. I might hit your hip. I might even hit your head by mistake, heaven forbid."

"Yeah, yeah. I get the point," said Taggert, breaking into a sweat. "What's the rush? Why can't he wait till next week?"

"I don't know and I don't care. All I know is he wants thirteen large from you this afternoon—four o'clock at the latest."

"That doesn't change anything," said Taggert, clenching and unclenching his fingers. "I still don't have it."

"But you *will* have it this afternoon," said Collins, stone-faced.

"Saying it doesn't make it so."

"I guess you want to say good-bye to your knees."

"You don't seem to understand."

"No. *You* don't seem to understand," said Collins, jabbing his forefinger into Taggert's face. Collins surveyed Taggert's unkempt apartment, expressing contempt with his craggy visage. "You need a wife or something to clean house for you."

Taggert massaged his brow and his closed eyelids, trying to figure out where he was going to get thirteen grand.

"I don't have time to stand around all day gabbing with you," said Collins and turned to leave.

"Wait a minute. See if you can get Sledge to give me three more days to get the cash."

26

Collins opened the door. "It's nonnegotiable. I'll be seeing you this afternoon to collect on your debt. And I'll be driving the same car with the Louisville Slugger in the trunk in case you're thinking about welshing."

"How about *two* more days?" said Taggert, gritting his teeth.

"Why do you hate your knees so much? What'd they ever do to you?"

Collins already had his foot through the door and wasn't even looking at Taggert.

"One more day," said Taggert, clutching at straws.

"Are you going deaf in your old age?" said Collins, wheeling around to face Taggert.

"I'm only fifty. I can hear fine. All I'm asking for is one more day."

"My Louisville Slugger is waiting for me in my car. Before Louis is ready for action I'll have to wipe the stale brains off the barrel of the bat. I don't want to get them on your knees if you don't have the dough this afternoon. A clean bat is a happy bat."

Taggert felt like he was going to be sick.

"See you later, alligator," added Collins, traversing the cement patio.

Taggert closed the door and wondered how he was going to get his hands on that kind of money, by four o'clock, no less. Not to mention that he still felt played out, deprived of a good night's sleep.

He shrugged. If he wanted an easy life, he wouldn't have become a gambler. No gambler could win all the time. You had to learn how to deal with failure—and losses of many bucks. Winning wasn't the toughest thing. It was the dealing with losing. That was the life.

The phone shrilled. The noise grated on Taggert's already-frayed nerves. He debated whether to answer it. He approached the phone that was bleating on the kitchen table. The caller ID couldn't ID the caller. Taggert decided to take the call.

It was Collins, fit to be tied.

"Did you rat me out to the cops?" he said.

"What are you talking about?" said Taggert. "Why would I do that?"

"Then what are those cops doing milling around your place? I saw them arriving when I left."

Taggert had no idea what was going on. He put down his handset on the kitchen table, cut across the room to the window that gave onto his patio, and peeked through the drawn miniblinds.

Collins was right. Two cops in black uniforms were making for Buckholtz's door. He could see them walking past his four-foot-high, vine-entangled, weathered wooden fence that encompassed his patio and Buckholtz's, their faces set. Sporting shades the lead cop, the taller of the two, commenced banging on the door with his fist. The other cop, a black guy in his thirties with a flat nose and flaring nostrils, swiveled his head, inspecting the surroundings, a scowl on his face.

Taggert returned to his kitchen and snapped up the handset.

"Those cops are next door," he said. "Not here."

"You didn't call them?"

"No."

"I'm watching you, Taggert. You better be on the level."

"Something's going on next door."

"I don't care what's going on. Just get the cash by four o'clock."

Collins slammed down his handset.

Taggert flinched. He hung up and returned to peeking through the miniblinds.

He could discern neighbors constellating in front of the fence that girdled Buckholtz's apartment as the cops pounded on Buckholtz's door. He started when he heard a loud crash.

All business, the cops were kicking down Buckholtz's door and charging into the apartment, guns at the ready.

Fired by an adrenaline surge, Taggert sprang to his bedroom, threw on some clothes, and hustled outdoors. He joined the crowd of rubbernecking neighbors that were gawking at Buckholtz's apartment.

"What happened?" he asked a middle-aged woman in a terrycloth bathrobe with pink curlers in her hair.

Mouth twisted, she gave him the once-over. "You look like something the cat dragged in."

Taggert sighed. *Not you, too*, he thought. *You and Collins with your wisecracks. This is getting old. You're not exactly a fox with those pink curlers stuck in your hair, lady. More like the bride of Frankenstein.*

What he said was, "I had a bad night."

"The cops just busted into Buckholtz's apartment."

"I can see that. But why?"

"I guess we're gonna find out," she said, picking up on the lead cop striding out of Buckholtz's apartment.

"This is a crime scene," the thirtyish cop said, face florid. "Everybody stay back."

Maybe he had high blood pressure, decided Taggert, taking in the cop's ruddy complexion. It didn't look like sunburn.

"What happened, Officer?" said Pink Curlers.

"The tenant here was murdered."

Pink Curlers gasped. "Oh no!"

Taggert inched closer to the cop. "How'd he die?"

"Who are you, sir?" said the cop, eyes squinty.

"I'm his next-door neighbor."

"Did you hear anything suspicious here last night, Mr. . . . ?"

"Taggert."

"I heard the usual yelling between him and his girlfriend," said Pink Curlers before Taggert could answer.

The cop turned toward the frowning woman. "You heard a fight?"

"So what else is new?"

"Does that mean you heard a fight?"

"It means I heard a lot of 'em. What'd she do? Up and kill him?"

"She's the one who called it in. She said she called him this morning and couldn't reach him. She thought something was hinky and called us."

"Working on her alibi, huh?" said Pink Curlers, giving the cop a shrewd look.

"I doubt she did it, ma'am."

"Why not? They were at each other's throats night and day."

"What about?"

"Everything and anything. I don't know how she could stand him. Some days I'd see her walking around with a shiner. She'd wear sunglasses to hide it, but I could still see it under the rim of the lens. He treated her like dirt. Why she kept coming back to him for more I'll never know. I don't blame her for killing him. It was self-defense, if you ask me."

"I shouldn't be telling you this."

Smiling for a change, Pink Curlers winked at him. "You know you want to," she coaxed.

"The killer was strong. He was so strong that when he throttled Buckholtz he crushed the poor guy's windpipe." The cop screwed up his face. "You don't want to see what's left of his throat." He paused. "Did you know the victim well, Ms. . . .?"

"Deetz. Sheila Deetz. Make sure you spell that right. D-E-E-T-Z. No, I didn't. I just heard him and his girlfriend at it tooth and claw all the time. Frankly, I made a point of staying away from the guy."

The cop produced a small notepad and scribbled on it with a pencil that had teeth marks in its yellow paint.

Taggert slunk away behind the fence while the cop was staring at his pad.

Taggert didn't want to give any statements now. He had no time for it. He had to scare up thirteen grand by this afternoon, or Collins would put him on sticks. And Taggert didn't want Collins to see him talking to the cops. Collins would draw the erroneous conclusion that Taggert was snitching on him. Collins might be skulking nearby for all Taggert knew.

Taggert didn't exactly feel sorry for Buckholtz. The guy was a lush and a rude, noisy neighbor who pounded on his girlfriend. Whoever had killed him had done the world a favor. Now maybe

Taggert could snag a decent night's rest. He could do with some serious rack time right now. He still felt wiped out from last night.

He had no time to sleep, though.

He wondered why he felt bone tired. Just because he couldn't sleep well? He had gone through sleepless nights before without incurring this debilitating exhaustion as a result.

Sitting down on the edge of his bed he racked his brains trying to dope out what he was going to do. He had five hundred bucks to his name. The bangtails were running today at Santa Anita. He could lay down bets on the horses with the five c's. But, dare he think it? What if he lost? To win thirteen grand, he would have to bet long shots. And throw in a pick six, exactas, trifectas, superfectas, super high fives, rolling pick threes, all manner of exotics . . . Not a good recipe for success. It was either that or rob a bank. Another low-percentage solution.

He squeezed his head between his hands and shut his eyes. A fire engine's siren blared on the street outside, slicing through his ears like a red-hot poker and dragging silence in its wake.

It was easier to think now that the siren was gone. But he still couldn't come up with a solution to his dilemma.

Unable to keep his eyelids open, he lay back on his unmade bed. He needed to grab ten or fifteen minutes of z time. It would hone his mind so he could figure out a way to glom onto the shekels.

He fell asleep in less than a minute. He dreamed about killing Collins, the bastard. In his dream Taggert sent Lizard Man to kill Collins. Lizard Man could take out Collins using only his hands, the same way he had scragged Buckholtz last night.

The shrilling phone jerked Taggert awake. He stumbled out of bed to the kitchen.

Taggert couldn't believe it, but he felt even more exhausted than before his brief nap. He had thought the nap would refresh him. Instead it had enervated him. He glanced under heavy eyelids at his wristwatch. He hadn't slept more than an hour.

Groggily, eyes blurry, he reached for the handset. It tumbled to the floor, thwacking against the linoleum. He muttered a curse, bent over, retrieved the handset, and raised it to his ear.

"Hello! Hello!" barked the voice.

"Hello?"

"What did you do that for, dickhead?"

"Do what?"

"Slam the phone down."

"I dropped it."

"My ears are still ringing. Damn it."

It was Sledge. Through his fogged-up mind Taggert recognized Sledge's tobacco smoker's husky voice.

"I didn't mean to do it," said Taggert.

"Where's Collins, you pathetic loser?"

"How do I—"

"I sent him over there an hour ago."

"I—"

"He should be back by now. Where is he?"

"I—"

"Did you do something to him?"

"No. Let me—"

"Spit it out."

"Let me answer," burst Taggert at last. "He left here about an hour ago."

"He should be here by now," said Sledge more to himself than to Taggert. "Did you get his message about your four o'clock deadline?"

"Yeah."

Sledge hammered his handset down into its cradle.

Taggert winced at the crack on the line. He hung up.

He felt so weak he could barely muster enough strength to continue standing. Sighing, bracing his hands against the tabletop, he sat down on the torn vinyl chair at the kitchen table.

What was going on? he wondered. Why did he feel so feeble? His nap seemed to have exhausted him even more. Why would sleep wear him out? It made no sense. He thought about it.

Maybe his dreams were wearing him out. That made as much sense as sleep wearing him out. How could a dream sap your energy?

He weighed what Sledge had told him over the phone. What had happened to Collins? Not that Taggert cared. He wished something *had* happened to Collins. It would be fine with Taggert if he never saw Collins again.

The phone blared again.

Taggert cringed. He was sitting right next to the instrument. He never got phone calls. He could go weeks without his phone ringing. Even his girlfriend Irene texted and e-mailed him rather than calling him. Today the phone was ringing off the hook.

Warily, he lifted the handset.

"One of my men just reported back to me," said Sledge. "He found Collins dead. Was that your handiwork?"

"How could it have been me? I've been asleep for the last hour."

"Collins was strangled in his own car. What do you know about that?"

Taggert couldn't believe his ears. "Nothing. It's news to me."

"You had nothing to do with it?" said Sledge suspiciously.

"I was asleep, I told you."

"Why should I believe you?"

"Because it's the truth."

"He said he was gonna rough you up, and maybe you decided to fix his wagon. Is that how it went down?"

"No."

"Whacking Collins ain't gonna save your bacon, anyway, buddy. You still owe me thirteen lousy grand by four o'clock. No, make that *three* o'clock, loser."

Sledge slammed down the receiver again.

Taggert whipped his handset away from his ear so the crack wouldn't reverberate through his ear. Not in time, though. He still heard the smack of plastic on plastic.

He felt more confused than ever. Now Collins was dead. Murdered like Buckholtz. The two had never even met each other, as far as Taggert knew, and yet they had both died at the hands of a strangler.

Of course, in Collins's line of work as an enforcer, it was only natural that he should die violently. Buckholtz was a drunken lout and no doubt had a carload of enemies. Still, that they should both die from strangulation was extraordinary, and it suggested that the same killer had done away with the pair of them. And Taggert had dreamed of their deaths. The irony was not lost on him.

Maybe he could see into the future via his dreams.

He didn't have time to think about this. He had Sledge to deal with. And Sledge wanted thirteen grand from Taggert. Which Taggert didn't have. Taggert's headache became worse just thinking about it. How was he going to get out of this mess? Sure, Collins was dead. But what was to prevent Sledge from hiring another enforcer to work Taggert over?

Played out, Taggert was having trouble holding his head up. He felt like he was dying, for Christ's sake. If going to sleep was killing him, he didn't want to go to sleep. He might not wake up the next time. But he had to sleep, sooner or later. If it *was* the dreams that were killing him, then he would have to prevent himself from dreaming. How could he do that? Could he hypnotize himself not to dream?

Taggert had a more immediate problem. He had to get the dough for Sledge. Taggert looked at his watch. He had four hours left to get the money. He didn't feel like he had enough strength to drive to the track and lay down bets. Even if he placed the bets, there was no guarantee he'd win thirteen large. The odds were, indeed, stacked against him, especially since he had to bet long shots to make enough money with his measly five c's.

He heard urgent rapping at his front door. He hoped it wasn't the cops.

Pressing his hands against the tabletop for leverage, he propped himself to a standing position. He shambled like an old man to the door on his rubbery legs and opened it.

Irene slammed into his apartment. Worked up, she paced around the room in her dress and high heels, blowing off steam.

"What happened to you?" she said.

"What?"

"I got back from my mother's. You were supposed to pick me up at LAX two hours ago. I waited and I waited and I waited."

*Christ*, he thought. He had forgotten all about it. What with all the excitement around here and his exhaustion it had slipped his mind.

"I forgot," he mumbled. "Why didn't you call me?"

"I've *been* texting you and e-mailing you for the last hour and a half. Why didn't you answer? I had to take a cab here."

Taggert clutched his brow in dismay. He could not recall where he had put his smartphone. He had gone to a movie yesterday and muted the phone. The phone must still be muted. No wonder he hadn't heard any texts or e-mails coming in.

"I've got too much on my mind," he said.

"That's no excuse," she said, curtailing her pacing to wheel around and confront him with her large liquid black eyes for the first time. Her wrath melted into worry at the sight of his face. "You look awful. What happened to you? Is there something wrong?" She stared into his droopy eyes with concern.

"I can barely stand up."

He sidled a few steps before collapsing into his easy chair, which groaned under his weight.

"Are you sick?" said Irene and massaged his shoulder.

"I'm having these dreams where I send somebody out to kill people, and they end up dead. I have no energy. I can barely move. And I owe money to a loan shark at three o'clock. How am I gonna pay him?"

"What have you got yourself into, Phil?"

"The question is, how am I gonna get myself out of it?"

"How much money do you need?"

"Thirteen grand."

Irene shook her head. "I can't help you."

"I'm not asking you to. I was going to the track to see if I could win the dough, but I'm so worn out I don't think I could make it to Santa Anita."

"How is going to the track gonna help you? That's what got you into debt in the first place."

"How else am I gonna pay him off?"

Taggert sniffed her subtle perfume. The fragrance calmed him after a fashion.

She turned away from him and fell to pacing again, this time in thought rather than ire. "Do you really believe this nonsense that you can kill people with your dreams?"

"My next-door neighbor got strangled last night after I dreamed up somebody to kill him."

"It must be a coincidence. How can dreams kill anybody?"

"But it happened again today. I dreamed about Lizard Man killing Collins. And Collins ended up strangled like Buckholtz."

"Lizard Man. He sounds like some sort of golem."

"If I don't cough up the money for Sledge today, he'll break my knees. How can I pay him if I can't even walk? He'll be signing my death warrant if he kneecaps me."

Irene thought about it. "Maybe you're going about this the wrong way."

That was what he liked about Irene, decided Taggert. She had a head on her shoulders. That and her insatiable carnal demands—which he could in no way fulfill in his current condition.

"What do you mean?" he said.

She stopped pacing and faced him. "Forget about the money."

"Forget about it?" he said, bugging out his eyes. "Haven't you been listening to me?"

"Let's think outside the box."

"What are you babbling about?"

"This golem you dreamed up."

"Lizard Man?"

Irene nodded. "Why not dream that he kills Sledge?"

"I forgot to tell you. Every time I have one of these dreams, I'm exhausted when I wake up. It's like the dream is sapping my energy, like it's killing me a little bit at a time."

"It's either that or get your knees smashed."

She had a point, decided Taggert. If Sledge was gone, it would solve Taggert's problems. His financial problems, for the time being anyway. And it would save his knees. It wasn't like he had a slew of choices at this point. It was nearing three o'clock.

The phone rang, breaking his chain of thought.

He halted to the phone in the kitchen and answered on the third ring. Fumbling the handset for a moment, he said, "Hello."

"You know what they say?" said Sledge. "Nice guys finish last. I'm tired of being a nice guy. You got till two o'clock."

Sledge slammed down his receiver.

Wincing, hanging up, Taggert cursed.

"Who was that?" asked Irene.

"I got till two o'clock to get the money." He glanced at his wristwatch and shook his head. "I'll never be able to win that amount at the track in time."

He staggered back to his easy chair and plunked down in it.

"Gambling isn't the solution," said Irene. "It's the problem."

Taggert broke into a cold sweat. She was right, of course. It would be a long shot, to say the least, if he could win thirteen g's with five c's. Who was he trying to kid? It looked like he had run out of options. Like it or not, he would have to summon Lizard Man. Nevertheless he had problems with that solution.

"Dreaming up Lizard Man again would be committing murder," he said. "Now that I know my dreams can kill, dreaming about his murder would be the same as murdering him with my own hands."

"How do you figure that? You had no qualms about murdering Buckholtz. Why suddenly do you have pangs of conscience?"

"It's different now. Don't you see?"

"How?"

"When I dreamed about Buckholtz's murder, I had no idea that dreaming it would result in his death by strangulation. If I dream about Sledge's murder, I'll be murdering him in cold blood."

"But *you're* not killing him. Lizard Man is."

Taggert shook his head no. "I'm making Lizard Man do it. I'll be as guilty as somebody contracting a hit man for murder."

"No jury in the world would convict you without evidence incriminating you. And there *won't* be any evidence against you if your golem commits the murder."

Taggert shut his eyes and pressed his eyeballs with his index finger and thumb. He cudgeled his brains, seeking a solution.

"I'm not a murderer," he said.

"I never said you were, Phil."

"But you want me to become one."

"I don't want you to become anything. I'm saying, if you can dream this guy Sledge dead, it'll save your skin, and nobody'll ever convict you of murder. Just think. You have the power to kill without ever being caught."

"It's not a power I want. I just want the guy to leave me alone."

Irene shook her head in frustration. "You just don't get it, do you? He's never gonna leave you alone, as long as he's alive. You'll be into him for the rest of your life, if you don't get rid of him. Once you owe people money, you become their slave."

She was right, he knew. There was nothing else for it. In a bind, he would have to conjure Lizard Man to whack out Sledge. Sledge was a son of a bitch, anyway. He deserved killing. How many men had Sledge ordered clipped in his line of work? Scads of them, for sure. Icing a murderer was more an execution than a murder. Thinking it through Taggert came to terms now with Sledge's death at the hands of Lizard Man.

Taggert gathered himself, staggered to his feet out of his easy chair, and made for his bedroom.

"I'm going to sleep," was all he said.

Watching him Irene nodded.

Taggert was asleep as soon as his head hit the pillow on his bed. He concentrated on conjuring Lizard Man as he drifted off. He willed Lizard Man to strangle Sledge. The dream seemed so real . . . the beefy Lizard Man with his particolored neck and his peroxide Mohawk striding into Sledge's house . . . Sledge sitting

38

all alone in his study, smoking a cigarette . . . the feel of Sledge's throat in Lizard Man's catcher's mitts of hands . . . the sound of Sledge coughing to death, eyes popping out of his head . . . face crimson at first then purple then blue . . . all so real . . .

"Phil," said Irene, shaking his motionless arm with concern, eyes welling with tears as she took in his wan face. "Phil, wake up!"

But Taggert had escaped his problems, never to be bothered by Sledge, nor by anyone else for that matter, again.

Lizard Man, on the other hand, was alive and stalking out of Sledge's house, a jack-o'-lantern sneer carved on his face.

Bryan Cassiday

# Through These Eyes

I was watching a video on my computer of me stabbing a roly-poly bald guy in the neck and then lapping down his blood like a dog slurping up water from his bowl when Sarah came into my apartment, letting in the night air.

She never knocked. She always let herself in without any invitation from me.

"I hate you," she said.

"I hate *you*," I said, glancing over my shoulder at her as she stood in front of the door, the knob in her hand.

It was weird, but that was how we greeted each other whenever we met.

Clad in a cranberry hoodie and jeans, five eight in her bare feet, she was casting around the room with her liquid green eyes that gazed through butterfly glasses. It was almost like she didn't see me. But how could that be? I was sitting at my laptop not more than fifteen feet from her.

Maybe she was drunk again. Drinking impaired her vision. She insisted on driving even when she was blitzed, although I repeatedly warned her not to.

She hated my driving. She loved to chew me out for going out of my way to avoid making left-hand turns in intersections without traffic lights. Was it my fault she never took driver's education?

I hoped she couldn't see the laptop image of me killing the blubbery man with the blood sloshing out of his neck coating my tongue that I was sticking out in anticipation. The guy, who had a partially sunburned face and skin peeling off his bent nose, was squinting like he was used to wearing spectacles and couldn't see without them. Or maybe it was because he had a knife sticking out of his neck.

He was sitting in a room with his hands tied behind his back as he sat and bled out. I recognized neither him nor the room.

Sarah stood, doorknob in hand, for a few seconds then left, shutting the door behind her.

What was that all about?

I didn't waste too much time thinking about Sarah's idiosyncrasies though, not with this video of my bloodletting playing out before my eyes. What the hell was going on? I didn't kill anyone. Who was this bald guy with the sunburn and the double chin? I never saw him before, and I certainly never stabbed him to death.

But there he was in living color, bare-chested, sitting bound in a chair, screaming mutely, as I slit his throat and drank his blood. Was this some kind of sick joke? Did I star in a snuff movie that I had no recollection of?

I couldn't get my head around it.

It was true I hadn't been feeling well the last week or so. It was hard to describe. It felt like worms were squirming through my body trying to eat their way out of my flesh. Like I would see them any minute oozing and squiggling out of my pores like thick hairs. My stomach rumbled at the revolting thought.

Maybe I was coming down with the flu.

And now this. A video of me killing a tubby guy. I had no memory of it.

Leaning toward the laptop's monitor I scrutinized the video image. I closed the image and tried to determine who had e-mailed the video to me. It had come from one of those do-not-reply addresses. I didn't recognize the name of the sender, and I could not e-mail him and ask him where he had gotten the video.

I hadn't been driving my cab lately thanks to my enervating illness. Needless to say, it was costing me money. However, I didn't feel up to logging in eight hours a day or more driving passengers around the city. The traffic congestion in LA was bad enough when I felt well. There was no way I could handle it all day being sick.

My stomach was a mess. I had the runs. What was I gonna do at work? Pull over at a gas station and go to the john every time I got sick? No fare in his right mind would put up with that. He would figure I was bilking him out of money by deliberately extending the ride and driving up his time on the taxi's meter.

I kept staring at the video playing before me, feeling sicker by the minute. Who had sent it to me and why? I hadn't gotten a blackmail note with it—not yet anyway. Maybe that would come later. My heart jackhammered as I sweated with fear. I fancied I could hear my heartbeat echoing in my ears, beating a deafening tattoo on kettledrums.

Why was I so scared?

I had nothing to fear. That wasn't me in the video. I hadn't knifed anybody. My heartbeat dialed it down a notch as I came to this realization. The killer might have looked like me, but it couldn't be me. I hadn't done it. Some joker must have hired an impostor to double for me in this movie and then e-mailed it to me to scare the bejesus out of me. *And it was working.* The son of a bitch.

But who would do such a thing?

Lapping up a guy's blood? The very idea of it made me sick to my stomach. I cringed at the image of my drinking the blood onscreen.

I kneaded my contorted face with my hand, trying to figure out what to do. Maybe I should try to clock in some hours at work just to get my mind off both my sick self and this nauseating video.

I hadn't been going out much ever since I had come down with my illness. Breathing fresh air might do me a world of good. Locking myself up in my apartment like it was a jail cell wasn't helping my mental health any.

What if I just put in a couple of hours at work today, instead of working a full eight? That might perk me up. In any case, it would preoccupy my mind and prevent me from dwelling on my illness to the point of obsession.

I didn't really have much of a choice. I needed the money. The rent would be due in another week and I didn't have enough cash to cover it.

I put my laptop in sleep mode.

I stood up muzzily and all but fell down. I had to grab the chair-back beside me in order to maintain my balance. My illness was sapping my strength more than I had realized. In my condition, maybe I couldn't even drive to work, let alone drive passengers around the traffic-congested city.

I dreaded to think it, but maybe I was coming down with rabies. A hooker I had been with a week ago had bitten me. Could you contract rabies from a human bite? Why not? You could get it from a dog bite, that was for sure.

But what were the chances she had rabies? Slim and none. Not in today's age. I could get tetanus maybe, but not rabies. I doubted I had tetanus, aka lockjaw. My jaw wasn't locking up. If the chippie had rabies, why hadn't she acted like a psycho frothing at the mouth when I had been with her? The fact was she hadn't.

But then again maybe she was a carrier, a modern-day Typhoid Mary. Maybe Bambi the hooker could carry rabies and infect her tricks without being infected by it.

I told myself to cut it out. My imagination was working overtime, flaring up with never-ending thoughts racing through my head.

I heard clicking on the ersatz hardwood floor. I turned my head to see Rodney, my Jack Russell terrier clattering toward me on his noisy claws. I patted his head. He yawned and wheezed with delight.

I drove from my apartment in Venice to the taxi station in LA, eager to forget about the video and my sickness.

Spotting my coworkers Lou and Tino at the time clock I said hello. Lou was a tall guy in his thirties who wore a truss courtesy of back problems. The truss kept his back rigid and made him look like he was strutting around. He wasn't preening. It just looked that way because of the truss.

Tino, a slight guy with thick lips, was a twentysomething Guatemalan that was always grinning. Nobody could figure out why. He had a big sloppy grin like that of a slaphappy dog. He would stick his toothy grin in your face when he was talking to you and compel you to back away to fend him off as he invaded your space.

They said hello to me but looked like they didn't know who I was. It was like they were politely saying hello to a stranger who walked up to them on the street.

I had been getting the feeling for a long time that Lou didn't like me anymore because I had stopped playing poker with him and his pals at his condo. I used to play, but I lost so much money, it was hurting. Maybe Lou was giving me the fisheye now on account of my not showing up anymore at his Thursday night poker games.

I thought I could hear Tino mutter behind my back, "Who was that?"

I figured I was imagining it. The three of us had known each other for going on four years now. Of course, they knew who I was. They must have been talking about somebody else.

I headed for the restroom. My stomach was acting up again, twisting into knots.

I swung open the wooden door to the men's room, entered, bellied up to the sink, and peered at my face in the mirror. The faucet in front of me was dripping. The drips made hollow sounds as the water slid down the drain.

The mirror revealed no secrets. Why hadn't Lou and Tino recognized me? I looked the same as ever, except I had more bags under my eyes, which looked hollow like I was a reptile staring out from under a rock. What could you expect? After all, I was sick.

Buckling his belt Phil the middle-aged dispatcher lurched out from one of the stalls with a grunt. He cast a glance in my direction but didn't acknowledge me. That was par for the course with Phil. He usually ignored me. Which was fine with me. All he ever did was carp about everything.

"One day closer to retirement," I heard him say, but he was halfway through the men's room door at that point and I didn't know who he was talking to. He may have been talking to himself, for all I knew. He did that a lot.

I resumed looking at my face's reflection in the mirror. My face seemed to have a greenish cast to it. But maybe it was the fluorescent lighting overhead. One of the tubes in the fixture was blinking like it was set to burn out.

"Who was that?" I heard someone say in the hallway beyond the restroom door. It sounded like Phil's voice.

I scrutinized my face in the mirror. On closer inspection I realized it wasn't a bag under my eye but a thick flake of wedge-shaped skin like a callus on the verge of falling off. I picked at it. It was squamous to the touch, with a grey color. Startling me it fell off in my hand. I could smell it. It stank of putrescence.

Pulling a face in disgust I flicked the dead skin into a trashcan that stood between the end of the sinks and the paper-towel dispenser.

I examined my face in the mirror again. I saw that the area beneath the dead skin that I had removed was grey and scaly, similar to the patch I had tossed in the trash. Maybe I was turning into a fish. I snickered at the thought.

I tore myself away from the mirror. It must be this disease, whatever it was. It was affecting my skin as well as my stomach. I had to get out of the head. Too many mirrors to look at. That was the trouble with mirrors. Every time you saw one you thought about yourself. And in my case I thought about my disease.

I bored through the restroom's swinging door into the hall. I didn't feel like working. I didn't think I could handle it tonight.

I drove back to my apartment.

Rodney was waiting for me at the door wagging his tail. He wanted to go to the beach. He had that look in his eye. He liked going to the beach at night and loping around on the sand.

I decided to take him. It was a mild night out. A walk in the fresh onshore breeze might be just what the doctor ordered.

I strode to the closet, retrieved Rodney's leather leash, and clipped it to his collar.

We walked four blocks to the beach. The fresh air helped. I started feeling better after a fashion.

At last we walked onto the sand and pulled up beside a knot of barbecue pits. Two of them were still smoldering with dying red embers, though nobody was present. The barbecuers must have left recently.

I unclipped Rodney's leash and he ran free. I slogged through the sand after him under the blue moonlight, which reflected off the black ocean to my left carving a shimmering river of light that led to the endless horizon.

Kicking up sand with his paws, Rodney was charging ahead of me like he knew where he was going, not taking time to look back at me. He wasn't heading toward the water. He was moving parallel to it.

I followed him, drinking in the mild night air redolent of brine, feeling better as I plodded through the sand, listening to the waves crashing then bubbling like bacon frying. At last they frothed in their death throes as they fanned across the moist dark sand that swallowed them.

To my surprise, Rodney balked and fell to yelping ahead of me. Something had caught his attention, but I didn't know what. I couldn't see anything up ahead through the gathering gloom. He just stood there barking at the sand in front of him.

I traipsed up to him. For the life of me I didn't know why he was raising such a racket. All I saw was sand in front of him.

Then he commenced digging in the sand with his front paws furiously working.

"What'd you find, boy?" I said, puzzled by his odd behavior.

He was digging away like he was on a mission.

Then he halted and barked twice. He dipped his head into the hole he had dug, snatched something in his teeth, and withdrew it.

With revulsion I beheld it in the moonlight.

46

A human hand with bites taken out of its flesh was wedged between Rodney's teeth. Rodney couldn't remove the hand any farther from the hole because the hand was attached to an arm, which was also gnawed with bite marks.

Tugging the hand with the strength of his entire body, muscles quivering, Rodney growled in frustration at not being able to pull the hand out any farther.

I stooped down on my haunches and scoped out the wounded hand and arm. Those bite marks hadn't been made by crabs on the beach. It looked like the handiwork of human teeth.

What kind of psycho would eat another person? I could think of only one answer. A cannibal. A cannibal must have killed the guy, devoured parts of him, and then buried him here so that nobody could find the corpse.

But that didn't explain Rodney's actions.

Rodney acted like he knew exactly where the cadaver was buried. He had headed straight toward it like a bee to a blossom.

How could he know where the corpse was buried? He couldn't have smelled it, not with all that sand covering it. It had been completely obscured by sand when we arrived. It was true Rodney was a terrier and had a keen olfactory sense. But how could he sniff a corpse buried head to toe in sand from fifty feet away?

I could not reach any other conclusion. Somehow Rodney had known in advance where the stiff was buried.

I got down on my hands and knees and scooped more sand away from the corpse, searching for the head. I wanted to know who this guy was.

Rodney saw what I was up to, dropped the hand from his mouth, and pitched in helping me excavate. It didn't take long for me to find the head. I brushed the sand off it. The face, like the body, was, for the most part, gnawed to the bone. I recoiled at the ghastly sight.

Then I resumed clearing the sand off the face. Even with the bite marks that mutilated it, I recognized it. My breath caught in my throat.

It was the guy in the video. The guy I had supposedly knifed.

White as a sheet, I drew away from the corpse, getting to my feet and staggering backward in the sand. That would explain why Rodney had known where to look for the corpse. He had seen me bury it.

My stomach fell to boiling. I was feeling sick again.

But something funny was happening. Instead of feeling sick to my stomach at the sight of the butchered corpse, I began feeling hungry. And I was thinking of Sarah at the same time. *I wanted to eat Sarah alive.*

In a transport of terror at the thoughts I was entertaining, I slewed around and bolted away from the half-buried stiff, plowing through the sand with my churning legs.

Gulping for breath, tongue hanging out of my mouth, I made it to the barbecue pits and stumbled around trying to figure out what to do. My throat felt parched, my mind on fire.

My vision was blurring. It was as though I was seeing the world out of somebody else's eyes. Somebody who saw the world in a polar opposite way to mine. Somebody who was hungry. Somebody who was starving for the taste of living human flesh in their salivating mouth.

I had no choice. I knew what had to be done. I had to get rid of that somebody.

Out of the corner of my eye, I caught sight of an iron poker canting against one of the sooty concrete barbecue pits. I snagged the poker and with it stirred the dying embers that lay smoldering in a grey heap in the base of the pit. I heated up the poker's iron shaft, waiting with bated breath for its black tip to turn red-hot, praying for it to happen before I lost my resolve.

You see, if I gouged my eyes out—or whoever's eyes they were—with the burning poker, I would not be able to find and butcher Sarah.

# Identity Crisis

When Brendan Malone got the severed finger in a box on his doorstep, he knew the sender meant business.

But what was the point? wondered Brendan, a UCLA liberal arts student, staring at the finger that lay in a corrugated cardboard box on his family's living-room coffee table next to a book by Aleister Crowley. The baldheaded Crowley's face in a black-and-white photo on the back of the book's jacket glowered up at him as Brendan regarded the bloodless digit that looked like it was fashioned out of wax. His family hadn't even received a ransom note. What was the point of mutilating his sister Sylvia? He clutched his head between his hands in confusion and anguish.

"Why are they doing this?" he said.

"To prove they have her," said Lydia, his mother, equally perturbed, limpid blue eyes welling with tears.

Dressed in a shift, she had straight blonde hair that reached several inches down her back.

"We never doubted they had her," said Brendan. "But who are they? Why do they feel they have to prove they have her?"

"Because they're idiots."

"They're animals," said Malone's father, Michael, an architect, angrily. "That's why they mutilated her. That's what animals do. Animals don't think."

"Either that or they're sadistic brutes," said Sophie, who, unlike her mother, wore her blonde hair short. It didn't even reach down her neck. "Maybe they did it for the fun of it."

Brendan, Michael, Lydia, and Sophie, Sylvia's twin sister, were gathered around the round walnut coffee table in the living room in Michael Malone's modest Tudor-style house in Glendale. Like Sylvia, Brendan and Sophie were in their twenties, while Michael and Lydia were middle-aged. Glendale was a peaceful, horsy neighborhood. Frequently when the Malones peered out their windows they would see neighbors riding on horseback along the shoulders of the woodsy, sweeping roads, the horses' hooves clop-clopping on the asphalt amongst scattered eucalyptus leaves.

Startling everyone the family cat, Nestor, who had brindled fur, a black tail, and prominent whiskers, bounded onto the coffee table and strutted around the box holding his tail erect.

"Get down from there, Nestor," said Brendan and tried to latch onto the cat.

Too deft for Brendan, Nestor dodged his hands, leapt off the table, and scurried across the carpet, tail held high.

"Maybe that's not her finger," said Sophie, staring at the finger in horror, ignoring Nestor's antics. "How do we know it isn't somebody else's?"

"It's hers," said Lydia, voice tremulous. "I recognize the scar below the fingernail. She cut herself there while crashing her tricycle when she was five years old. She was lucky she didn't lose part of her finger."

Indeed, a jagged white crescent of a scar curved underneath the width of the fingernail a few millimeters below the cuticle.

"I can't stand looking at it," said Sophie and buried her face in her hands.

"If they don't give us a ransom note, how are we supposed to know what they want?" said Brendan.

"How do we know she isn't already dead?" said Michael, scowling.

"They must know if they kill her they won't get any money out of us."

50

"We still don't have proof she's alive. That finger only proves they have her. She might be dead."

"Why do you always have to assume the worst, Michael?" said Lydia.

"Let's not kid ourselves. Sylvia's prospects aren't good."

"That doesn't mean we should give up."

"Who's giving up? I don't want us to get our hopes up too high just to have them dashed."

"I knew we should have called the police as soon as we got that box," said Sophie.

"The kidnapers said they would kill Sylvia if we did," said Michael.

"It's not too late to call the cops."

Rattled, Michael smoothed his recently trimmed hair back, eyes unfocused behind his horn-rimmed spectacles. "I don't know if we should risk it."

"The question is, why did they kidnap her?" said Brendan. "If we can figure that out, maybe we can figure out what to do."

"I'm calling the police," said Sophie, reaching for the phone on the coffee table.

"No, don't," said Michael. "Hold your horses. Let's think this over. What if the kidnapers have somebody watching our house? If they see the cops here, we're cooked."

Sophie stopped reaching for the phone. "We need to do something. What if they cut off another of Sylvia's fingers?"

"But what's the point?" said Brendan, kicking the sofa near him in an access of pent-up rage. "Why are they mutilating her?"

"I told you," said Michael. "They're animals. Maybe this is some kind of bestial game to them."

Brendan shook his head no. "I don't think so. They must want something from us. But what?"

"Probably money," said Lydia. "What else would they want?"

"Then why us?" said Sophie. "We're not exactly the 1 percent. How much do they think they can squeeze us for?"

"And why don't they tell us how much?" said Brendan. "How are we supposed to know the amount?"

Bryan Cassiday

Grimacing, Lydia clenched her eyes shut. "I don't know."

"It's the waiting that's driving me nuts," said Sophie. "What are they going to do next? What do we do in the meantime?"

As if on cue, the phone rang.

Nerves frayed, everybody in the room started.

"We don't know that's them," said Michael, gazing at the shrilling phone.

"I hope it is," said Lydia. "I want to get this over with."

Brendan strode to the phone and reached for it.

"Wait," said Michael. "Maybe it's better if we don't answer it."

"How do you figure?" said Brendan, balking.

"If we play hard to get, it'll send them the message we can't be pushed around."

"Or maybe they'll kill Sylvia," said Lydia.

The phone rang again, sounding insistent, not to be denied.

"We need to know what they want before we can hatch a plan," said Brendan and snagged the handset.

"No," said Michael, gesturing to Brendan, but it was too late.

Disregarding Michael, Brendan doggedly lifted the handset to his ear. "Hello."

"Did you get the package we left at your door?" said an electronically altered voice.

"We got it," said Brendan, trying to sound firm, like he wouldn't allow himself to be strong-armed.

Despite his youth, he felt this was the proper way to handle the situation, especially after what his father had just said about being pushed around.

"Then you know we're serious," said the voice.

"What the hell do you want?"

"We want Sophie."

"Are you nuts?" Brendan exploded, tightening his grip on the handset pressed to his reddening ear. "You got Sylvia, and now you want Sophie, too?"

The rest of Brendan's family stiffened at his outburst and eyed him anxiously.

52

"You misunderstand," deadpanned the voice.

"Then tell me," said Brendan.

"We want to make a trade. Sylvia for Sophie."

"What?" said Brendan, bewildered.

"You heard me."

"And what if we don't agree?"

"Sylvia dies. You got an hour to think it over," said the voice and hung up.

"What was that all about?" said Michael, expression intense, watching Brendan replace the receiver in its cradle.

"They told me what they want."

"Well?"

"They want Sophie in exchange for Sylvia."

Michael bugged out his eyes behind his glasses. "What kind of sense does that make?"

"I'm repeating what they said is all."

Speechless, Sophie gawked at Brendan.

Lydia walked over to Sophie and draped her arm around Sophie's shoulders. "Don't worry, dear. We're not giving you to anyone."

"They said they'd kill Sylvia if we don't agree," said Brendan under his breath.

"I told you," said Michael. "We're dealing with psychos. They're certifiable."

"Now do we call the cops?" said Sophie, voice cracking.

"We need to think this out," said Michael, pacing around the room in his khaki trousers like a man possessed.

"I'm tired of all this thinking and shilly-shallying," said Brendan. "It's getting us nowhere. Let's *do* something. Let's get guns and go after these bastards."

"Don't go off half-cocked. You don't want to get us all killed, do you? We need to choose the best response before we go cowboy."

"Shooting the bastards *is* the best response."

"And what if we end up shooting Sylvia while we're shooting them? Did you ever think of that?"

53

"It's better than sitting here doing nothing," said Brendan in frustration.

"I don't get it. What's the difference between having Sylvia for a hostage or having Sophie?"

"Makes no sense. Do they think we'll pay more for Sophie?"

"Maybe they don't want money," said Sophie.

"Then what the hell *do* they want?"

"Why me? Why do they want me instead of Sylvia? We're identical twins. There's not a whole lot of difference between us."

"I've been thinking about that," said Michael, pulling up. "Maybe the fact you're twins had something to do with their sending Sylvia's finger to us."

"They sent her finger to us to prove they had her and she was alive," said Brendan.

"It doesn't prove she's alive, unfortunately."

"I hope you're wrong about that," said Lydia.

"Well, it proves they have her," said Brendan.

"Or *had* her," said Sophie.

"But maybe there's more to it than that," said Michael. "The fingerprint ID'd Sylvia. It proved Sylvia wasn't Sophie."

"I thought Sylvia and I have identical fingerprints because we're twins."

"That's not true," said Lydia. "I asked your doctor that once. He said fingerprints are formed when you're an embryo. The different pressures from amniotic fluid and other things in the womb form the ridges in your prints. Even though you have the same DNA as Sylvia, you don't have the same fingerprints. Everybody's fingerprints are unique."

"Then they must've wanted me all along, and they messed up when they kidnaped Sylvia," said Sophie.

"That's what it looks like," said Michael.

Sophie couldn't get her head around it. "Why do they think I'm more valuable to you than she is?"

"I have no idea."

"And what do they want in exchange for Sophie, if they get her?" Michael asked Brendan.

"They didn't say."

Brendan's smartphone pinged inside his trouser pocket, signifying the arrival of an e-mail. He scooped out his phone and checked the incoming e-mail. There was a picture of an hourglass in the e-mail along with the words *Your time is running out.* Brendan didn't recognize the sender's address. He figured the e-mail had to be from the kidnapers.

"What's up?" said Michael.

"They're harassing us with e-mails," said Brendan.

"Why do they hate us so much?" said Lydia.

"This isn't about hate," said Michael.

"Are you sure?" said Brendan. "Maybe it's about revenge."

Michael shook his head. "I can't imagine why anyone would hate us that much. They must want something."

"How could they think Sylvia was me?" said Sophie. "Why didn't they just ask her who she was when they took her?"

"Why should they?" said Brendan. "She looks just like you. It doesn't help that both of you wear your hair the same. They figured it was you. Maybe they don't know she has a twin."

"Let's sort this out," said Michael.

"Let's stop sorting and start doing," said Brendan in annoyance. "All this thinking is getting us nowhere."

"When Sylvia told them she wasn't Sophie, they probably didn't believe her," Michael went on. "Then they took her fingerprint, found out she was telling the truth, cut off her finger, and sent it to us."

"How could they have equipment to check fingerprints unless they work for the government?"

"You think the government's in on this?" said Sophie.

Michael waved her off. "Maybe it wasn't her fingerprints but the scar on her finger that gave Sylvia away."

"That still doesn't explain why they want me," said Sophie.

"We're going around in circles," Lydia told Michael in frustration. "We don't know why these idiot lunatics want Sophie."

"Why do you call them lunatics?" said Brendan.

"Because they're not demanding a ransom. If they don't have any motive, they must be crazy."

"Maybe they do have a motive. We just don't know what it is yet."

Michael paced around the room, absorbed in thought. "Let's say we agree to the trade."

"What?" said Sophie, not believing her ears.

"We'll say we agree just to stall for time, Sophie. You don't want them to go on mutilating Sylvia, do you?"

"No."

"Then what?" said Brendan.

"I don't know yet," said Michael.

Brendan threw up his hands. "Talk, talk, talk. All we do is talk."

"This whole thing seems way too complicated," said Lydia, frowning. "They kidnap the wrong girl. Then they want to make a switch for Sophie. What happens after they get Sophie?"

"Good question," said Michael.

"Are we going to have to go through this whole charade again when they want to swap me for money?" said Sophie, baffled and exasperated.

"They're not laying their hands on you, Sophie," said Lydia.

"Why go through all this rigmarole?" said Brendan. "Why don't they just tell us how much they want for Sylvia? Why even bother switching Sophie for Sylvia?"

"My head's aching just thinking about it."

"The only thing I can come up with is, they don't want a ransom for Sophie once they get her," said Michael.

"So they plan on keeping me?" said Sophie in a fit of pique.

Brendan's smartphone pinged. He fished it out of his pocket and consulted the screen. He read the new e-mail from the kidnapers.

"What do they want?" asked Michael, watching Brendan.

"They want us to leave Sophie in room 20 at the Motel 6 in Arcadia," answered Brendan, reading the e-mail. "The room will be empty. She's to go there alone. If they see cops, they'll kill

Sylvia. The kidnapers will take Sophie and leave Sylvia in the room in her place."

"I can't believe this is happening to me," said Sophie, flicking her thumbnails against her forefingers. "Nothing like this ever happens to me."

"We won't let them get you, Sophie," said Lydia, holding Sophie.

"I'll take a gun and meet the bastards in the motel room," said Brendan.

"What if they've got somebody watching the room?" said Michael. "If they see you go in there, they might kill Sylvia in retaliation."

"We've got to do something," said Brendan and pounded down the air with his fist.

"I could take a gun with me," said Sophie.

"But we don't know how many kidnapers there are," said Michael. "You won't be able to deal with a bunch of them by yourself. There could be dozens of them, for all we know."

"Do you really think there could be that many?" said Sophie, voice quavering.

"I don't know what we're dealing with. There's no way of knowing how many of them there are."

"There must be something we can do," said Brendan.

"If we can figure out their motive, maybe we can get a handle on this," said Michael.

Brendan glanced at his wristwatch. "We don't have time. We have to start for the Motel 6 in a few minutes."

"Sophie's not going," said Lydia. "You're crazy if you think I'll let her go to that room."

"Let me take her place," said Brendan.

"They'll see you're not Sophie right off the bat, if they're watching the motel. And we know they must be."

"I'll dress like a girl."

"Don't be ridiculous. They'll see your face."

"I'll wear a hoodie and big sunglasses."

"Then what?" said Michael.

Bryan Cassiday

"I'll take a gun with me. That's the only way to deal with these animals."

Michael thought about it, face screwed up. "It might work," he said, gnashing his teeth. "You're gonna be in a lot of danger if you do this, Brendan."

"I'm sick of this," said Sophie. "Let's call the police and let them handle it. What's to stop the kidnapers from killing both Brendan and Sylvia?"

"Me," said Brendan.

Michael blew out his cheeks. "We're dealing with too many unknowns and variables."

Brendan sighed. "No plan is perfect. We have to take our chances. Unless you have a better idea."

Michael left the living room and disappeared into his study.

"What did I say?" said Brendan, watching him go.

Moments later Michael returned, a wooden box not much larger than a cigar box in his hand. He placed the box on the coffee table and opened the lid. Inside was a Glock 17 semiautomatic.

"Do you know how to shoot this?" said Michael.

"Yeah," said Brendan. He had seen it done a million times in movies.

"You better wear a dress or a skirt if you want them to think you're a woman."

"Then you better shave your legs," said Sophie, suppressing a giggle. "They see hairy legs on you, the jig is up."

As much as he hated to do it, Brendan went to the bathroom, pulled off his jeans, got out his electric razor from under the sink, and shaved his legs. It was hard enough being a man. Now he had to learn how to be a woman. Somebody knocked on the bathroom door. He cracked it. Lydia handed him a skirt through the opening.

"This is one of my old skirts," she said. "I hope it fits. And you need this, too," she added, handing him a bra.

Brendan accepted the clothing and closed the door. He put on the skirt and bra. They seemed to fit, if tightly. He looked at

58

himself in the mirror. He felt like an idiot. He didn't know how long he could walk around in this ridiculous getup. Something wasn't right, he noticed. His hair.

As if reading his mind Lydia knocked on the door again and produced a blonde wig. "Here's one of Sophie's wigs."

He donned it. He didn't look as grotesque now, but he wasn't in any sense of the word pleasant to look at. He looked even worse than a spavined hooker. He would have to use a hoodie to cover most of his face when he appeared in public.

As he entered the living room he heard a wolf whistle from Sophie. He gave her the finger.

"You need lipstick," she said, dug some from her purse, and handed it to him.

Sneering, he grabbed it and returned to the bathroom. Peering into the mirror over the sink he daubed the vermilion lipstick onto his lips. He groaned at the sight. He was sickening to look at.

He returned to the living room, compressing his lips to smooth the lipstick over them.

"Are you sure you want to go through with this?" said Michael.

"I'm waiting to hear a better idea."

"They're never gonna believe you're me," said Sophie. "You're too tall." She paused. "And too pretty." She laughed.

"In a pig's eye. As for being tall, I'll hunch over when I have your hoodie on."

"I'll give you my pink one."

"I can't wait to get this over with."

"Let's have a talk first," said Michael.

"Here we go again with the talking," said Brendan. "We don't have time for it, Dad."

"This won't take long."

Michael nodded for Brendan to follow him into Michael's drafting study where he designed buildings.

Grudgingly, Brendan followed.

"If you wore high heels, you might look more feminine," said Sophie, watching him walk away.

"I'd break my neck," Brendan said over his shoulder. "I'm gonna need to be able to run. Things could get hairy."

He entered the drafting room after Michael. They stood near a desk that had a drafting board with a building's blueprint unrolled on the board. On the blueprint lay a T square, a pair of compasses, a ruler, a pencil, and a calculator. A shiny articulated metal lamp rose from the desk, the unlit lightbulb aimed down at the blueprint.

"I just want to tell you one thing," said Michael, closing the door behind them. "Being a man is about not being scared. Being fearless is the one thing that makes you a man."

Brendan rolled his eyes. He couldn't help it. It wasn't like this was the first time he was hearing one of Michael's manhood speeches.

"I've been one for a while," said Brendan, "in case you haven't noticed."

"I also wanted to tell you I'm going with you."

"I can handle this alone."

"You need backup, just in case things go sideways. I can cover you."

Michael strode to a closet and withdrew another Glock from the top shelf. "If there's more than one kidnaper, you're gonna have problems. This isn't a cakewalk."

Brendan shrugged. He was in no mood to argue. "OK. Suit yourself."

Ten minutes later, armed with the Glock, Brendan was driving the family Prius to the Motel 6 in Arcadia, Michael in the seat beside him.

They parked on the side of the street opposite the motel.

Michael remained in the car, slumped down in his seat, peering over the dashboard, trying to be inconspicuous scoping out the Motel 6 and the street in front of it for signs of an ambush, as Brendan strode toward room 20 in white jogging shoes. Michael wished Brendan would shorten his strides to look more feminine. The way Brendan was walking now made him look like a truck driver in drag.

60

Pink hoodie raised to mask his face, Brendan crossed the parking lot to room 20. Wary at first, he stood in front of the door, straining to hear movement in the room. He didn't hear anything. He couldn't see the interior, as the drapes were drawn shut. Glancing over his shoulder toward Michael, he indicated he was about to enter.

He tried the doorknob. It turned in his hand. Circumspectly, he cracked the door. He edged inside, one hand on the Glock in his purse.

His gaze instantly lit on a large red pentagram drawn crudely with red paint on the carpet. Puzzled, he stared at it. He hoped it was drawn with paint and not with blood. He didn't want to go there. He saw no sign of Sylvia, or anyone else for that matter.

Pentagram. Had Satanists kidnaped her? he wondered. Worshipers of black magic? Witches? Who was he dealing with?

He stole across the carpet toward the bathroom. For all he knew somebody was hiding inside it. He couldn't discern all of it from his vantage point as the door hung half open, obscuring his view. Reaching the door he pushed it open, eyes flitting about the bathroom casting around for a kidnaper or Sylvia.

All he saw was a message scrawled in red lipstick on the medicine-cabinet mirror over the sink. He read the message. It gave him a start as the tap leaked into the sink. The words chilled his blood.

*We're at your home.*

*Jesus Christ!* he thought. It was a trick! The whole thing was a setup. A ruse to lure him and his father here, while the kidnapers descended on his undefended house and snatched Sophie from under the noses of the unarmed pair of Lydia and Sylvia.

Paying no attention to the pentagram on the carpet, he slewed around and tore out of the room for all he was worth. Waving his arms at Michael, knees churning, he bucketed across the parking lot to the Prius, face flushed.

Eyes bulging, Michael said, "What happened? Did they kill Sylvia?"

"It's a setup," said Brendan, climbing into the driver's seat, gasping. "They're at our home."

"Sons of bitches," snarled Michael.

Brendan pulled away from the curb, tires shrieking in protest, and rocketed down the street.

"We'll never make it in time," he said, face beading with sweat as he hung a right onto the 210 westbound ramp.

"Step on it," said Michael.

"I don't want to get busted," said Brendan, glancing at the rearview mirror for cops.

"We can get there in fifteen minutes with any kind of luck."

"That's pushing it."

"I'm beginning to think we should've let the cops in on this," clucked Michael, furrowing his brow.

"The kidnapers said they'd kill Sylvia. We had no choice."

"How did they know we wouldn't be at our house?"

"They must have somebody watching it," said Brendan, white knuckles on the wheel as the Prius shot down the freeway. "They saw us drive away from the house."

"But you're in disguise. They're supposed to think you're Sophie."

Brendan shrugged tensely. "I guess they didn't fall for it."

"Who are we dealing with?"

"It may be some kind of black magic cult."

Michael searched Brendan's face. "Why do you say that?"

"They drew a pentagram on the carpet in the motel room."

Michael clutched his temple. "Satanists? Human sacrifices and all that whack-job Black Mass babble? That's the last thing I want to hear."

"Was Sophie involved in that bullshit?"

Michael shook his head. "Not that I know of. I have no idea how they got onto her. Watch the road," he said, bracing his arm against the dashboard with a grimace.

Brendan all but rear-ended the four-by-four in front of him as it slowed down. Cursing, he crushed the Prius's brake pedal.

"Why is the traffic slowing down?" he said.

"Maybe there was an accident."

"We don't have time," said Brendan, drumming a tattoo on the steering wheel. He swung off onto the next exit, eyes wild. "We'll take surface streets."

"Let's take it easy. We can make it."

Just shy of fifteen minutes later they were at the house.

"How are we gonna handle this?" said Brendan, pulling over to a curb, not sure if he should turn into their empty driveway, which would tip off the kidnapers to his presence.

"They may've left already," said Michael, scrutinizing the house for any sign of activity inside. "The driveway's empty."

"Maybe they parked on the side of the street," said Brendan, noticing cars parked nearby.

"We can't wait around. We have to go in."

Michael threw open his door, as did Brendan. They piled out of the car and hustled across the street into the driveway.

They burst up the cement stairs two steps at a time past the riotous fuchsia bougainvillea that climbed one side of the stairway. They stopped at the front door. Brendan opened it.

They walked in, not knowing what to expect.

Eyes alert, Brendan whipped his Glock out of his purse.

They didn't see anybody in the living room.

"Are we too late?" said Brendan, hopes sinking.

Michael withdrew his automatic from his waistband with one hand, held his finger to his lips with his other to silence Brendan, and stole across the living room, Brendan in tow.

Brendan pricked up his ears at the sound of what sounded like chanting emanating from somewhere in the house.

When Michael and Brendan turned the corner, a heart-freezing sight greeted them.

In Michael's bedroom, three chanting figures in scarlet cowls, their heads hidden from view, were holding a gagged, struggling Sophie pinned to the carpet, while a fourth figure stood hovering over them with a wicked-looking scimitar gripped at its handle with two hands, the tip aiming down at Sophie's chest. Beneath them on the rug was painted a pentagram, which Brendan

63

recognized as being similar to the one in the Motel 6 room. Sitting on the bed Nestor riveted his green eyes on the proceedings.

"Nutbags!" screamed Michael in disbelief, training his Glock on the figure with the scimitar. "Drop the knife!"

Somebody fell to rapping urgently on the inside of the locked bedroom-closet door, screaming, "Let me out!"

It was Sylvia.

The hunched figures clasping Sophie continued chanting, ignoring Michael's words and Sylvia's yelling.

"She is the chosen one," the figure with the scimitar chanted in a low female voice a shade above a whisper.

"I'll kill you! I swear it!" cried Michael.

"Don't, Dad!" burst Brendan, believing he recognized the dagger holder's voice.

"The chosen one must be sacrificed this day this hour this minute," said the figure with the scimitar. "The firstborn must be sacrificed to Satan. It is Satan's will."

The hunkered-down figures pinning Sophie continued chanting ominously. It sounded like Latin to Brendan, but it could just as well have been gibberish.

"I'm warning you," said Michael, face contorted. "I *will* shoot you if you don't drop that knife."

The figure holding the scimitar turned slowly toward Michael. As Brendan had suspected with dread, it was Lydia's face framed in the scarlet cowl's folds.

In a transport of fear and rage, Michael hadn't recognized her voice as it chanted. Now that he saw her face he felt his arm going limp as he clutched the Glock. He blinked several times as if the act of blinking might banish the nightmare he was beholding.

"For Christ's sake, Lydia," he managed to say at last, "what are you doing?"

Lydia gazed back at him with distant eyes, like they weren't seeing him. "The firstborn must be sacrificed to prove my faith in Satan. It is Satan's will. Sophie was born seconds before Sylvia and belongs to Satan. Sophie is the chosen one. So mote it be."

"Are you on drugs? Think about what you're doing! You're killing our child!"

Lydia roused from her trance for a moment. "How do you think you got your job? Do you really think being good at your profession is all there is to it?"

"What are you rambling about?"

"You have to be willing to sacrifice everything to be successful—even your own child."

"Put the knife down and try to make sense."

Lydia's eyes resumed their thousand-yard stare. Her voice became monotonic. "You must leave us alone. You weren't supposed to be back by now."

With that she turned toward the writhing Sophie below her and prepared to plunge the scimitar through Sophie's chest.

Face streaming with sweat, adrenaline coursing through his system, Michael clenched his teeth and shot Lydia through the chest.

At the crack of the gunshot, the three other robed figures released Sophie and fled out of the room with Nestor, who bolted off the bed, as the bleeding Lydia slumped to her knees, releasing her hold on the scimitar, whose haft thudded against Sophie's shoulder as it fell. Wincing, Sophie rolled away from Lydia in terror.

"I don't understand," was all Michael could say.

# The Lucifer Wasp

It wasn't until the second day after the occurrence that Roderick Simmons knew the full extent of his malady.

Simmons was a fifty-one-year-old entomologist. He became an entomologist late in life. It wasn't until his wife Esmeralda died from a wasp's sting that he showed any interest in bees, in caterpillar wasps in particular. The tragedy of her death precipitated a sea change in his personality.

Before Esmeralda's death Simmons had been an easygoing, approachable teacher of algebra at a Los Angeles high school and had shown not the slightest interest in bees. Esmeralda's death changed all that.

Ten years ago to the day, Esmeralda had died from a caterpillar wasp's sting because she was allergic to bee venom. The sting triggered an anaphylactic reaction in her as she had been hiking in the Santa Monica Mountains. She had been hiking alone and had neglected to take her cell phone with her.

When paramedics, alerted by other hikers, finally did find her, they determined from her symptoms what had happened to her. She had an itchy rash on her face, and her eyes and her throat were swollen. From her symptoms they could infer that she had been allergic to bee venom and that some sort of bee had stung her. Once the bee had stung her, they conjectured, her blood pressure had dropped and she had lapsed into unconsciousness within thirty minutes after the bee attack. She died soon after.

They located the bee that had stung her lying dead beside her throat. Esmeralda had managed to swat the creature with her hand and kill it as it had stung her throat. It turned out it was a caterpillar wasp that had killed her.

Overcome by the loss of his wife, Simmons became somewhat of a gloomy hermit, quit his job, and devoted the rest of his life to the study of entomology, in particular the study of wasps, in order to develop a serum that would cure people of their allergy to bee venom. He discovered that immunotherapy with Hymenoptera venoms did not work for everyone. He needed to find a serum that *did* work for everyone. He didn't want anybody to end up like Esmeralda had in the prime of her life.

Clad in a doctor's white smock, he was studying a caterpillar wasp under an electron microscope in his home lab when his teenage daughter Helena walked in. He looked up at her with his doleful brown eyes that seemed too wise for his years, as if pain had conferred wisdom on him. If not for the striking expressiveness of his eyes, his Roman nose would have dominated his long face that was creased with a multitude of wrinkles.

"You need to take time off and relax," said Helena. "You can't keep working 24/7. It's not good for you."

He eyed her cherubic rosy face that she had inherited from her mother. Helena's sandy hair fell in wavy hanks to her shoulder. She was wearing stonewashed jeans and a sleeveless Guns n' Roses silkscreened apricot blouse. Her pale green eyes were studying him with concern.

"I can't think of anything else but my work as long as I know another person could wind up like your mother because of an allergy to bee stings," said Simmons.

"That's no excuse for not doing anything but work all the time."

A spring breeze blew in from the open window, stirring the white lace curtains. It was a beautiful sunny day outside, the air cleaned by the onshore wind. He would like to go sit in their peacock chair outside in their garden and relax in the sunlight, smelling the roses, he realized. But he could not relax.

He had to develop an immunotherapy that protected everybody from death by bee sting. Now that Esmeralda was dead, his job was all that mattered to him—except for Helena.

"You need to go to school," he chided Helena gently.

"Hello. I just got back from school. It's like the afternoon outside. Maybe you should look out the window once in a while. You got a bad case of tunnel vision."

He had not realized it was that late. His all-consuming work devoured his attention to the exclusion of anything else. "Then you need to do your homework."

"I don't work 24/7 like you. I'll do it later." She paused, twitching her button nose, which she had inherited from her mother, in an idiosyncratic way she had when she discovered something she thought nobody else knew. "I know what your problem is."

"Which is?"

"You need to start dating again."

Recalling Esmeralda he turned away from Helena. "I don't have the time."

"It's not natural to work constantly."

"It's what I do."

"You're turning into a different person."

"I have different priorities nowadays. That's all."

Helena shook her head. "No, it's more than that."

"You're overreacting."

"Whatever."

Simmons wished she would stop using that word. She must use *whatever* over fifty times a day now that she was a teen.

Helena glanced at the dead wasp under Simmons's microscope and pulled a face. "I hate hornets and yellow jackets. I'd get sick if I had to look at those things all day long. Yuk."

"I want to make sure you never die from their sting."

"You made me take immunotherapy for five years after Mom died. How can I possibly die from a bee sting?"

"That's the problem. There's no immunotherapy that's a hundred percent effective. I'm working on one that will be."

"You worry too much."

Maybe she was right, he decided. But he had to keep working. It's what kept him going. If not for his work, all he had was emptiness in his life, with Esmeralda gone. Nobody could take Esmeralda's place, not even, sad to say, Helena, though he doted on the child. It simply wasn't the same thing. He didn't want to think about it.

"Out of the mouths of babes," he said.

"You keep treating me like a child," she said in a fit of pique. "I'm not a child anymore."

"You're not a child, but you're still young."

"I'm just trying to help you."

"I know that," he said, smiling at her.

"It's gonna mess you up if you keep looking at ugly hornets all day long. You're gonna start to look like a hornet."

"It's technically not a hornet. It's a caterpillar wasp." He clapped his eyes on the wasp under his microscope. "It lays its eggs inside a caterpillar and enslaves it to its will. When the baby wasps are born, they burrow their way out of the caterpillar to freedom, eating the caterpillar alive."

"Yuk! Not only is it ugly, it's evil. That's horrid."

"Caterpillar wasps are parasites and feed off their hosts."

Helena covered her ears. "I don't want to listen to this."

"This is the same type of wasp that killed your mother."

"Give it a rest. You're becoming obsessed. Do you ever look at yourself in the mirror?"

Simmons peered through the microscope at the female wasp's ovipositor, which the creature used to lay eggs and sting its victims. It was a female that had stung Esmeralda. Only the female wasp could sting.

Simmons started as he heard a knocking at the bungalow's front door.

"I'll get it," said Helena and flounced out of the laboratory.

Bryan Cassiday

A few minutes later, Harvey Congreve entered the room. He was a bearded middle-aged math teacher who worked at the high school where Simmons used to work. Congreve walked with a limp on account of a foot injury that he had suffered during a car accident he was involved in as a teenager. He wore thick-framed black glasses that sat awkwardly on his bulbous nose.

"Hello, Harve," said Simmons, tearing himself away from his studies.

"Long time, no see, Roderick."

Helena had not returned with Congreve, Simmons could see.

Simmons sighed. "I don't get out much anymore."

"It's plain to see you should."

"What do you mean?"

"Can I be frank?"

Simmons shrugged noncommittally.

Congreve took Simmons's gesture for an affirmative and gazed at him. "You look like hell."

"Flattery will get you nowhere."

"I'm not joking, Roderick. Your hair's all scroungy. Your complexion's pale. You look flat-out sick." Congreve paused. "You need to get out more and socialize."

"I have too much work to do."

"There's a time to work and a time to play."

"Is that why you came to see me? To cheer me up?"

What Congreve and Helena were both saying to him was true enough, of course, decided Simmons. Simmons knew his personal life was a train wreck. He would be the first to admit it. He had never recovered from his loss of Esmeralda.

"Have you ever thought of marrying again?" said Congreve.

"Not you too." Not only was his daughter on him about that but so was Congreve, decided Simmons.

"What?"

"Nothing. I don't want to go through that again."

"Through what again?"

"Another wife's death."

70

Congreve shook his head vehemently. "Just because Esmeralda died prematurely doesn't mean another wife would. That's ridiculous."

"I'm married to my work."

"That's no answer."

Simmons resumed peering through his microscope. "I have to find the vaccination."

"What vaccination? What are you working on anyway?"

"I'm trying to find a vaccination against the venom in bee stings. A vaccination that will prevent anyone who is allergic to bee venom from dying."

Congreve cleared his throat. "They already have immunotherapy."

"It's not a hundred percent effective."

Congreve scratched his ear that curved out of his head like a large seashell. "How do you plan on doing this?"

"By developing a new species of wasp whose venom counteracts wasp venom when inoculated into a human."

"Good luck with that," said Congreve wearily. "Talk about impossible goals."

"Nothing is impossible if a man sets his mind to it."

"But you shouldn't have to sacrifice your life for it. And that's what you're doing, Roderick. Can't you see? You have no life. Frankly, I don't know how you keep sane," said Congreve, scoping out the lab that was cluttered with specimens of assorted types of wasps and bees, both living and dead.

The living ones were flying around in large rectangular glass aquarium-type structures, which muted the insects' buzzing, Congreve noticed.

"What makes you think I'm sane?" said Simmons with a half smile on his thin lips.

"This is nothing to joke about," said Congreve, slewing around on his heel and staring at Simmons again. "I'm worried about you."

"I'm just doing my job—like anybody else. What's to worry about? We all have our jobs, and that's how we spend our lives—

doing them. How does that make me any different from anybody else?"

"Because your health is suffering, man. Are you blind?"

"The results of my research will save the lives of millions of people. How can conducting such research be detrimental to my health?"

"Because you're obsessed with it. Absolutely nothing else matters to you."

Grimacing, Simmons massaged his furrowed brow. "It's hard for me to accomplish any work when I'm constantly interrupted. First Helena. Now you."

"We're both concerned about you—and rightly so."

"I'm fine. There's nothing to worry about."

Congreve paced around the lab in thought, dragging his lame foot behind him. "Are *you* allergic to bee venom?"

"No."

Congreve spun around awkwardly and confronted Simmons. "Then why are you so obsessed with immunotherapy?"

"It's not about me."

"I understand about Esmeralda—"

"Helena is allergic to bee venom," cut in Simmons.

"That still doesn't mean you have to sacrifice your life to find some mythical vaccination for this allergy."

"There's nothing mythical about it. I'm on the right track. I know it."

"I have a psychiatrist friend . . ."

"Good for you."

Disappointed with Simmons's response, Congreve hitched over to a glass bee container that incarcerated a singular-looking Day-Glo orange and black striped wasp. Congreve scowled at the wasp.

"A cuddly-looking thing, this one," he said. "I don't believe I've ever seen one like this."

Simmons turned away from his work to find out what Congreve was looking at. "You haven't."

"How can you be so sure?"

"That's the new species I created from crossbreeding a caterpillar wasp with a yellow jacket."

"You're joking."

"I'm dead serious."

"It's impossible."

"Nothing's impossible, if you set your mind to it—like I told you before."

Wanting to get a closer look at the insect, squinting, Congreve nudged the translucent perforated plastic lid that covered the wasp's prison so he could peer inside. The wasp was crawling along the plate-glass container's side, picking up its skinny black feet every so often and licking them.

"This is fantastic," said Congreve, jaw dropping with awe.

"Don't get too close to it."

"What do you call it?"

"A *Vespa Lucifer* or just plain Lucifer wasp."

"Why, may I ask?"

"Because of the bright orange of its thorax."

"I noticed that right of way, of course."

"It looks like it's on fire. Like a falling star, like Lucifer, the fallen angel."

Congreve pulled his head away from the container and slid the plastic lid back into place. "You need to write a paper about this and announce your discovery to the world."

"Not till I find a vaccination for bee venom that works for everyone."

Congreve grunted in disapproval of Simmons's decision and limped toward the lab's door. "You need to let the scientific community know about your creation ASAP."

"I'll let them know when I'm good and ready to let them know."

Congreve grunted again. "Suit yourself. But I don't agree with your decision. It's important that there are no secrets in science. As soon as an important discovery is made, it should be shared with the world. Science belongs to the entire world, not just to one person. You can't hog science to yourself. It flies in the face of all that's moral."

"I don't want any media attention now. It would interfere with my studies. As soon as other scientists and the media get wind of this, they'll be all over me like—like a swarm of bees, so to speak, and I'll never get anything done."

"There are no secrets in science," said Congreve, the doorknob in his hand. "Science is for the benefit of the entire human race."

"I'm getting closer every day to my goal. It's within my grasp. I know it," said Simmons, eyes becoming fiery with the intensity of his ambition. "Then I'll let the world know."

"I have to go now. Take care of yourself. Nothing's worth working yourself to death for. When you're dead, nothing matters."

Congreve departed and closed the door behind him.

Simmons knew that he was on the verge of concocting a serum that would be 100 percent effective against bee allergies. He could feel it in his bones.

He didn't notice that the orange and black Lucifer wasp was making good its escape from its enclosure by squeezing through the crack left between the glass box and the lid that Congreve had improperly closed.

Simmons worked for two hours straight without a break, then, feeling drowsy, succumbing to his rigorous work schedule, laid his head on the tabletop. No sooner had his head touched the table's surface than he fell asleep.

#

He awoke screaming.

He had no idea how long he had been sleeping. All he knew was his eyelid was burning up. He clutched it and was shocked to find that it was swollen. He bolted to his feet and pelted into the small bathroom that communicated with the lab.

Peering into the medicine cabinet's mirror over the sink, he froze in bewilderment at the sight of his right eyelid. A fiery red, it had swollen to at least three times its original size and had shut his eye. He winced for the excruciating pain and wondered what had happened to him and how to treat his malady.

He leaned closer to the mirror to inspect his eyelid. He fancied he could make out a tiny red dot in the middle of the swelling. It looked like something had stung him, he decided.

He heard a buzzing emanating from the lab. He ducked back into the lab and cast around the room for the source of the sound, unable to see very well thanks to being blinded in one eye. Despite his reduced vision, he was able to make out a wasp flying about the room.

Approaching the wasp warily lest he be stung again, Simmons realized it was the orange and black Lucifer wasp he had created. Somehow it had escaped its confinement. He glanced at its container. Indeed, it was now empty.

The wasp must have stung him while he was sleeping, Simmons decided. But how had it escaped? Afraid of being stung again, he kept his distance from the wasp, which continued soaring about the room, bouncing off the exposed beam ceiling now and then.

Simmons made his way to the wasp's glass container and tumbled to what had happened. The box's lid was askew and did not fully cover its top. He recalled that Congreve had been fiddling with the lid before leaving and must have accidentally left a gap by means of which the creature had escaped its captivity.

The pain in Simmons's throbbing eyelid was unbearable. Hornets had stung him before, but he had never experienced such keen pain, which must have been due to the sensitivity of the site of the sting—his tender eyelid. But it also felt like the stinger was continuing to drill into his eye, past his eye, and toward his brain. But that was impossible, he decided.

Hearing the wasp buzzing above him, he realized he must catch it or kill it before it stung him again. Some bees died after stinging their victims, but obviously this wasp went on living after its attack. It might even be able to sting him again, for all Simmons knew. After all, it was a new species that he had invented. Who knew what it was capable of?

Simmons could not take any chances. He had to capture the creature. He could not bring himself to kill a new species, especially one that he himself had created. It was the only one of its kind, a prototype. It would be a crime to kill it.

*Christ!* he thought, what if Helena should walk into the lab while the wasp was flying around free? He could not risk her being stung. The Lucifer wasp's venom seemed many times more toxic than any other bee venom he had heard of. His stung eyelid continued to throb and burn without letup.

As if on cue, he heard high heels clacking toward the lab's closed door. He pegged to the door and locked it, dreading that Helena would enter. The rattling of the doorknob confirmed his suspicion that Helena was standing outside trying to gain entry.

"Dad, I need to speak to you," she said, frustrated by the locked door. "Why is the door locked?"

"I'm busy now," said Simmons. He conjured a lie. He didn't want her to worry about his being stung. "I'm using formaldehyde in here. I don't want you to come in and breathe it."

"How come you can breathe it and I can't?"

"I'm wearing a mask."

It was true he had a gas mask in here which he used when he was dealing with certain toxic chemicals in his experiments, but he wasn't wearing it now.

"OK," she said reluctantly. "I'll come back later."

Standing beside the door he heard her footfalls clack away down the corridor and fade into the distance.

Now to deal with the wasp, he decided, cringing as he heard it homing in on him from above. He sprang to the opposite corner of the lab to evade the creature, careful to avoid running into his worktable in his frantic haste.

He scoped out the room, casting around for the wasp. He had no idea where it had secreted itself. One minute it was inches from his head, the next it was gone. Mute, motionless, he pricked up his ears, trying to pick up on the wasp's ominous buzz. Nothing. Neither sight nor sound of the creature.

He realized the pain in his eyelid had subsided to a degree, but it was still swollen shut. He didn't have time to worry about it. It was just a bee sting. It would smart and be swollen for a while then it would go away. He needed to return to his work, to find a vaccine that would immunize everybody from bee venom.

He canvassed the room warily one more time, seeking the Lucifer wasp. He had no desire to be stung again. The creature was nowhere in sight. He scoured the walls on which dead bees and hornets of all stripes hung mounted on wooden plaques. Then he pored over the rectangular glass containers that were sitting on wooden shelves that lined the walls. The containers imprisoned living wasps. Still no sign of the Lucifer wasp.

He resumed sitting in front of his microscope, which was trained on venom that he had extracted from a dead caterpillar wasp and mounted on a slide. Becoming absorbed in his studies he lost track of the time.

The next thing he knew it was dark outside.

He stood up and stretched. His legs had fallen asleep. He needed to get his circulation going. He walked around the room to exercise his legs and stimulate the flow of his blood to get it coursing through his legs again.

Though it was suppertime, he didn't feel hungry. In any case, he would rather work than eat. Eating held no attraction for him.

He wondered what his wounded eye looked like. He was feeling more pain, but not from the eye this time. The pain was located deeper inside his head, almost like a murderous headache. Maybe that was what it was, he decided.

He entered the bathroom and flicked on the light. Taken aback, he recoiled at the sight of himself in the medicine cabinet's mirror. His swollen eye had changed color. It looked a ghastly ocher, and its size had not subsided, though its soreness had. He could not understand it. The swelling should be going down. And the yellow color made no sense to him at all.

His headache seemed to be getting worse.

Wincing, he opened the medicine cabinet, glommed onto a plastic bottle of Tylenol, and downed several of the pain-killing caplets with a glass of tap water. He killed the light in the bathroom and returned to his lab.

He needed to get back to work. Nothing else mattered to him.

He startled at a flurry of rapping on the lab's door.

"What is it?" he asked, annoyed at the interruption.

"Supper's ready," answered Helena through the door.

"I'm not hungry tonight. I don't have time to eat."

"What are you saying? Of course, you have time to eat."

"Not tonight, honey. I have a headache. I think I'll call it a day soon and sleep here tonight."

"Why are you talking crazy?" Helena tried to open the locked door. "Why don't you unlock this door?"

Simmons didn't want her to see him in this condition. It would worry her for no reason. After all, it was just a bee sting. It would be better tomorrow, and he would see her then. Damn, but his head still ached—despite the Tylenols he had gulped down. No matter. Even in pain, he could work. He would work through the pain.

"I'll see you tomorrow, honey," he said. "Have a good night."

"Sometimes you're impossible," she said, clacking her high heels more loudly than usual, it seemed to him, as she left.

Simmons stretched out on a sofa in his lab and fell asleep.

Unfortunately, he felt no better the next day. His head still ached. It felt like somebody was driving a hot poker through his swollen eye into his brain. He felt weaker now, too. Maybe he should stay in bed all day, he decided, sitting up groggily on the sofa and cradling his head in his hands.

A diving gull squalled over his bungalow's roof. The gull's wail burned through his ears, grating on his nerves and exacerbating his headache. Grinding his teeth in pain, Simmons flinched.

He peered out the window. Sunlight percolated through the glass into his lab, illuminating carefree dust motes that floated and swirled aimlessly. Watching the gamboling motes he wondered where the Lucifer wasp was. Where had it taken refuge?

Getting stung by it once was enough. He had no desire to be stung again. Its venom must be several times more toxic than an ordinary wasp's, whose sting could not possibly inflict the onslaught of pain he was now feeling inside his head courtesy of the Lucifer wasp.

He bolted to his feet. Time was wasting. He had to get back to work. Since the Lucifer wasp's venom was more toxic than other wasps', it would be the perfect choice to create a vaccine from, one that would protect everyone from death by bee venom, he decided. He made for his desk.

But the pain in his head was crippling him. He raced to the bathroom, downed a handful of Tylenol caplets (more like half the bottle), and gulped them down with water. Not a good idea, he decided afterwards. He probably shouldn't have taken so many. He didn't want to OD on the stuff. But the pain in his head was intolerable.

He glanced up at the mirror.

His breath caught as he set eyes on his face's image. The swelling in his yellow eyelid was even more pronounced than it had been last night. It was simply a bee sting, he told himself. He could not let it interfere with his work.

He returned to his microscope and resumed his studies.

And was immediately interrupted by a rapid series of knocks on his door.

"Yes?" he said, looking up with irritation from his microscope's lens.

"Breakfast is ready," said Helena.

"I'll eat later."

"But you didn't have any dinner last night. You must be starving by now."

"I think I'm coming down with a cold," he lied. "I don't want you to catch it."

"At least drink some orange juice. You need vitamin C for a cold."

"I'll have some later. You go on to school now."

Bryan Cassiday

"Are you sure you're OK?" she asked, concern inflecting her voice.

"Just a little head cold. I'll be fine." He groaned as a pang stabbed through his head.

"What was that? Are you in pain?"

"Just a paper cut. It's nothing."

"Want me to call the doctor for your cold?"

"No," he snapped. "I'll be OK, honey. I'll take it easy today and catch up on my rest."

"All right," she said, voice hollow. "I'm off. Good-bye."

"Good-bye, dear."

Increasingly fatigued, Simmons managed to make it through the day without spotting the Lucifer wasp.

On the second day after the wasp had stung him, things took a dramatic change for the worse.

He was awakened by the buzzing of the wasp corkscrewing above his head. The wasp was so near his head that the buzzing sounded deafening. As crazy as it sounded, it looked like the wasp was trying to peek into his ear. He knew it sounded insane, but that's what it looked like to him.

Terrified at the creature's proximity to his face, Simmons sprang off the sofa and darted to the other side of the room. In his weakened condition, it was becoming difficult for him to move. However, the fear-triggered adrenaline coursing through his body changed that in a trice, invigorating him.

First and foremost, he needed protection for his head, he decided. He couldn't stand the idea of being stung in his face again. The pain in his head was already insufferable. Another facial sting would send him over the edge.

He thought of the gas mask he had stored in his closet. When dealing with formaldehyde he wore the mask sometimes to prevent himself from becoming sickened by the gas's noxious fumes.

He threw open the closet door, scoffed up the gas mask, and snugged the mask on his head. The pressure of the neoprene mask squeezing against his puffed-out eyelid smarted, but he preferred such pain to being stung again in the face. The very idea of

80

another sting in his face, especially near his eye, sent a frisson of dread down his spine.

He sat down in front of his microscope.

The pain in both his eye and his head combined with his neglecting eating took their toll on him, enervating him. He fell asleep.

As Simmons slept, the Lucifer wasp alighted on his gas mask's hose and fell to eating through the rubber.

The better part of fifteen minutes later the wasp had chewed a hole in the rubber hose large enough for it to pass through. Unbeknownst to Simmons, the wasp entered the hose and flew through it until the creature entered the area between Simmons's face and his Perspex faceplate.

Jerked awake by the pain, Simmons screamed in agony as the wasp stung his other eyelid. Terrified out of his wits, he clutched the gas mask, tore it off his head, flung it to the other side of the room, and gingerly felt his newly stung eyelid, which was pulsating and swelling with pain.

Maddened by the pain and blinded by the two stings, he pegged around the room hysterically, tripped over one of the table legs, slammed his head into the floor, rolled over, and passed out.

#

A tad over three hours later, Helena and Congreve knocked urgently on the lab's door, apprehensive of Simmons's condition.

"He hasn't come out of the lab for two days," Helena said, biting her lip. "I'm worried about him."

"Does he usually lock the door?" said Congreve, trying without success to twist the doorknob.

"No. Hardly ever."

"What do you think's wrong with him?"

Helena shrugged. "He said he has a cold."

"A cold wouldn't prevent him from answering the door."

Helena nodded. "I'm certain something's happened to him. We need to get in there."

Congreve inspected the doorknob and saw no keyhole. "Isn't there a window in his lab? It seems to me I remember one."

"Yeah."

"Maybe we can see what's going on in there through the window."

"Follow me."

She headed outside through the bungalow's front door, Congreve in tow.

They reached the lab's large window, which was almost as big as a picture window and bordered by a rhododendron on each of its two sides. Bright burgundy-hued bougainvillea crept up the side of the house to the shelving eaves as if on a lattice and arched over the window's lintel. A scrub brush squatted between the two rhododendrons, blocking anyone from standing directly in front of the window.

However, Congreve could peer over the bush and into the lab.

Knocked for a loop at what he saw, he picked up on Simmons's body that sprawled on its back on the floor near the desk, Simmons's face a twisted mask of agony with his eyes bugging out of his head. But that was nothing compared to what Congreve made out next.

He could see that Simmons's head was swollen to at least twice its size on account of its bulging ocher eyelids, which gave it the aspect of a monstrous fly's head, or wasp's head, for that matter, and out of one of Simmons's bloody ears several baby fluorescent orange and black wasps were crawling like inquisitive hatchlings.

Despite his paroxysm of shock at the lurid sight, Congreve was able to recall that Simmons had said that he had crossbred a caterpillar wasp with a yellow jacket when he had created his so-called Lucifer wasp.

From the sight of Simmons's swollen eyelids, Congreve deduced in horror that, instead of stinging a caterpillar like one of its parents would have done, the Lucifer wasp had stung Simmons in his eyelids and deposited its eggs behind Simmons's eyes. The tiny wasps had then proceeded to eat their way through his brain and out his eustachian tube.

## The Fine Print

MacKay had no idea he was on the road to hell. It all started out innocent enough. All he wanted was some luck. He wanted fate to smile on him for once in his life. Was that too much to ask for? He had had it up to here with bad luck, and no luck wasn't much better.

He had gotten off the Greyhound bus at a dusty pocket town called Las Cruces de Sangre on the American side of the Mexican-American border. The entire town couldn't have been more than a few blocks long.

The bus pulled out after dropping him off, kicking dust into his eyes and blowing heat into his face as he stood on the corner surveying what passed for a town. He got off here on a whim. He had been fired from his truck-driving job by his dickhead of a boss whose only desire in life, other than greed, was to treat his employees like dirt.

That was two days ago and MacKay wanted to blow off steam in some godforsaken hole in the wall where he could be alone and far enough away from his boss that he wouldn't be tempted to murder the so-and-so. The guy was crying out to be blown away, decided MacKay.

With that in mind MacKay headed from San Diego to the border. En route, he clapped eyes on Las Cruces de Sangre. It looked like the middle of nowhere. A perfect destination where he could disappear for a week and pull himself together.

Other than the odd saguaro, manzanita, and Joshua tree amongst the sage in the desert flatland that surrounded the town, there wasn't much to look at.

Eyes tearing from the dust the bus had churned up, he hitched up his jeans at the bus stop and made a beeline for the edge of town.

The town had one gas station.

The gas station had two gas pumps. A hand-printed Out of Order sign hung askew from twine on one of them. An antique red Coke machine stood in front of the owner's cramped office which had a doorway so narrow you had to turn sideways to pass through it. Next to the office was a dusky service bay devoid of cars at the moment.

MacKay strolled over to the Coke machine.

"What can I do for you, my friend?" said a Mexican guy in his thirties who wore his black hair combed back tight in a ponytail.

Grinning, he emerged from the office and eyed MacKay.

MacKay couldn't interpret the grin. Grins weren't always friendly. They could, in actuality, be bared teeth. Which had nothing to do with geniality, as any wolf could tell you.

MacKay dug coins out of his trouser pocket and poked through them on his palm. He slotted four quarters into the machine one at a time. A red aluminum Coke can tumbled down to the bottom aperture in the machine with a thud. MacKay withdrew the can from the machine. The can was cold to his touch.

"You got a hotel in this town?" he said.

The gas jockey pointed. "The second block. On your left." He scoped out MacKay. "Where's your luggage?"

"I don't plan on staying long."

MacKay yanked the ring top off of the soda can and took a swig of Coke. A bloated bluebottle buzzed around his head, searching for a place to land.

"Suit yourself," said the gas jockey, watching MacKay saunter into town.

MacKay ambled past a café and a barbershop. Next door was a nail salon. Beside that was a Starbuck's. The barista eyed him expectantly. He paused. He thought about going inside but he didn't feel thirsty after the Coke. He polished off the Coke, crumpled the can in his hand, tossed the can in a wastebasket on the sidewalk, and kept walking.

Still no sign of a hotel.

Next up was a small store with a tinted black display window. He tried to peek inside, but the tinted glass thwarted his view of the store's interior.

On the plate glass in white letters was printed The All in One Store. In smaller letters underneath the name of the store were the words If You Want It We Got It.

His curiosity piqued, MacKay opened the plate-glass door, which was also tinted black, and entered the poky store. An old-fashioned bell on the top of the door chimed as he entered.

Items of all shapes and sizes cluttered the dim-lit store. He didn't see anybody inside, neither the manager nor a counterjumper. A mephitic fusty odor greeted his nostrils. Wincing at the stench he was weighing whether to leave the dive when a sixtysomething man clad in shorts shuffled into sight from the pitch-black nether recesses of the store.

Peering through round-lensed wire-rim spectacles he had a shock of white hair and wore a green headband.

"Hello, sir," he said. "My name is Ed. Can I be of service to you?"

MacKay shrugged noncommittally. "I'm just looking around."

"What do you really want?"

"How about some good luck?" he said with a laugh as he surveyed the gimcracks that crammed the shelves around him. "I'm fresh out."

"How much do you want?" asked Ed.

Bryan Cassiday

Amused at Ed's response, MacKay scoffed up a stuffed donkey on a nearby shelf and squeezed the animal's white belly. "As much as I can get."

"How badly do you want it?"

MacKay replaced the donkey on the shelf, annoyed at Ed's prolonging the joke. "It's not funny anymore."

"I'm not trying to be funny."

"That's good. Because you're not."

"Maybe you don't understand my question."

"What question?"

"I'll rephrase it. What's good luck worth to you?"

"Are you still harping on that? I told you, the joke's over. I'm not in a very good mood today."

"Why is that, sir?"

"None of your business," said MacKay and fell to pacing around the poky confines of the room, up one narrow aisle and down the next.

He found it difficult to move in the place because of the jumble of merchandise scattered throughout the store.

"Good luck is an expensive commodity," said Ed. "Can you afford it?"

"Can we stop with the jokes? If I wanted a comedy routine, I'd go to a nightclub."

"What makes you think I'm joking?"

"Pretending you can sell good luck? How gullible do you think I am?"

"I sell anything you want. Didn't you see the sign outside?"

MacKay gave Ed a look. "Did you ever hear of false advertising?"

"There's nothing false in that sign. I have everything you could possibly want in my store."

"Like good luck," said MacKay ironically.

"Like the sign says: if you want it, we got it."

MacKay screwed up his face. "Why does it smell in here?"

"I don't smell anything."

"You've been in here too long."

86

Ed became impatient. "Do you want to know the price for good luck, or not?"

"OK. Sure. Tell me the price," said MacKay to humor the geezer.

"Are you sure? It's steep."

"I promise I won't faint when I hear it."

"First off, I must tell you we don't sell good luck per se."

"How about that?"

"Bear with me, sir. You need to make a specific request as to what exactly you want as a result of your good luck."

"OK. I'll play along with this gag. I want $20 million."

Ed's deep-set eyes bored into MacKay's. "Then you need to kill somebody."

"Is that all?" said MacKay with a guffaw.

"That's quite enough," said Ed, face grave. "Don't you think?"

"I think you're pulling my leg."

"But it's true."

Tired of the joke, MacKay said nothing.

"Hardly anyone ever comes in here," said Ed. "Did you know that?"

"I can't imagine why. Did you ever hear of air freshener?" said MacKay, pulling a face. "You might actually get a couple of customers once in a while if you used it."

Ed ignored the comment. "What customers we get tend to be ones who are down on their luck."

"Is that some kind of snide comment about me?" said MacKay, voice edged with anger.

"Not at all. I'm simply stating the facts."

MacKay cooled off. "I thought you were trying to say something."

"Then let's get back to business. Are you willing to kill somebody for $20 million?"

"Just wait a minute. Now where is this 20 million bucks? How do I know you got it?" MacKay scoped out the store's interior. "I hate to be blunt, but it doesn't look like you got two cents to rub together."

"There must be a misunderstanding. I don't pay you the money."

"Then where does it come from?" MacKay canted up his head and eyed the ceiling. "Does it just rain down on me?"

"You get what you pay for: good luck. As a result of the good luck, you will receive $20 million."

"Like I said, it'll just rain down on me," scoffed MacKay.

"The decision is yours."

MacKay wanted to find out what kind of a racket this clown was running. "Who am I supposed to kill?"

"If you sign the contract, I'll tell you."

MacKay was tempted to sign it, just to call the guy's bluff. This had to be a world-class scam. And then of course there was the fact that he had been canned and didn't have a job . . . another reason to sign the contract. Being unemployed he could certainly use 20 million clams.

His cell phone rang.

He answered it.

"Where are you, Mac?" asked his wife Dani.

Nervously, MacKay paused in thought before he answered. He didn't want Dani to know he had been fired.

"I'm away on a business assignment," he answered.

He hated lying to her, but he didn't want to tell her yet that Tubbs had fired him. He knew the news would upset her, so he was putting off telling her as long as possible. Not only would the news upset her, it would infuriate her.

"Why didn't you tell me before you left?" she said.

"It's just a job. Nothing to be concerned about."

"So you won't be home for dinner tonight. Is that what you're saying?"

"I'm not gonna be able to make it to dinner. I'll be away all night."

"This isn't good news."

In his mind's eye he could picture the strained smile she used on him when she wasn't happy.

"I'm sorry, Dani, but it can't be helped."

He was never any good at saying he was sorry. The words seemed to stick in his throat before they came out. As mad as she was at him now, she would be even madder if he told her the truth about his losing his job, he knew. Even worse, she might break into tears.

"I don't know why I need to tell you this, but your job should take second place to certain other things," she said.

Squirming in discomfort MacKay was breaking into a sweat. He didn't want to prolong this conversation. She was making him feel like a heel.

"I'll make up for it," he said. "I'm getting a bonus for this job."

What bonus? he wondered. It wasn't like he was getting severance pay. Tubbs had paid him squat when he gave MacKay a pink slip. Why did he say bonus? The more he lied, the farther he put his foot in his mouth. He needed to keep his trap shut.

"Well, at least that's something," said Dani. "But you shouldn't just take off, leaving me in the dark."

"I know. My bad. I better get back to work now."

"Try to get back here as soon as you can."

"Definitely. I will. Good-bye."

He ended the call and put away his smartphone before she had a chance to prolong their conversation.

He could kick himself. He had blown it. He was trapped in his own lies. Not only would he not show up for dinner with her tonight, now she would be expecting extra money thanks to his so-called bonus. He closed his eyes and massaged his forehead.

"Are you all right?" said Ed.

"No, I'm not all right," snapped MacKay, "if it's any of your business."

"I wouldn't be worried, if I were you. Twenty million dollars solves a lot of problems."

"I don't have $20 million."

"You will have soon, after you sign on the dotted line."

Ed angled to the cashier's cluttered counter, reached behind it, and produced a contract.

"All I have to do is kill somebody for it, huh?" said MacKay. "And then it'll rain C-notes."

Ed plucked a ballpoint from an empty Dundee orange marmalade jar that now held an assortment of pens and pencils in lieu of marmalade on the counter. With one hand he offered the contract to MacKay, with the other he offered the pen.

MacKay stood there looking at them.

"This is what you need," said Ed, continuing to hold the pen and contract in front of MacKay.

"What I need is some good luck."

"And you'll get it if you sign this contract."

"What are you? Some kind of witch?"

"I'm simply a store owner."

"If you can produce on this deal, you're more than just a store owner."

"Then let's say, I'm a go-between and leave it at that."

"I feel like calling your bluff, Ed, and putting you in your place," said MacKay, taking stock of the pen in Ed's hand.

Ed held the pen closer to MacKay. "Please do."

MacKay was no murderer. He had never murdered anybody in his life. He had gotten into a couple of fistfights in bars in his twenties. That was about it. And he had lost both fights. He had never served in the armed forces. He didn't even own a gun.

He was a truck driver, not a killer. He drove an 18-wheeler for a living. He didn't know if he could kill another human being. He had no desire to kill anybody. Well, maybe his ex-boss. But MacKay knew he would never do it.

This was insane, he decided. Why was he even considering signing the stupid contract?

Because he could use the money now that he was unemployed. Driving gigs were hard to come by with the meltdown of the economy these days. It wasn't the greatest job in the world anyway. It was exhausting, monotonous, and he had to log ten or more hours a day just to make ends meet. What was he waiting for?

He accepted the contract from Ed and skimmed it in the dim light. He flipped through all seven pages of the stapled document. Who was he trying to kid? He wasn't a lawyer. These endless clauses couched in legalese were greek to him. He laid the document on the countertop and snagged the pen from Ed's hand.

MacKay might as well sign it if it meant he had a chance at $20 million. If he didn't get the 20 million, he wouldn't have to kill anyone—and the odds were he wouldn't get the money. This guy Ed didn't look like he had more than a hundred bucks to his name what with this cheap shop he owned full of discarded knickknacks and garage-sale rejects that nobody wanted.

"Why is this contract so long?" said MacKay.

"Lawyers," said Ed with a dismissive wave of his hand.

Against his better judgment, shaking his head, MacKay signed and dated the contract. For all intents and purposes, it wasn't worth the paper it was printed on. The whole thing was a joke. Why not go along with it? He wanted to call Ed's bluff to see what would happen.

"So where's the 20 million smackers?" said MacKay.

"I'm sure I don't know. Your luck will soon change for the better and then you'll receive the money. It won't be coming from me."

MacKay smirked. "Yeah." He paused. "Well, if you're not keeping up your end of the bargain, I don't have to keep up mine."

Ed read MacKay's signature on the contract. "But you *will*, Mr. MacKay, when the time comes."

MacKay was making to leave when his cell rang. He answered it.

It was Dani. She sounded excited.

"You won't believe what just happened, Mac. I got a call from your father's lawyer. Apparently, your dad died and he left you a humongous life insurance policy worth $20 million."

Phone in hand, MacKay stood there in a daze. A confused welter of shock, grief, astonishment, joy, and even fear overcame him. He was having trouble absorbing the news.

"Honey, are you there?" said Dani over the phone. "Did you hear what I said?"

"Yeah, I heard," he managed to croak through a dry throat. "Look, I'll get back to you, Dani."

With that he ended the call and pocketed his mobile.

"I heard your wife," said Ed. "The ball's now in your court, Mr. MacKay."

"You want me to believe you had something to do with this?"

"After you signed the contract you received $20 million. That was the deal."

"But you had nothing to do with it. It's just a coincidence."

"There's no such thing as coincidences in life."

"So my father died because I signed this contract? Is that what you're saying?"

"Not at all. I'm saying you signed the contract and got good luck in the form of $20 million. It's your turn to fulfill your end of the bargain."

"You expect me to believe you had something to do with my father's death?"

"I expect you to kill somebody and fulfill our contract."

Ed reached behind the counter, withdrew a buff manila folder, and laid it on the countertop. He opened the folder and snapped up a black-and-white headshot of a middle-aged man.

"It was dumb luck," said MacKay. "That contract had nothing to do with it. And it's not exactly good luck to have my father die."

"But it's good luck for you to get the money."

MacKay was never very close to his father. Still, MacKay never wished for his father's death.

"It's a coincidence," said MacKay, shaking his head. "You had nothing to do with it."

"You signed the contract and got good luck just like it says in the contract. There's nothing to argue about." Ed showed the photograph to MacKay. "This is your victim."

MacKay glanced at the photo without interest. "You don't expect me to go through with this?"

Ed dug a car key fob out of his trouser pocket. He tossed the fob on the countertop.

"The victim, Herbert Samuels, is living at a mansion on Catalina Island," he said. "His address and other details are in the dossier." He slid the manila folder across the countertop toward MacKay. "Drive there today and take him out by tonight."

"Drive what? I came by bus."

"Those are the keys to the car you'll be driving. Everything you need to fulfill the contract is in the car's trunk."

MacKay shook his head. "This is crazy."

"After you kill him, cut off his head and take a picture of it with your cell phone."

MacKay felt nauseous thinking about it. He heard his stomach growling.

"I never agreed to cut anybody's head off," he said.

"I need proof that Samuels is dead. If you read the contract close enough, you would have seen that the only way the contract can be fulfilled is with proof of the victim's death. Not only must you kill the target, you must prove to me you did so."

Face contorted, MacKay ran his hand through his hair, trying to come to grips with the situation. What if he took the car, didn't kill Samuels, disappeared, and never came back to this godforsaken town? he wondered. Ed would never find him. Even if Ed sent the cops after him, they'd never find him. He could skip the country with his $20 million. But Ed *wouldn't* send the cops. He'd never show them this contract to murder somebody. Such a contract would put Ed in the joint if the cops saw it.

"I know what you're thinking," said Ed. "You're thinking about cutting and running. Forget it. If you renege on the contract, you won't get the money."

"I already have the money. You heard Dani."

"You have it *now*. But your luck will change if you renege. And you can kiss your $20 million good-bye."

Flummoxed, MacKay didn't know what to do. He wanted to get out of this mess, but he wanted to keep the money as well. Torn by conflicting emotions, he had to make a decision. Was Ed really responsible for getting the $20 million or was it a coincidence? Could Ed take the money away as he said? Then MacKay would be back to square one—out of work and out of luck. Which was out of the question.

He decided he better go through with the deal. If this guy Ed could make good luck, he could also make bad. It meant he had some serious mojo that didn't bear thinking about. MacKay had had enough bad luck to last him a lifetime.

"Who is this Samuels fellow?" asked MacKay. "Why do you want him killed?"

"Why do you care? The less you know about him, the better, if you ask me. Ignorance about the target will make it easier for you to kill him. He's just a face in the crowd."

"What if the cops catch me?"

"They won't, unless you're a complete idiot about this."

"Why won't they?"

"The reason most murderers get caught is on account of motive. That's how the cops find out who did it. In your case you have no motive. You don't know the victim from Adam. Just don't leave any fingerprints. Use the gloves in the trunk of the car when you kill him. And be sure to wear the rubber galoshes in the trunk over your shoes. The keys to Samuels's house are secreted inside one of the rubbers."

"Why the galoshes?"

"They'll distort the size of your foot."

"Is that all?"

"No." Ed reached into his trouser pocket, withdrew a remote control like the ones used for garage openers, and handed it to MacKay. "Here's a remote to open the security gate on his driveway." Ed produced a key. "And here's the key to his house."

"You think of everything," said MacKay and pocketed the remote and the key.

"We're not virgins at this."

MacKay started. "How many people have you had blown away?"

"There's a thriving black market for murder for hire."

"Where's the car?" said MacKay, snagging the key fob and the manila folder off the countertop.

"It's the black Crown Vic parked at the meter on the street in front of the store."

MacKay stalked out of the shop. He couldn't get out of there fast enough. He saw the car immediately. Using the key fob he popped open the trunk. He picked up on a Beretta semiautomatic lying inside, a silencer screwed into its barrel. A pair of blue latex gloves lay under the pistol grip. Beside the pistol was a pair of extra large galoshes. And beside them lay a carry-on.

He thwacked the trunk shut, unlocked the driver's-side door with the press of a button on the plastic fob, and scooted behind the steering wheel.

Shutting the door he was gratified to see the car was equipped with GPS. He fired the ignition, turned the GPS on, and programmed it for his destination. It would take him close to three hours to get to Long Beach. From Long Beach Harbor he would take the ferry to Catalina Island. He would need to get to Long Beach by four o'clock to catch the ferry. Consulting his wristwatch he figured he could make it.

He peeled off out of Las Cruces de Sangre, burning rubber with his rear tires. The Crown Vic had more power than he had expected.

He took the 805 north to the 5 to the 405 to Long Beach. Traffic started getting heavy on the 405 when he hit the rush-hour commuters.

Nevertheless, he managed to reach Long Beach Harbor in time to book passage on the ferry to Catalina Island. The teenage brunette cashier was wearing a white yachting hat and a T-shirt that sported a silk screen of a ship's steering wheel with eight spokes. He paid her in cash. That, too, had been provided in the Crown Vic's trunk by Ed.

Carry-on in hand, MacKay ascended the gangplank and boarded the bobbing Catalina Express ship that was moored to the wharf. An onshore ocean breeze negotiated by bawling seagulls swept across the dock. One of the gulls swooped down toward him and snapped its wings near his ears as he was boarding, startling him.

With all of the passengers aboard, the crew cast off.

While he sat in one of the enclosed airplane-style seats, MacKay paid the purser for a Coke with the voucher the teenage cashier had given him for a drink when he had purchased his ticket.

The ferry docked at Catalina Island in an hour and change. It wasn't even dark yet, MacKay noticed as he disembarked. Applying Chap Stick to his lips the leather-faced bosun said good-bye to him and the other passengers as they paraded down the gangway off the ship.

MacKay grabbed a complimentary map on the wharf, studied the map, and made for the town of Avalon. Tourists milled everywhere, snapping photos and gawking at the souvenir shops and restaurants that lined the wharf.

Having consulted the map MacKay decided he needed transportation to Samuels's manse. He discovered he had a choice between bicycles and golf carts for transportation.

He rented a golf cart with a torn vinyl seat. He didn't know how long it would take him to waste Samuels, but he wasn't going to hit Samuels till it was dark, so he rented the vehicle for four hours. MacKay would scope out Samuels's digs in the residual daylight before he went in for the hit.

He rode the tacky golf cart along the narrow roads up to the town's residential section that loomed above the main drag on a bluff with domiciles carved into the hillside. He followed the map to Samuels's palatial mansion.

Whoever this Samuels guy was he was loaded. His pink adobe mission-style mansion with an orange pantiled roof

96

sprawled on the hillside with its own fifteen-foot-high steel security gate.

MacKay rode past the front of the residence in his golf cart, pretending to be a tourist taking in the sights as he cased the house. At dusk he returned to the wharf and ate dinner at a restaurant on the shore waiting for it to get dark.

Waves crashing underneath his feet, he ordered an Alaskan halibut and a pinot grigio to take the edge off. To put it bluntly he was scared. He was in no hurry to murder Samuels. A tad of Dutch courage might be just the ticket. He was sitting on the restaurant's weathered wood-planked patio watching the sun descend behind the island's beige-columned round casino. Beneath him he could see the waves crashing and frothing onshore through the interstices between the planks in the floor.

Why was he going through with this insanity? he wondered. Did Ed really have as much juju as he claimed he did, or was he nothing but a con man? Could Ed track him down if MacKay hightailed it without killing Samuels? MacKay didn't know. All he knew now was he had $20 million which he didn't have before he signed Ed's contract. If he didn't fulfill his end of the contract, that 20 million bucks might vanish as quickly as it had appeared.

If this was an elaborate scam by Ed, MacKay couldn't figure it out. He decided it must be what it looked like: a once-in-a-lifetime deal that he had to grab or forever lose out on the big bucks. If killing was the only way to score a fortune, so be it.

Doubts continued to nag at the back of his mind though. He wasn't fully convinced he was doing the right thing. After all, he was committing murder for Christ's sake. He shrugged. To hell with it. He decided to act.

He paid for his supper with cash and drove his golf cart back to Samuels's house.

Lights were on inside. He figured that meant Samuels was home. Did Samuels live alone, or did he have a family? MacKay wondered. A family would complicate matters. The point was MacKay wasn't a professional assassin. Without experience in this type of endeavor he was going in blind. He would have to play it by ear.

He pulled to a halt at the side of the street in front of the security gate and slipped on his gloves and rubbers. His rubbers looked like clown shoes on account of their enormous size. He had to be careful he didn't trip over his own feet.

Using the remote he opened the security gate. He turned off his golf cart's headlights. As the gate swung open he drove onto the driveway that swept toward the mansion's entrance.

After he killed Samuels, MacKay knew he would have to hide the body so it wouldn't be found for at least twenty-four hours. That would give him time to get off the island. If the murder was discovered before that time, the authorities might very well cancel all of the ferry trips to the mainland while they hunted the shooter, stranding MacKay on the island.

He worked himself up to waste Samuels. MacKay wondered if it would be easier for him to whack the guy if he pictured Samuels as his sadistic ex-boss. As it stood now, MacKay had no incentive to waste Samuels other than the monetary one. MacKay imagined that he was in reality carrying out the killing of his ex-boss.

MacKay parked the motor cart near the bushes, out of sight of the front door and the windows. He decided to use the back entrance. That way the neighbors would not see him enter the house in the lamplight on the front porch.

Beretta in hand, he stole toward the backdoor. The backdoor was dark. It was so dark he had trouble locating it. The entire backyard lay in shadows. Nobody would see him enter here.

Satisfied nobody was watching him, he inserted the key in the lock with difficulty in the dark, opened the backdoor, and crept into the dim-lit kitchen. He all but tripped on his clown rubbers. Cursing to himself he eased the door shut behind him.

Heart thumping, he heard voices emanating from the depths of the capacious house. He was a rank amateur at murdering people. He had no idea what he was doing. He ought to beat it on a dime, if he knew what was good for him.

Despite misgivings he edged through the kitchen, heading in the direction of the voices. He skulked through the hallway that led out of the kitchen. The voices sounded nearer. He caught sight of light flickering on the wall in a nearby room.

The voices were coming from a TV set, he realized as he recognized a familiar commercial playing. He poked his head around the doorjamb to peek into the room.

A man was lying on a couch half awake, watching the sixty-inch flat-panel HDTV screen. MacKay recognized Samuels's face from the photograph Ed had showed him.

MacKay stepped into the TV room, trained his silenced Beretta on Samuels's head, and, imagining he was killing his ex-boss, squeezed the trigger. Nothing happened. Befuddled, MacKay inspected the pistol. The trigger wouldn't pull. He spotted a lever near the grip and decided it must be a safety. He flicked it.

He leveled the pistol at Samuels's head again. Samuels woke up, snapping his eyes open at the sight of him. MacKay squeezed the trigger. The gun offered a muffled pop. The bullet missed Samuels. Frantically, teeth clenched, MacKay fired three more times as Samuels, wide-eyed, made to bound off his sofa.

One of the rounds caught Samuels in the side of the head, spinning him around. He fell off the sofa and slumped to the carpet in a motionless heap.

MacKay darted out of the room. He had to know if anybody else was inside the house. Going from room to room, gun at the ready, he inspected the rest of the house, hoping against hope that he would not run into anyone. His luck seemed to be holding. He didn't see anybody. Even after he inspected the upstairs rooms he detected no one.

He returned to the TV room, flipped Samuels over on his back, and, using his smartphone, snapped a picture of Samuels's lifeless face. Then, in dismay, MacKay recalled he was supposed to decapitate Samuels before he took a photo of the head to prove Samuels was really dead.

Bryan Cassiday

Why hadn't Ed provided him with a machete or an ax? wondered MacKay. Too big for the carry-on, he decided. He would have to get cutlery from the kitchen to use on Samuels's neck.

MacKay pegged to the kitchen and cast around for a large knife. His eyes fell on a meat cleaver hanging on the wall under a cupboard near the sink. He snagged the cleaver and belted back to the TV room.

He didn't look forward to decapitating Samuels. The very thought of it sickened MacKay. What about the blood? It would get all over the place. But Samuels was dead. Corpses didn't bleed, MacKay knew. Therefore, there shouldn't be much blood when he beheaded Samuels.

Grimacing, MacKay swung the cleaver and severed Samuels's throat. It sounded like an ax blade splitting a watermelon. Blood splattered the carpet, but not much. The throat wasn't completely severed, MacKay saw to his consternation. He had to give it another whack with the cleaver to finish the job.

The head fell free from Samuels's neck with a thump and rolled over a couple of times on the carpet.

Appalled at what he had done, MacKay stepped back from the decollated cadaver and gasped for breath.

Pulling himself together he used his smartphone to snap a photo of the head that lay on its temple, its eyes staring vacantly, on the carpet.

He snapped up the TV's remote from the coffee table near the sofa and switched off the TV set. How was he going to hide this bloodbath? he wondered. If somebody entered the house, they would see Samuels's corpse as soon as they passed the TV room.

He locked the TV room's door behind him as he left. It was the only way he could think of to cover up the crime.

In the hallway's light he inspected his clothing to make sure no blood had splashed onto him. He didn't see any. He washed off the cleaver in the kitchen sink, wiped the blade dry with a dishtowel, and hung the cleaver back on its hook in the wall.

He skulked out the backdoor through the backyard to the front of the house where he had parked the golf cart. He mounted the driver's seat, removed his clown rubbers, and drove back to the center of Avalon, where he returned the golf cart, removed his latex gloves, and rented a room in a tumbledown waterfront hotel, paid for in cash.

That night, using his cell, he booked the first ferry out of port to Long Beach the next morning. He called it a night, went to bed, and tried to sleep, but couldn't. He kept turning over restlessly like a lathe, worrying somebody would find Samuels's corpse and alert the cops, who would shut down the island before MacKay could escape from it.

He got out of bed feeling exhausted the next morning. He grabbed a bite to eat at a nearby café and hustled to the dock to catch the ferry, carry-on in hand.

On tenterhooks, he stood waiting at the dock, hoping they wouldn't cancel the ferry. He felt too agitated to sit down. So far, so good, he decided. Hopefully, nobody had found Samuels's corpse yet.

MacKay fetched a sigh of relief when they commenced boarding the ferry. He wasn't home yet, though. The ferry still hadn't pulled out of the harbor. Until they put out to sea, MacKay could not unwind.

At last the ferry set out for Long Beach. Calmer now, he watched Catalina Island disappear in the offing as the ferry hove through the ice-smooth sea. But he knew the cops could hold the ferry and detain the passengers when it docked at Long Beach Harbor if Samuels's corpse was discovered while MacKay was at sea.

MacKay was one of the first passengers off the ship when it docked at Long Beach. Not wasting any time in the city he collected the Crown Vic and drove back to Las Cruces de Sangre.

He parked on the street in front of Ed's shop. He needed to go inside and verify Samuels's death with the photo he took of Samuels's head.

MacKay stretched when he climbed out of the car, limbering up his stiff legs and aching back. He entered Ed's shop on shaky pins.

Ed was standing at the counter.

"Who was that guy Samuels?" said MacKay, taking out his smartphone and displaying the photo of Samuels's head to Ed.

Ed nodded at the picture. "He was the guy who signed the contract before yours."

"Why did you want him killed?"

"He refused to execute his next victim."

"What next victim?" said MacKay, becoming alarmed.

"He stopped killing after his tenth victim."

"I don't get it."

"Don't worry. It gets easier after your first kill. Remember what Stalin said. 'One death is a tragedy; one million is a statistic.'"

"What's this 'next victim' bullshit you're babbling about?" said MacKay, eyes bulging in horror.

"Didn't you read the fine print?"

# Infestation

The silence was deafening. It was like snow falling, entombing Los Angeles in ponderous layers of quiet. And yet it wasn't snowing. It was a warm spring day. And this was Los Angeles. It never snowed in Los Angeles.

Sitting beside the window in his apartment, Sully could feel the warmth of the sunlight as it struck his wrist. From the direction of the sun, it was about five o'clock in the afternoon, he figured. It was a good way to tell the time of day, especially when you were blind.

*But why was it so quiet? he wondered. The question kept niggling at the back of his mind. Where was the endless sound of traffic beneath his window?*

Not that he really needed to know the time of day, since he had no job to go to or anywhere that he had to be. He had lost his sight in a car accident while returning home from a night of pub-crawling in Hollywood. He should have had a designated driver with him, but he had gotten pie-eyed alone. Monday morning quarterbacking was always twenty-twenty. There was no sense in crying over spilt milk. He could not set back the clock and he wasn't going to spend the rest of his life wallowing in self-pity because he went on a toot one night.

He simply had to learn how to adapt to his new life of being blind. It had been all of five years since his accident and he believed he was getting along pretty well, considering the circumstances. It wasn't every blind man who could live alone and take care of himself, in spite of his handicap. That was something to feel proud of. And he did feel proud. Lonely in his separation from humanity, but proud nonetheless. He was beating the odds every day he got by on his own and made it through another day.

There was something odd about today, though. The quiet. The interminable quiet. No traffic. No garbage truck picking up trash.

There weren't any sounds. It was stone quiet—like three feet of snow had fallen on the city.

He cupped his hand around his ear to amplify his hearing. It did no good. He still heard nothing. He shook his head in disappointment. Was he going deaf? he wondered. On a normal day he could hear dogs barking, cars whooshing underneath his window, buses chugging by, brakes squeaking to a halt, tires shrieking, the shrill of an ambulance's siren, planes flying overhead, pedestrians chattering on the sidewalk underneath his window . . .

What had happened to them? he wondered, becoming apprehensive now. Something definitely wasn't right today.

The sun was still out, though. He could feel its warmth on the back of his wrist, reassuring him of its presence. He chuckled to himself at the thought. *As long as the sun's shining, all's right with the world*, he thought. So what if he could not see it? He could feel it. That was the most important thing. Feeling.

But the deadly quiet was unnerving.

The refrigerator clicked on and fell to humming. He startled at the sound. At least, the refrigerator was working. The power was on. But where was everybody? He reached for the transistor radio on the coffee table in front of him.

Flicking on the radio's dial, he got white noise. He tried another station with the same result. No matter which station he tried, he got static. He turned off the radio, the static grating on his nerves.

As he tried to figure out what was going on, he heard a commotion beyond his door in the stairwell. Two or more persons were rushing up the stairs. One guy was ascending two steps at a time. Some kind of an emergency, Sully decided, heartbeat accelerating.

He flinched as a flurry of fists commenced pounding on his locked door.

"Help!" cried the person.

Apprehensively, Sully got up and made his way to the door, as the frenzied rapping continued.

"Who is it?" he said, reaching the door.

"Help us, mister!"

"What's wrong?"

"They're trying to kill us!"

"Who is?"

"Open the door before they get here!"

It was a woman's voice this time, Sully realized. So there were at least two of them, as he had suspected.

"Who's trying to kill you?" said Sully.

"We don't have time to talk about it. Open the door or we're dead!" said the woman. Her voice became more frantic. "They're coming up the stairs!"

How could he trust these strangers? Sully wondered. He had no idea who they were. They could be burglars trying to escape the police, for all he knew. On the other hand, he had not heard any police sirens. If the police were near, he would have heard a siren.

Then he heard what sounded like growling gibberish. He didn't know how else to describe it. He heard guttural sounds that didn't form words. There was something ominous and nerve-racking about the harsh grunts emanating from the stairwell. They were animal sounds. Something not human, anyway, decided Sully.

The rapping on his door became more frenetic.

"They're almost here, mister! Let us in!" cried the woman.

She sounded young, in her twenties, Sully decided.

Bryan Cassiday

He unlocked his door and opened it. He had no idea what was
going on, but these people were in trouble. There was no doubt of
that.

The two strangers barged past him, all but knocking him over
in their haste to enter his room. They slammed the door behind
them and locked it as a mob of howling, grunting people that
sounded more like animals than people crashed against it, trying to
get in.

"Is that door gonna hold, Roy?" said the woman.

"I hope so," said Roy. "It looks pretty solid."

Roy sounded about the same age as the woman, Sully decided.

Sully could smell the rank odor of sweat mixed with fear in
the room. The air fairly crackled with the anxious tension of the
two strangers.

"What's going on?" he asked. "Who are those people out
there?"

"Don't you know what happened?" said the woman.

Sully shook his head.

"He doesn't know, Beth," said Roy.

"Don't you ever look out your window?" Beth asked Sully.

"No."

Sully didn't know whether he should tell them he was blind.
At this point, he wasn't sure they could be trusted. After all, he
had no idea who they were. They were two complete strangers
that had barreled into his room, reeking of panic.

"I was asleep," he said.

They would probably find out sooner or later that he was
blind, but he decided he would not tell them yet.

"How can you sleep through something like this?" said Roy.
"And why are you wearing those shades inside?"

"They relax my eyes."

"I guess you haven't been outside lately, have you, mister?"
said Beth.

"No, I don't get out much these days. My name's Sully."

"You're old, Sully, but not *that* old. What are you? Scared to
go out? Do you have agoraphobia?"

106

"I'd be scared, too," said Roy. "The way things are now."

"That's understandable, because you're a coward," said Beth.

"What are you talking about?" said Roy, bristling.

"You ran away. That's your answer to everything. Running away."

"I could kick the shit out of your ex-boyfriends any day of the week."

"Settle down," said Sully.

He had no desire to listen this quarrel, especially since it reminded him of his ex-wife, who had left him a year before his accident. She had called him a coward because of his drinking. She had said boozing was a coward's way out. She could really get under his skin, he had to hand it to her. This Beth was riding Roy the same way, and Sully didn't want to listen to it.

"Who put you in charge, old man?" said Roy. "You got your head buried in the sand like an ostrich. You don't even know what's happening out there."

"What *is* happening out there?" asked Sully.

"Take a look outside your window."

Sully knew that would be pointless. All he could see was blackness wherever he looked. He decided to sidle toward the window, though, so they would not suspect him of his handicap.

He pretended he was gazing out the window. Even though he was blind, he knew its approximate location.

"What do you think?" said Roy.

"So?" said Sully.

"So? Is that all you can say? Like it's just another day or something?"

"Why are you getting so excited?"

"See, he thinks you're a coward, too," said Beth.

"Shut the fuck up!" cried Roy.

Sully could sense someone walking toward him. He figured it was Beth, since he could smell perfume. It was a subtle fragrance. He liked it—as long as you leached out the pungent reek of sweat and fear from it.

"Open the window," she said.

107

"Why?" said Sully.

"You can't, can you?"

"Yeah, I can."

Sully reached for the window. He felt the glass pane then lowered his hands to feel the wooden transom. Crouching, he placed his hands underneath the transom and shoved upward. The window opened with a crack as it slid against its sash. An overpowering stench wafted into his nostrils from the street. Gagging on it he felt like retching.

"You still think it's just business as usual today?" said Roy.

"Sully, come here," said Beth.

Sully wondered what she wanted. He stepped in the direction of her voice. He felt her removing his black sunglasses from the bridge of his nose.

He heard her gasp at him as she beheld his sightless eyes.

"Look, Roy," she said.

Sully heard Roy stride over to her side.

"Give him those things back," said Roy in disgust. "No wonder he's clueless about what's happening. Blind as a bat with those messed-up eyes."

Beth replaced the shades on Sully's nose.

"I can see you're gonna be a big help," she told him.

"A blind guy," said Roy. "That's all we need."

"What's that stink?" said Sully, becoming nauseated by the stench from the sidewalk below.

"It's those things down on the street. They're the same things that chased us up to your room."

"What things?"

"There's some plague going around. When people contract it, they lose their minds and start cannibalizing everybody in sight, spreading the disease."

Nonplussed, Sully didn't know what to say. He could not get his head around it. He could not relate to it. He had never encountered anything like this before in his life.

"What's that god-awful stink?" he said, pulling a face.

It was Beth who answered. "That's them. First, they get the disease and die. Then they become reanimated and try to devour everybody who's alive. They're living corpses. That's the stink of death."

"You said they lose their minds."

"Yeah, you're right. My bad. They have no minds to speak of after they die. How can you lose your mind, if you don't have one?"

"How is the disease spread?"

"Nobody knows—"

"Why are you asking these stupid question?" cut in Roy. "The bottom line is, we gotta get as far away as we can from the infected. That's all that matters."

"Then let's go," said Sully.

"How? Haven't you been listening, old man? The infected are everywhere. They're down on the streets. They're outside your door. Can't you hear them?"

Sully could, indeed, hear a barrage of rapping on his door.

"Are you sure that door's gonna hold?" asked Beth, fear edging her voice.

"I don't know," said Roy. "All I know is, we gotta get out of here. This whole area is infested by the infected."

"What's that?"

"What?"

"The lights went out."

Sully realized he could not hear the refrigerator humming anymore.

"Just what we need," said Roy. "A power outage."

"Is it getting dark?" asked Sully.

"That, too," said Beth.

"Do you have a phone, pops?" asked Roy.

"I have a cell phone," answered Sully.

"Figures," said Beth. "Cells aren't working. We already tried ours."

"No landline, pops?"

"No. It's cheaper to have just a cell. Are the landlines working?"

"Might be. We haven't been able to get to one to find out."

"Who are you gonna call?"

"Police. 911. Whatever."

"I can't help you."

"Do you have a gun?"

Sully didn't know if he should answer. If Roy wanted a gun, it might be to use it on him. But, then again, if Roy was going to mug him, he wouldn't need a gun to do it. After all, Sully was blind and defenseless. If he said he had a gun, it might deter Roy from assaulting him—if that was Roy's intention. Somehow Sully didn't think it was, not if everything Beth and Roy had said was true about the disease that was going around. Then again, you never knew with people. Beth and Roy might not be above robbing him. Sully would not call himself paranoid, just cautious. He decided to tell the truth.

"No, I don't," he said.

"Fuck," said Roy.

"Why would I have a gun? I can't see to shoot it."

"Don't smart-mouth me. I have a good mind to belt you."

Sully could feel Roy advancing on him, could feel Roy's breath on his face.

"I don't know what good a gun would do us, anyhow," said Beth. "There are so many of them out there. Maybe we could kill six of them. So what? Then what? How do we get past the thousands that are still left out there?"

"Well, what's your solution?" said Roy, turning on her.

"We need to reach a phone and call for help."

"Just how do we do that?"

It sounded to Sully like these two would be at each other's throats in a matter of minutes the way they were going at it hammer and tongs.

"It's better than your idea," said Beth.

Roy laughed harshly. "How are we gonna get to a phone with all those flesh eaters out there?"

"There must be a way."

"Like how?"

"Maybe we could break into an adjacent room."

"Like we broke into this room?" scoffed Roy.

"Why not?"

"We wouldn't be in here if pops hadn't let us in. We're not much good at B&E."

"We could still try."

"And what if the tenants in those rooms are infected? Then what? Did you ever think of that?"

"I have an idea," said Sully.

"Yeah?" said Roy in a snarky voice. "Let's hear it. It couldn't be any worse than any of the other ideas I've heard so far."

"There's a phone both at the end of the block."

"Great. A lot of good that does us! It's just at the end of the block. That's all. An inch is as good as a mile the mess we're in."

"Would you stop being so sarcastic?" said Beth. "Is that your idea of sounding tough? It just makes you sound like a loser."

Sully heard Roy spitting.

"You're the expert on losers," said Roy. "What about that last boyfriend of yours?"

"I'm tired of listening to you bitch."

"We're never gonna get out of here if you two kill each other," said Sully.

"What do you know?" snapped Roy. "You can't even see. You're the most hopeless, useless person in this room."

"Knock it off, Roy," said Beth.

This Roy was giving Sully a swift pain. The pair of them, Roy and Beth, were obviously at the ends of their ropes thanks to the crisis of the epidemic. Sully had to take that into consideration. But just because they were upset, didn't give them the right to denigrate him. To hell with them. Still, all of them had to work together to figure a way out.

"What if I can reach the phone booth?" said Sully.

"I hate to tell you this, pops, but it's pitch-dark out now," said Roy. "Just how are you gonna see—"

"I don't need to see," Sully cut in.

"You think you can make it to the phone in the dark?" said Beth.

"I go down those stairs once a day for my walk. I know them like the back of my hand. And I know where the phone booth is, too."

"Even if you *can* get there in the pitch-black, you're forgetting one thing."

"I'm listening."

"The zombies, or whatever you want to call them. They're everywhere. They'll tear you to pieces."

Sully pricked up his ears. "I don't hear them at the front door anymore."

"He's right," said Roy. "It sounds like they left the door."

"Well, they're still on the street," said Beth.

"I can get past them," said Sully.

"You're dreaming, pops," said Roy.

Sully headed for the door. "I can."

"How, you crazy old coot?"

"I'm not that old. I'm only in my sixties."

"That's plenty old. A lot of people die before they reach your age. You're blind and you're old. I don't see how you can do much of anything."

Sully reached the door, pressed his ear against the painted wood, and listened for noise in the hallway. Hearing nothing he unlocked the door and cracked it.

"What are you doing?" said Beth, a tinge of fear in her voice.

"I'm gonna go to the phone and call for help."

"How are you gonna get past the flesh eaters? Haven't you heard a word we've said?"

"I'm walking past them."

"And they're gonna just let you walk right by them, pretty as you please?"

"Yep."

"Why?"

"Because, just like you, they're handicapped."

"What are you babbling about, pops?" said Roy.

"They can't see in the dark." Sully paused, suddenly unsure of himself. "Can they?"

"I think you're right about them," said Beth. "I don't think they can."

Sully wished he knew what these two newcomers looked like. Somehow he figured they were good-looking, from the way they sounded so cocksure of themselves. Then again, maybe their arrogance was merely a sign of their youth. It didn't really matter what they looked like. They could not see him now either, on account of the dark, which gave him an advantage. He could find his way through the dark, whereas they and the infected could not.

More than anything, he wanted to get out of this room. Being stuck in here with these two lovebirds chewing each other out all the time was driving him batty.

"You're as nutty as a fruitcake, pops," said Roy. "You'll never reach the phone booth in one piece."

Opening the door wider, Sully wondered why he was risking his life to help these two carping strangers. The bottom line was, he was helping himself at the same time. He figured it was the right thing to do to help his fellow man. They were all in this mess together, like it or not. He would reach the phone and call the police for help for the three of them.

Once in the hallway, he closed the door behind him. He heard Roy or Beth lock the door behind him.

*The ingrates*, he thought. They hadn't even wished him good luck. Why was he bothering to risk his neck to save that crass couple?

The corridor reeked of a stench like rotting garbage combined with raw sewage and a trace of spoiled milk thrown in. It was all he could do to keep himself from gagging. He made for the stairwell. He didn't hear any of the creatures moving in the corridor or on the stairs. However, he thought he could hear shuffling on the ground floor at the bottom of the steps.

113

Bryan Cassiday

As he edged down the stairs, it dawned on him that he must be a fool to be walking straight into a nest of zombies. What was he thinking! How did he know they would not be able to see him? How did he know anything about them? He only knew what Roy and Beth had told him. And what did they really know?

He shuddered with cold, feeling alone, overcome by angst as he realized the true nature of his predicament. He froze, wondering if he should continue. He had not passed the point of no return yet. There was still time for him to turn back.

To what? To Roy and Beth? To hopelessness?

He decided to continue his mission.

The infected sounded louder now, as he descended the creaky steps. The creatures must have been milling around, grunting and snarling at each other.

He balked on a tread, wondering if he should continue his foolhardy trek. What if he caught their disease as he mingled among them? he wondered. Even if he could not see them and they could not see him, he still might be able to catch their disease. Maybe the pathogen was airborne. Maybe all he had to do was breathe the air the infected were exhaling for him to become infected.

Standing here would not solve any problems. He had to either continue his journey or retreat back to his apartment.

He decided to keep descending the whining steps. He wished they would not make so much noise. The treads and the risers were constructed of aged wood that bellyached whenever stepped on. What if the creatures heard him? He wondered if their hearing was as acute as his. His had been sharpened by years of blindness. In any case, he kept going and reached the ground floor.

He could feel ambient air stirring near his face as the creatures roamed around in the lobby. They did not seem to react to him. Surely, they could see him now on account of his proximity to them—if they could see him at all in the darkness.

He did not sense them reacting to his presence.

He continued angling toward the front door of the apartment house.

114

Accidentally, he bumped into one of the creatures. A Michelin man. Sully felt its beer belly. He froze in his tracks, petrified with fear. Had the creature seen him? If not, maybe it could smell him. Christ, what was he thinking when he decided to risk his life on this harebrained trip to the phone booth!

He heard the creature shamble away. Maybe it thought it had bumped into one of its fellow creatures when it had collided with him, decided Sully.

He decided to keep moving toward the door. However, his collision with the Michelin man had disoriented him. He might have gotten spun around during his impact with the creature and, as a result, might not be facing the door anymore.

He knew this route by heart, but that was only if he did not encounter any obstacles that might divert him from his course.

There was nothing for it. He resumed making his way to the door that gave onto the street. At least, that was where he thought he was heading.

Could the creatures smell him? he wondered. Apparently not. None of them was attacking him. It was a wonder they could smell anything at all with that noisome odor they were exuding.

He reached the front door—at least, he thought it was a door. Unless it was a wall. He felt around for a doorknob. Where was the doorknob? he wondered, splaying out his hands and sliding them across the wooden surface. It should be around here somewhere. He continued moving his hands along the wood in quest of the knob.

The forefinger on his left hand struck something made of steel, jamming his knuckle. It had to be the doorknob, he decided. He grasped it, twisted it, and opened the door that led to the street.

As he opened the door, he felt a mild breeze gust into his face, a breeze freighted with the stench of thousands of the dead. He screwed up his face with revulsion. He had no time to regurgitate. He had to keep going. He had to make that emergency call.

He walked onto the stoop then down its cement steps to the sidewalk, where he could sense scores of creatures maundering around, hissing and groaning. Reaching the sidewalk he struck out for the end of the block where the phone booth was located.

He walked with tiny steps, feeling his way. After all, garbage and who knew what else could be strewn all over the sidewalk. The city had to be a mess with these creatures swarming all over it.

He was going to make it! He could feel it in his bones. The creatures were paying no heed to him. Even when one of them fitfully bumped into him, the creature did not launch into an attack. As Sully had suspected, the creatures must not be able to see him in the darkness.

Estimating he was the better part of twenty-odd feet from the phone booth, he took larger steps, but took them gingerly, feeling with his toecaps for detritus that might be littering the sidewalk.

He heard a loud electronic buzz overhead, which startled him. He hoped it wasn't what he thought it was. It sounded like it might be a sodium streetlight humming to life—which would mean it would be shedding light on him as he padded across the sidewalk.

A nearby creature grunted louder in Sully's direction. Could the creature see him? wondered Sully. He sensed it advancing on him. It was so close to him now he could smell its rancid breath and feel its deathly coldness on his cheek, the breath of a corpse caressing him.

Sully took a gamble. Fearing lest the creature attack him, he removed his sunglasses, playing a hunch. Maybe it would work . . .

He had the distinct impression the creature was staring into his sightless eyes, trying to figure out if he was living, and all it could see was the blind, glazed eyes that reminded the creature of itself. Like looking into a mirror.

And the creature snorted at him.

And let him go.

And Sully knew, as surely as he knew anything, that the creature had made a mistake. Sully wasn't one of them, not yet anyway. He was still alive.

# Holder's Coffin

De Quincey could not believe there was blood leaking out of the bottom of the coffin. After all, the corpse inside the coffin was dead. How could there be fresh blood?

De Quincey had been a mortician for going on twenty years now. This was unheard-of.

He was standing in the funeral parlor in LA on a mild day in October, baffled, as he watched blood leaking out of the bottom of the mahogany coffin and dripping onto the hardwood floor under the bier. It was a beautiful day outside with the balmy Santa Ana winds whispering through palm fronds and eucalyptus leaves under a pristine blue sky, and here he was in the middle of a graveyard spending his entire life surrounded by rotting cadavers like he did day in, day out.

Was he dreaming this? he wondered. It was giving him the willies watching the blood impinge on the floor. He could even hear the drops plinking on the hardwood like water dripping out of a leaky faucet into a sink. The inference was undeniable. There could be no other conclusion. If the corpse inside the coffin was bleeding, it must still be alive.

De Quincey's heartbeat fell to jackhammering at the thought. He had no desire to open that coffin. But if that corpse was still alive, De Quincey knew he should open the coffin's lid to let in air for the immured victim to breathe. Otherwise, the inhabitant of the airtight coffin really would be a corpse in no time, dead by suffocation.

De Quincey dug his smartphone out of his trouser pocket and summoned his assistant Herb. The son of one of De Quincey's few friends who happened to be a landscaper by trade, Herb was all of nineteen years old. De Quincey hired him as a favor to Herb's father. Herb wasn't the sharpest tool in the shed, but he was strong and, like a horse, had no trouble moving coffins around.

Clad in stonewashed jeans and a T, Herb entered the parlor at a jog and made his way down the middle of the aisle that bisected the dozen rows of folding wooden chairs that had been arranged for the corpse's wake that had taken place inside of an hour ago. Not that they needed a dozen rows. It turned out they needed only the first two rows to accommodate the guests to the wake. And even those rows didn't fill up. The corpse, one Bram Holder, had few friends and relatives—sort of like De Quincey, realized De Quincey.

He didn't want to think about it. He sometimes wondered how he got out of bed in the morning. Burying cadavers wasn't his idea of a dream job, but it kept a roof over his head and food in his belly. As for these wakes he attended, he didn't believe in any of the accompanying mumbo jumbo that went with them. He believed in the ashes-to-ashes and dust-to-dust part, and that was as far as it went. When you were dead, it was over. Game, set, match. Kaput. Nothingness.

Looking at corpses day after day bummed De Quincey out. He was becoming obsessed with death. Almost to the point of killing himself, but, then again, what was the point? What was the point of any of it? Life was pointless, but so then was death. So what was the point of killing yourself? And now he was seeing blood dripping out of coffins. *Christ!* Was he losing it, or what?

"What's up?" said Herb, trotting up to De Quincey. "You sounded jacked up on the phone. I've been meaning to ask you, how come you never come over to our house and have a beer?"

"I didn't call you here to socialize."

"Just asking," said Herb, shrugging in apology.

"I don't drink."

"My dad says you're a lone wolf. How come you don't have a wife and family?"

"Why are you so nosy today?"

"Beats thinking about stiffs all day."

"What does?"

"Getting to know more about you. Working in a graveyard all my life would send me up the walls. So what gives?"

"Hmm?"

"How come you don't have a wife and family?"

"You want to know the truth?"

"Yeah. Of course."

"I have no idea."

Maybe it was because he had spent twenty years of his life working in a graveyard with a bunch of moldering, stinking corpses for friends, decided De Quincey. That might have had something to do with his dearth of social contacts and a family.

The dripping of the blood from the coffin interrupted his thoughts and seized his full attention.

He cut his gaze toward the blood seeping out of the coffin less than six feet in front of him. "Do you see what I see, Herb?"

"Jeez! What the hell? Is that blood?"

"It ain't Kool-Aid."

"Is the guy still alive in there?"

"A stiff can't bleed."

"Then he must be alive." Herb rushed over to the coffin. "We need to get the poor guy out of there."

"Think about it, Herb. Do you really want to open that coffin?"

"If somebody's alive in there, we've got to. He'll suffocate."

"Shhh," said De Quincey, holding his index finger to his lips.

"What?"

"What's that scratching sound?"

"I don't know."

"It's coming from inside the coffin."

Herb winced. "Sounds like a guy dragging his fingernails across a chalkboard."

"Shut up."

"What?"

Cocking his ear De Quincey held up his hand to silence Herb. De Quincey could hear something else.

"It sounds like somebody's screaming in the coffin," he said under his breath, gnashing his teeth.

"Jesus wept."

"Do you hear it?"

"I'm not sure. It could be the wind howling. It's kicking up a ruckus outside. And now that I think about it, that scratching could be coming from the branches thrashing against the sides of the mortuary."

"It's coming from inside that coffin, I tell you."

"What are we gonna do?" said Herb, bug-eyed.

"Can you imagine being buried alive? It must scramble your brains. He could be nuts by now."

De Quincey was trembling. He wondered why he was so scared. Why didn't he go over to the coffin and help Herb open it? De Quincey hated to admit it, but fear was holding him back. No matter how hard he tried, he could not take a step toward the coffin. His legs wouldn't work. It made no sense. It shouldn't be paralyzing him with fear like this. He needed a drink.

Herb hesitated at the side of the coffin, face working. "I'm not sure I want to go through with this."

The door to the mortuary burst open and slammed against the wall. Coiled with tension, De Quincey and Herb all but jumped out of their shoes. Withered brown leaves from the lawn skittered across the floor down the aisle toward De Quincey, clacking like crabs' legs along the hardwood.

"We've got to," said De Quincey, getting a hold of himself. "We can't let him die."

"Help me," said Herb, attempting to pry open the lid. "It won't budge. It feels like it's locked or something. Did you lock it?"

De Quincey screwed up his face in thought. "I must have. I don't recall."

"Come over here with the key."

"This can't be happening. How can a coffin weep blood?"

"Because the guy in there's alive," said Herb, tearing his fingernails on the heavy coffin lid that would not budge.

At last De Quincey found the strength of will to move his feet in the direction of the bier. He sidestepped the puddle of blood that was expanding on the floor. The plinking of the drips in the puddle waxed louder the nearer he got to the coffin.

Reaching the coffin he fumbled for the key in his trouser pocket. The key seemed to be stuck on something in there. He latched onto the key and gave it a good yank. Attached to the key ring, its teeth ensnared in the ring, his comb snapped out of his pocket with the key. He disengaged the comb from the key and replaced the comb in his pocket.

"Hurry!" said Herb.

Still reluctant to open the coffin, De Quincey nevertheless inserted the key's shank into the lock and twisted. The lock snicked open.

Frantically, Herb clutched the coffin lid and flipped it open.

De Quincey reeled in shock. He could not believe his eyes. Clasping his brow he tried to comprehend what was happening.

The coffin was empty.

"I don't get it," said Herb, scratching his head. "Where is he?" He glanced at the dripping blood. "How can there be blood if nobody's inside here?"

"Can't you smell it?" said De Quincey, grimacing at the stench.

"Yeah. Phew! What is that?"

"The stench of a rotting corpse."

"It's coming from the coffin," said Herb, leaning toward it then abruptly pulling back. "But there's nothing in there."

"I can see that."

"Then why does it stink so bad? And why that dripping blood? This is creeping me out."

"Look at the inside of the lid."

"What the—"

The glossy royal purple damask that insulated the coffin lid hung in tatters.

"It's like somebody tore it apart," said De Quincey.

He stepped toward the lid to get a better look at it. Brushing aside the damask he peered at the mahogany coffin lid. Scratches marred the wooden lid's interior surface, scratches like fingernails might make. Appalled at his discovery, he looked gaunt, face frozen.

"What's the matter?" said Herb, watching De Quincey.

"There are scratch marks on the inside of the lid."

"The guy inside must've tried to scratch his way out when he came to."

Something inside the coffin caught De Quincey's eye. He leaned down into the coffin and picked up the tiny object that lay on the damask lining.

"What's that?" said Herb.

"One of his fingernails, it looks like," said De Quincey, raising it to his eyes and scrutinizing it.

"What are we gonna do?" said Herb, getting jittery, shifting back and forth on his feet.

"Call the cops. This may be a crime scene."

"But there's no corpse."

"Not here, anyway."

"What are you saying? That the guy climbed out of here, left blood on the coffin, and died somewhere?"

"It's possible."

"How could it be a crime if he was already dead in the first place?"

"But he wasn't already dead, apparently. Just because he was pronounced dead doesn't mean he actually *was* dead."

Herb massaged his chin in thought. "How could he climb out of a locked coffin?"

"It can be unlocked on the inside without a key. Just twist open the lock. It works like a door to a house."

Herb shook his head in confusion. "Why would a coffin be constructed with a lock that opens from the inside? The corpse is dead. What's the point?"

"This is a special coffin. It was constructed in this fashion in case the victim wasn't really dead. He suffered from catalepsy and feared being buried alive."

"Catalepsy?"

"It mimics death. Even a doctor can't distinguish a cataleptic trance from death."

"Then that so-called corpse is stumbling around the graveyard right now?"

"It looks that way."

"He must be half out of his mind if he was locked up in that coffin for who knows how many days."

"Did you call the police?"

Herb pulled out his cell phone and did so.

"Let's take a look outside," said De Quincey.

"Do we have to? I don't know about you, but I don't want to run into this guy if he's out there."

"He may need our help," said De Quincey, even though he felt as edgy as Herb.

De Quincey ushered Herb outside the mortuary. They surveyed the cemetery that stretched out before them on gently rolling hillocks studded with tombstones that stuck out of the grass like oversized cleats.

The dry air desiccated De Quincey's throat as he inhaled it. The drought-stricken wilting palms and eucalyptuses looked sere and brittle, as if they might snap like matchsticks any moment in the wind and explode into flames. Eucalyptus leaves rattled over his head. Curling at its edges the bark on the nearby tree trunk looked like chapped lips.

De Quincey ran his eyes along the cemetery grounds. No sign of anyone.

"If he climbed out of that coffin, how did he get by us without our seeing him?" said Herb, scoping out the grounds with squinty eyes.

De Quincey had no answer.

He picked up on a squad car with its bar lights flashing and its siren blaring highballing along the outskirts of the cemetery. The siren's keening seemed to ride the currents of the shifting wind like a surfer coasting on a ragged comber.

The black-and-white drove into the necropolis, negotiated the bottleneck that led to the mortuary, and pulled to a tire-shrieking halt in front of De Quincey and Herb. Open-mouthed, they watched the squad car disgorge its passenger.

A plainclothes cop pushing sixty lumbered out of the passenger's-side door with a grunt. Stocky with a barrel chest, all of five ten, he had greying hair. Wearing an off-the-rack fawn jacket and dark slacks he strutted toward De Quincey with the rolling gait of a stevedore.

"I'm Inspector Bolt, sir," he said. "And you are?"

"Patrick De Quincey."

"You called this in?"

"*I* did," said Herb. "I'm Herb Greensmith."

"What's this all about?"

"We think somebody may've been buried alive," said De Quincey.

"Let's check it out."

Clad in a black police uniform, the twentysomething brunette officer that had driven the squad car approached Bolt and nodded at De Quincey. De Quincey couldn't help but notice she wore skintight black pants and her thick black leather belt emphasized the narrowness of her waist.

"Officer Lupe Suarez," said Bolt, introducing the driver.

De Quincey led them to the bier in the mortuary. "See the blood dripping from the coffin?"

Bolt approached the puddle of blood and inspected it. Then he peered inside the empty coffin that still had its lid flipped open.

"So where's the corpse?" he said.

"There isn't any," said Herb.

"If there's no corpus delicti, where's the crime?" said Bolt, confronting De Quincey and Herb.

"Let me explain," said De Quincey. "We think somebody was buried alive in this coffin and escaped."

De Quincey took a pencil and a pad out of his jacket pocket. "What's his name?"

"Bram Holder."

"Hmm. That name sounds familiar," said Bolt, furrowing his brow. "I'll think of it later." He shrugged and wrote the name down on his pad.

"We believe that's his blood dripping from the coffin."

"Funny how it keeps dripping even when there's nobody in there," said Bolt, stooping to examine the puddle.

"Freaks me out," said Herb.

Groaning, wincing, Bolt straightened up. "My trick knee . . . So what's the crime?"

"He was buried alive," said De Quincey, nettled by Bolt's question.

"Is that a crime?" asked Suarez.

"Of course, it is. You can't go around burying people alive."

"False imprisonment," said Bolt, scribbling on his pad. "But what's this blood here got to do with it?" he said, gesturing with his pencil toward the puddle near his foot.

"He must've cut himself crawling out of the coffin."

"So where's"—Bolt consulted his notes—"where's this Holder fellow now?"

"We don't know."

Bolt snorted. "Not much to go on. We don't have any hard evidence that he crawled out of this coffin. Only your word for it."

De Quincey strode over to the opened lid. "The lining's in tatters. That's proof that he was in here. And the bottom of the lid's wood is scratched from his trying to claw his way out of the coffin."

Bolt followed De Quincey and pored over the shredded lining and the scratched coffin lid. He curled his lips like he was sucking a lemon.

"At what time did Holder escape from the coffin?" asked Bolt.

"I don't know," answered De Quincey. "I didn't see him do it."

"Did anyone witness his escape?"

"Not that I know of."

"It would help if we could establish the approximate time of his escape. Then maybe we could ask around and find out if anyone saw where he went. What about you?"

"I didn't see him get out," answered Herb.

Bolt hemmed and hawed. "I find it hard to believe that nobody saw him climb out of this coffin—if, in fact, he did climb out of here. Even if it's true, how come nobody saw him cross the cemetery? Certainly people would take note of a walking corpse."

"But he wasn't a corpse," said De Quincey. "He was buried alive."

"Without his testimony, we have no evidence that a crime actually took place." Bolt paused a beat. "Who locked him in the coffin?"

"I did."

"You, sir? You confess to locking a living man in a coffin?"

"No, no! That's not what happened."

"What *did* happen?"

"After the coroner pronounced Holder dead I locked Holder in the coffin."

"You thought he was dead?"

"The coroner signed the man's death certificate. What am I supposed to think?"

"Don't get excited, sir. I'm only trying to find out what happened. Some time after you locked Holder in this coffin, he clawed his way out and walked away. Is that it?"

Agitated, De Quincey commenced pacing around, trying to make sense of it all. "I know it sounds crazy."

"Then where is he?"

"It looks like this coffin's bleeding," chimed in Suarez, puzzled. "There's nobody inside, but blood keeps seeping out."

De Quincey and Bolt angled over to Suarez, who was standing staring in awe at the blood dripping out of the coffin.

126

Overwrought, De Quincey clutched his brow. "This can't be happening. Coffins don't bleed."

He crouched down on his haunches next to the puddle of blood and held his palm under the blood that was dripping from the coffin. The blood didn't drip onto his palm.

"You see," he said triumphantly, jumping to his feet. "It's not really happening. That blood didn't drip onto my hand. The blood's an illusion."

"Then what the hell's going on?" said Herb.

"This isn't happening," De Quincey said more to himself than to anybody else and slewed around so he faced away from the coffin.

He figured when he turned back around to face it, there wouldn't be any blood dripping out of it. The blood was a figment of his imagination. It had to be.

Taking a deep breath he turned around deliberately to face the coffin. He cast around for the puddle of blood on the floor. As he expected, there wasn't any blood. He sighed with relief. He was having a doozy of a nightmare, that was all. Except—

Except Herb, Detective Bolt, and Suarez were still in the room staring at him.

"What's this all about?" said Bolt. "Why'd you call us here?"

Searching De Quincey's face Inspector Bolt removed a pipe from his jacket pocket and inserted the black plastic pipe stem into his mouth. Without lighting up he fell to chewing the stem while cupping the pipe bowl in his hand.

"Is this some kind of gag?" said Suarez, scowling.

De Quincey checked out the coffin. The lid was still open, but he saw no sign of damage either to its interior or to its lining. No sign of a corpse having crawled out of the coffin.

"Don't you see?" he said. "It's not real. There's no blood. Nothing happened here."

"Then why'd you call us?" said Bolt. "That's the question. We ought to charge you with making a prank call to the police. Hey, wait a minute, now I remember your name. De Quincey.

You're the guy that was investigated about fifteen years ago, was it?"

"Want me to run him in, Inspector?" said Suarez.

"Hold on a second. This guy De Quincey was investigated for burying somebody alive in this mortuary. What was the name of that guy you buried alive?"

"Holder," muttered De Quincey, crestfallen. "Bram Holder. It wasn't my fault." He gritted his teeth in recollection of the tragedy. "It wasn't my fault."

Clutching his face with both hands, De Quincey collapsed to his knees on the floor, sobbing. *"It wasn't my fault."*

"I knew that name sounded familiar," said Bolt.

"What's this all about, Inspector?" asked Suarez.

"I was working over in the Hollenbeck division back then when I heard about it. De Quincey here buried Holder alive. The guy suffocated to death in his coffin. Holder's relatives wanted the DA to charge De Quincey here for false imprisonment."

"What happened?"

"The DA didn't file charges. It was the coroner who pronounced Holder dead. De Quincey had nothing to do with that. The relatives sued the city for negligence and won. If I remember correctly, the coroner later resigned in disgrace for botching the call on Holder."

"So what's the deal with today?"

"I don't know. De Quincey had a nervous breakdown after he found out he buried someone alive. He couldn't come to grips with it. He got over it eventually and returned to his job at this mortuary."

"Except for one thing."

"What's that?"

Suarez gazed at De Quincey who was hunched in a fetal position on the floor and beating the floorboards with his hands in a combination of sorrow, frustration, and anger at himself.

"Except he never really got over it."

# Brush with Death

Hocker got drunk before he killed himself.

That was the plan anyway. After all, who wanted to go on living during a zombie apocalypse? What was the point? There was nothing to live for. Just another day in paradise. As if that wasn't enough, his girlfriend had dumped him, to boot.

He was working on his third can of beer. The drinking part was easy—and fun as well. It was the other part, the self-destruction part that was tough.

There wasn't much call for hypnotists these days. Before the plague and the rise of the flesh eaters, he had eked out a living as a professional hypnotist. That was back in the day, when it was safe to walk the streets—which seemed like a million years ago. Actually it was less than two weeks ago. Not that it mattered. Everything was in chaos now. Civilization was collapsing. The infected flesh eaters were running amok on the streets slaughtering everybody in sight, devouring their flesh.

Hocker had taken refuge in an abandoned house that he had broken into in LA the better part of a week ago and was now sharing it with his best friend Max, the same best friend that had stolen his girlfriend Becky. Becky with her pageboy brunette hair and dimpled rosy cheeks. And her insufferable Pollyanna optimism. What could she see in Max? A disheveled hippie type pushing thirty who rode around on a Harley scavenging for food most of the time. Though he resembled a hippie with his shoulder-length scroungy hair, Max was more a redneck than anything.

Needless to say, Hocker would like to kill Max. But he didn't. He didn't want to be left alone on earth among millions of zombies. And then there was Becky. She wouldn't appreciate it if Hocker took out Max. No doubt she would never speak to Hocker again if he blew away Max. But Hocker still wanted Max dead.

If only there was another way to rid the world of Max other than murdering him himself, decided Hocker. He couldn't very well hire somebody else to do it, since living human beings were few and far between these days.

Hocker flirted with the idea of arranging an accident to befall Max, but couldn't dream up one that had an iota of a chance of working. In the end what difference did it make whether Max lived or died? decided Hocker. They were all going to die at the hands of the plague-infected flesh eaters.

*Be always drunken, nothing else matters*, thought Hocker. Wasn't that a line from the *Rubaiyat* of Omar Khayyam?

Clutching his can of beer Hocker got out of his chair, angled across the carpeted floor to the bay window, its monk's cloth curtains drawn, and gazed at the street below, where milky-eyed flesh eaters were staggering around with blood dripping from their jowls, searching for prey in the dying sunlight of a late afternoon in autumn. Hocker pulled back from the window, not wishing to be seen by the creatures.

He picked up on a man cowering behind a fluted green lamppost on the other side of the street. Clad in a suit, a loose tie askew about his neck, eyes bulging with fear, the guy looked to be in his forties with dark hair and a Vandyke. Hocker pegged him for an uninfected human.

Hocker sidestepped in front of the window and waved at the guy, who spotted him and nodded tightly. Hocker backed out of the window before the flesh eaters had a chance to catch sight of him.

Scoping out the scores of creatures lumbering in the street, the suit was debating when to make a dash for the safety of Hocker's house. As yet, the creatures had not picked up on him as he stood stock-still behind the lamppost.

Hocker didn't know how long that would last. He figured it was only a matter of time before the infected would clap eyes on the suit.

Hocker scampered to the front door, ready to unlock it the moment the suit arrived. Hocker peered through the judas in the door, watching the blood-splattered zombies on the street slog by, picking their way through the cars abandoned on the macadam. Miles and miles of creatures wherever you looked.

Hocker figured the suit needed to make up his mind on a dime to run for the house. It was either that or dally behind the lamppost and risk discovery by the infected.

Hocker couldn't blame him for being scared, but what was the guy waiting for? No matter when he scrammed, the dead would spot him as he crossed the street. Their numbers showed no signs of thinning out. If anything, they were increasing. He might as well take off now. Hocker wasn't going to stand here all day waiting to unlock the door for him.

Max chose to appear at that moment.

"What's up, Svengali?" he said, approaching Hocker from the kitchen, chewing on a granola bar, wearing jeans and a navy blue wife-beater. "Are you sloshed yet?" he asked, noticing the can of beer in Hocker's hand.

"There's somebody out there," said Hocker, facing Max.

"One of those things?" said Max, eyes wide.

"No. A person."

"Well, let him in."

"He's across the street."

Hocker turned back to the door. Peering out the judas he started as the suit bolted out from behind the lamppost across the street and dashed toward the house, slaloming between zombies and parked cars at a breakneck pace.

The sluggish creatures spotted him and gave chase, jerking after him like broken marionettes. The suit easily outstripped them. It was just a matter of dodging them. But a mob of them

131

was marching down the street in his direction cramming the macadam with a wall of lurching dead bodies.

A pack of stray dogs that was roaming the street fell to baying at the sight of them.

As long as he kept running, the suit would make it, decided Hocker.

Hocker unlocked and yanked open the door as the suit sprang up the stairs onto the stoop and barreled toward him, gasping for breath.

Flesh eaters constellated around the stoop and climbed its wooden steps, groaning in anticipation of a fresh meal, clumsy feet clunking on the treads and kicking the risers.

Hocker slammed the door in their faces after the suit shot into the house with seconds to spare.

Becky darted into the living room from the kitchen, drawn by the commotion and the banging of the door.

"What's going on?" She locked eyes on the suit stumbling into the room, his mouth gasping for breath. "Is he OK?"

"His eyes look clear," said Hocker. "He was hiding across the street."

Zombie fists thwacked against the locked front door.

"Now all those things are gonna want to get in here," she said, and bit her lower lip, which whitened under the compression.

"What did you want me to do? Let him get eaten on the street?"

"Never mind." She paused. "Can those things break down the door?"

Hocker approached the juddering door and peeked through the judas at the grimacing faces of the undead bobbing outside. "There aren't enough of them out there to break through."

"What if they get reinforcements?" said Max.

"Enough of them can't fit on the porch to burst through the door with their combined weight."

"What makes you the expert?"

"They're too slow and uncoordinated," said Hocker, his words punctuated with the nerve-frazzling thuds of zombie fists on the door.

"Excuse me if I don't believe you."

Slewing around to face Max, beer foaming and sloshing out of the can in his hand, Hocker looked graveled.

Ignoring him Max pelted toward a shellacked deal bureau in the living room and gestured to Becky. She headed over to him. He stood at one end of the bureau and motioned for her to stand at the other.

"Let's push it in front of the door," he said.

Straining, they slid the bureau across the thin-napped carpet. Putting his back into it, half-eaten granola bar in hand, Max did the lion's share of the horsing with Becky as cynosure.

They shoved the bureau against the door, which was vibrating in its frame as a flurry of thumps erupted on it. Max wiped the sweat off his face with the back of his arm as he released the bureau.

"That ought to hold," said Becky.

"For now anyway," said Max.

Becky turned her attention to the newcomer, poring over him to make sure he wasn't infected. "Who are you?"

"Val D. Maars," said the suit, straightening his magenta tie to a degree.

"The man from Mars, heh?" said Max, a lopsided grin plastered on his face.

Hocker noticed a drop of fresh blood on the carpet next to one of Val's grimy black oxfords. Hocker's eyes traveled up the length of Val's dark trousers, detecting a slight tear in the fabric on the thigh. If Hocker hadn't been looking for it, he wouldn't have picked up on the rip. Hocker didn't bring up the matter.

"Did any of the infected bite you, Val?" said Becky.
"No."

She approached him and stared into his eyes.

Val backed away from her gaze.

"Your eyes look clear," she said.

"Of course. Why shouldn't they?" said Val, adjusting his tie again.

"What'd you do before the plague?" asked Max.

"I was a salesman. What'd you do?"

Max didn't answer off the bat. "I was a survivor. Still am."

Val looked blank.

"Welcome to the end of the world," said Max.

"I would've been a goner out there if I hadn't seen you guys. There's hardly anybody left alive."

"Tell me about it."

"Have a seat," said Becky. "It's not like we're going anywhere."

Max polished off his granola bar and made for the kitchen. Becky followed him.

Played out, Val plunked down on a sofa and spread-eagled on his back.

Hocker sat beside him.

"What'd you used to do?" asked Val.

"I was a hypnotist," answered Hocker.

"No kidding? That sounds interesting. Were you a hypnotherapist?"

"No. I performed stage hypnosis for entertainment."

"What's that like?"

"During hypnosis, a patient's mind becomes detached from his body."

"How so?"

"It becomes suspended outside his physical presence."

Val snorted. "Sounds like a load of bull, I gotta tell you."

"Do you know what that means?"

Val yawned. "No."

"If you take it to its logical conclusion, it means that the patient's body could die and yet his mind could go on living, suspended in the air outside the corpse."

"You're putting me on," said Val, smiling.

"The mind is a marvel of complexity. The ordinary human doesn't use even half of it."

134

Max ambled into the living room, nibbling on a fresh granola bar. It was dusk outside. The living room lights flickered.

"Oh no," he said. "There goes the power again."

"And you've actually done this with one of your patients?" Val asked Hocker.

"No," answered Hocker. "Not yet. This would be a good time to put my theory into practice. Don't you think?"

"If the body dies and the mind lives, where does the mind go?"

"Since I haven't done the experiment, I don't know. I can only speculate. I believe the mind exists in an invisible state outside the body's husk."

"Why are you telling me this?"

"You would make the ideal patient for my experiment."

Val bolted upright on the sofa. "What are you talking about?"

"Because one of the flesh eaters bit you, and you're gonna die and turn."

"No, they didn't."

"Your leg is bleeding, and you have a tear in your trousers near the thigh." Hocker pointed at Val's foot.

Val looked down at his foot and, beside it on the carpet, picked up on drops of coagulating blood. "I didn't even realize it."

"One of those things bit you?" said Max with concern, overhearing their conversation.

"No."

"Then how come you're bleeding?"

Puzzled, Val shook his head. It took a while for him to answer.

"I must have gotten cut on some barbed wire," he said at length.

"Where'd you run across barbed wire? There isn't any in the street outside."

"It wasn't here." Val paused in thought. "It was . . . let me see. I'm trying to recall . . . I'm stressed out and can't think straight."

"You ought to be able to remember something like that. Getting cut. Sure."

"To tell the truth, I didn't even know it cut me, till you guys mentioned it. With all the excitement going on I didn't even realize. I was running for my life, for Christ's sake."

Max fished out a pocketknife from his trouser pocket and flicked open the blade. "It's easy to check out."

"Now I remember," said Val, eyes wide as he took in the open pocketknife in Max's hand. "It was at a hardware store."

Coughing, Becky entered the living room. "We're gonna survive this little plague and rebuild the city. It's just a matter of believing we can do it. It's all about believing in yourself."

Nobody said anything. Dead silence.

At last, knife in hand, Max said, "We got a problem."

"What?" said Becky, picking up on his knife. "What happened?"

"We think one of the infected bit Val."

"It's not a bite," said Val edgily. "Barbed wire cut my leg. I'm not infected."

"So what's wrong with that?" said Becky. "He may have tetanus, but not the plague," she told Max.

"One thing," said Hocker. "There's no barbed wire around here."

"I told you," said Val, face breaking into a sweat. "I was in a hardware store when it happened."

Holding out his knife Max approached Val.

"What are you doing?" said Val.

"We need to check out that wound on your leg," said Max.

"Why do you need a knife for that?" said Val, drawing back in his seat. "Are you calling me a liar?"

"I'm not calling you anything. If you're infected, we got problems."

"I'm not infected."

"Hold still!"

Stooping on his haunches Max stuck the knife's tip into Val's trousers a half inch above the torn fabric.

136

"What are you gonna do?" said Val, quailing in terror. "Cut off my leg?"

"Hold still and I won't cut you."

Max sliced through the trousers with his blade. Then he latched onto the trousers and jerked a flap of the cloth down, exposing the bleeding wound on Val's thigh. Max scrutinized the wound.

Hocker approached Val and scoped out the ripped flesh.

"I can't be sure, but I'd say it was teeth that did this," said Max.

"Whatever did it twisted the flesh and tore out a chunk like a dog does when it bites, so it's hard to see the outline of the teeth marks," said Hocker.

"That's because it wasn't teeth," said Val. "It was barbed wire that did it."

Max straightened up, knife in hand. "We can't take any chances."

"What are you gonna do?" said Val, face screwed up in panic.

Max nodded to Becky. They both left the room.

"What are they gonna do?" Val asked Hocker, who stayed behind.

"If one of the infected bit you, you're now infected," answered Hocker.

"Do I look like I'm infected?"

"No. Not now. It takes a while for the virus to enter your system."

"But how could I be infected, if one of the infected didn't bite me?"

Hocker ignored Val's question. "There may be a way to save you."

"I don't need saving."

"Yeah, you do. Max is gonna want to blow your brains out if you can't be cured."

"You and I both know there's no cure. And anyway, I'm not infected!"

"We can't take that chance." Hocker paused. "I have a theory, a good one if I do say so myself. I believe it'll work."

"Let's change the subject."

"I believe I can hypnotize somebody in extremis and prevent their mind from dying with their body."

Hangdog, Val grunted. "Sounds like science fiction to me."

"If I could save your mind from becoming infected when your body turns into a zombie, you wouldn't be a threat to us."

Val scoffed. "How do you figure that?"

"Because I could control you via hypnosis. I could hypnotize you into not wanting to eat us."

"You don't really think that hocus-pocus would work, do you?" said Max behind Hocker.

Startled, Hocker whipped his head around at the sound of Max's voice. "I didn't know you were there."

"I didn't want you to know I was here."

"What harm is there in trying?"

Max contemplated the gun in his hand. "If I shoot him in the head now, we won't have to worry about his turning."

"Think about it. If we're able to control him through hypnosis after he turns, we could use him to attack the other creatures."

"Only if it works."

"It would give us another weapon against the infected. He can attack the other zombies, but they won't attack *him* because they don't eat zombie flesh. They attack and eat only the living. I could hypnotize him to kill them. He could be our one-man wrecking crew."

"Like I said, only if it works."

"It *will* work. Why wouldn't it?"

"What if you can't hypnotize him? I've heard that some people can't be hypnotized."

"That's true. Certain types aren't susceptible to hypnotic suggestion."

"What if Val's one of those types?"

"I don't like you guys talking about me like I'm not here," said Val.

138

Hocker thought about Val, wondering if he would make a good subject for hypnosis. Val was a salesman who wore a suit to work. A conformist, he obeyed orders and dressed like he was supposed to for his job. In order to succeed at his job, he needed to please customers in order to convince them to buy his product. Basically, he wanted people to like him. In other words, he wasn't his own man. Therefore, Hocker concluded that Val would be a prime candidate for hypnotic suggestion, that Val didn't have the independence of mind to be able to think for himself and fight off Hocker's powers of suggestion.

"I believe I can hypnotize Val," Hocker told Max.

"It's a long shot. I say we whack him now," said Max, gripping his pistol, raising it, and training it on Val. "Why go to all the trouble of hypnotizing him?"

"We don't have to kill him yet," said Becky, walking up to Max from behind, clutching his raised arm, and lowering it.

"What's the point of waiting?"

"Maybe there's something to this hypnosis stuff. A tame zombie might come in handy as a weapon we could use."

"Can't you guys get it through your heads?" burst Val. "I'm not a zombie."

"Not yet," said Max, almost as an afterthought.

"What about how I feel? Did you ever consider that?"

"What do you mean?" said Becky.

"Maybe I don't want to go on living in a zombie body. Maybe I'd rather be dead than have my mind floating in space telling my zombie body what to do."

Max raised his gun again and brought the muzzle to bear on Val. "Works for me."

Val waved him off like he was washing a windshield. "Not yet."

"He's got a point," said Becky. "I wouldn't want my mind to go on living if I had a stinking dead zombie body."

"But we might be able to find a cure for the disease, while his mind is still alive outside his zombie body," said Hocker. "And then we could cure his body of the plague."

139

"Slim and none on that one," said Max. "Talk about wishful thinking."

"Any chance is better than none."

Max shrugged.

Suits were good to hypnotize because they were conformists at heart, decided Hocker. He was convinced Val would make a perfect subject.

"What do you say?" Hocker asked Val.

Val shook his head, trying to grasp the enormity of what Hocker was asking him. "Let me get this straight. You want me to become a zombie and hypnotize me just before I turn?"

"The fact of the matter is, you're gonna turn into one whether you want to or not. I don't *want* you to become one. It's the way it is."

"I told you I wasn't bitten."

"We think you're lying to protect yourself," said Max. "I can't say that I blame you. I'd lie about it too, if I got bit. I wouldn't want anybody to know."

"What if I say no?"

Max sighed and gazed at his pistol.

"Damned if I do and damned—," said Val.

"Does that mean yes?"

Grudgingly, Val nodded. He turned to Hocker. "When do you plan on putting me under?"

"Now's as good a time as any," said Hocker.

It was dark outside now, he noticed, but the flesh eaters at the door continued their rapping on it unabated.

"How do you feel, Val?" asked Becky.

"OK," answered Val.

"You look kind of peaked."

"Like you're seasick or something," said Max.

"That's because you guys are stressing me out," said Val. "The only reason I'm agreeing to this is to keep you from shooting me." Val did a double take. "You're not gonna shoot me after you hypnotize me, are you?"

"No," said Hocker. "If he shoots you, you're dead. Hypnosis won't save you. Nothing will. Hypnosis is your best bet for staying alive after you turn."

"Let's do it."

Hocker told him to sit back and relax. Hocker then exerted his powers of suggestion over him. Hocker withdrew a penlight from his trouser pocket, switched the light on, and held it steady ten-odd inches in front of Val's eyes.

"Watch the light," said Hocker. "Keep looking at it. Don't look away."

"Don't you need one of those hypnotic-eye gizmos?" said Val, staring at the penlight. "That thing that spins around with wavy lines?"

"And how about some *Twilight Zone* music?" said Max with a grin.

"Amateur hour," said Hocker.

Hocker was using James Braid's eye-fixation technique. More often than not, it worked on patients, Hocker knew. As Val's pupils became dilated from staring at the pinpoint of light, Hocker moved it closer to Val's eyes, telling him to close his lids.

"I don't think this is gonna work on me," said Val.

"You are entering a trance," said Hocker in a soothing voice. "You will do as I tell you. Listen to the sound of my voice."

Hocker could not care less about curing Val of the plague. Hocker had another reason for saving Val.

"Open your eyes," said Hocker.

Eyes glassy, Val obeyed, tuned in to Hocker's voice to the exclusion of everything else.

"How are we gonna know when he's dead?" said Max, eying Val.

"He'll stop breathing," said Hocker.

"Will he look like a zombie?"

"Good question. I would say yes. After all, the plague virus is circulating through his bloodstream even as he's hypnotized."

"What you're saying is, when he dies he'll become a zombie but he won't attack us because he's under your spell," said Becky. "Right?"

"That's about the size of it," said Hocker.

"How long's this gonna take?" asked Max.

"Not long. Note the greenish pallor of his face. His irises are losing their color, too."

"Will he be able to talk?"

"I don't know."

"Val, can you hear me?" asked Hocker.

"Y. . . e . . . s," answered Val in a guttural voice that emanated from the depths of his chest.

"What the hell was that?" said Max, flinching at Val's thunderous voice.

"Maybe he's dead now," said Becky.

Gingerly, Hocker reached toward Val's throat and felt for a pulse. "He's gone."

"How do you feel?" Hocker asked Val.

Mouth hanging ajar, Val groaned. The entire room seemed to rumble with the sound.

"What?" said Hocker. "I can't understand you."

Val's mouth continued to hang open. "I'm in pain," he said, without moving his lips. "I want to die," it sounded like he was saying. "Let me die . . ."

"How can he be talking?" said Max in awe. "His lips aren't moving."

"Can you understand what he's saying?" said Becky, face racked with confusion.

"Is this a trick? Are you some sort of ventriloquist, Hocker?" said Max, brandishing his gun.

"No," said Hocker. "I'm not doing it. Val's the one speaking."

"But you said he was dead."

"He is."

"Then how can he be talking?"

"His mind's communicating with us," said Hocker, waving his hands about his head excitedly. "Don't you see? My hypnosis worked. His mind's still alive, even though his body has been killed by the plague."

Val chose that moment to lurch to his feet.

Max backed away in apprehension, leveling his gun at Val.

"Don't shoot," said Hocker.

"Why not?" said Max, gun hand shaking. "He's gonna bite us."

"I'll tell him not to."

Hocker got to his feet and stood no more than a yard from Val.

"I'm . . . in . . . pain," said Val in a voice that came from the bowels of hell. "I can't stand the pain. Kill me."

Val prepared to walk.

"Stay where you are," said Hocker. "Don't move."

Val balked.

His head fell to suppurating and decaying in full view of Hocker, Max, and Becky. Reeking of death, putrefying flakes of skin sloughed off Val's face and tumbled to the carpet, revealing portions of neon white skull.

Hocker could barely breathe with the stench that Val's decomposing body was giving off.

"Jesus! The smell," said Max, pulling a face. "Let me kill him and put him out of his misery."

"No," said Hocker. "He's completely under my control. We can use him to help us fight the zombies."

Val groaned in pain. It seemed like the very rafters shook as the house shuddered at the roar of his voice.

"I can't stand that sound," said Becky, sticking her fingers in her ears.

"Kill me," it sounded like Val was uttering through his groans of pain.

Becky bugged out to the kitchen.

"Tell him to shut up," said Max.

"Stop groaning," Hocker told Val.

"I'm in pain," rumbled Val.

"I thought you said you could control him," said Max.

"I can," said Hocker, "but I can't control his pain."

Max cursed. "Let's put him down like a rabid dog."

"No! I'm telling you, we can use him to help us fight the creatures."

Val groaned again, his face's flesh continuing to molder and flake off to the ground, revealing additional chunks of skull.

"I'm in pain," he bellowed like a wounded lion in the jungle.

"Shut up!" said Max, grimacing at the nerve-racking sound of Val's voice.

Choking on the stench emanating from Val's corpse, Max belted to the kitchen. "I'm gonna puke."

Hocker watched Max take a powder.

"I'm starving," rumbled Val. "Ahhhh! . . . the pain."

"It's all in your mind," said Hocker. "You can't feel pain because your body's dead. You can't feel anything."

"Pain . . . pain . . ."

"Listen to me. Do as I tell you."

Hocker coughed on the reek of Val's putrescent flesh.

"Kill me," boomed Val.

"Listen to me."

"Let me die."

"I want you to kill Max," whispered Hocker so Max couldn't hear him. "Kill Max. Do you hear me?"

Val commenced shambling toward the kitchen. "Pain . . . pain . . ."

Exigent zombie fists kept up their drumbeat on the front door, demanding entry, unnerving Hocker.

Sudden darkness. Blackness steeped the room.

Hocker started. He froze.

Power outage, he decided. It wasn't the first time. It was a wonder it didn't happen more often what with the havoc the infected were wreaking on the streets and buildings outside. It was true the power had been going out fitfully, but it always came back on. Sooner or later it would go out for good. Maybe now.

He couldn't see a thing. He could hear, though.

He heard a scream in the kitchen.

Good, he decided. Max was dead. The bastard. He deserved to die for stealing Becky from him.

Hocker could kill Val now. Hocker had kept him alive only to waste Max. With Max gone, there was no reason to keep the wretched fool Val alive, or semi-alive, or whatever he was. Suspended somewhere between life and death, he was writhing in pain like a boar roasting on a skewer over a hot flame. The intensity of the pain Val must be feeling defied imagination. Hocker shivered just thinking about it.

Hocker had made up all that stuff about using Val to fight off the zombies, which had never been Hocker's intent. Hocker would have killed Max himself, but Hocker knew Becky would hate him if he did. That left Val to do it. It seemed the perfect solution to the problematic Max. Hocker was proud of himself for coming up with the idea. He experienced no qualms whatever about doing away with Max. Now the only problem was rubbing out Val.

If only the lights would come back on, decided Hocker, then he could waste Val. Hocker didn't want him hanging around. The zombie gave Hocker a serious case of the creeps with its hollow voice that reverberated from the grave.

The lights flickered back on.

Hocker sighed with relief and made a beeline for the kitchen. He felt a spring in his step, something he hadn't felt in a long time, now that he had disposed of Max. Hocker's desire to commit suicide had left him. Instead, he wished he had a gun to blow out Val's brains. Hopefully, he would find Max's gun beside his zombie-mutilated corpse.

But Max wasn't dead.

Paralyzed with fear, mouth gaping, he stood next to the aluminum sink in the kitchen watching Val tear Becky's throat out with his teeth as blood geysered from her carotid artery.

"Pain . . . ," rumbled Val as he chewed.

Aghast, Hocker snapped up Max's gun that was lying on the floor and shot Val in the back of the head. The bullet cracked

Val's skull and lodged in his brain. He dropped dead, sliding down Becky's collapsing, dying body to the floor.

Hocker watched in shock, overcome by a crippling mixture of fury and desolation at Becky's loss. In the darkness the dead idiot had killed the wrong—

"Kill me! Kill me!" rumbled Val's voice.

## Second Sight

He could not tell the doctor what he did for a living, decided Rattigan as he was walking into the psychiatrist's waiting room, wearing an aloha shirt, jeans, and scuffed white jogging shoes. After all, he was a hit man.

"Mr. Rattigan?" asked the bubbly brunette secretary looking up at him from the calendar on her desk.

"Yeah."

"Dr. Hemholz will see you now," she said, all smiles.

She had nice teeth, he noticed. Very white and very even. But he didn't care. What he cared about was that he thought he was going nuts. That was why he had made this appointment with the shrink. There was a first time for everything. He never thought he'd see the day when he made an appointment to see a headshrinker.

He opened the door to the psychiatrist's office and let himself in.

He was mildly surprised to see that Dr. S. Hemholz was a woman. Clad in a loose beige dress, she had long blonde hair that tumbled halfway down her back like sinuous tendrils of an exotic vine. Rattigan hadn't been expecting a woman shrink. Not that it made any difference. Why should it?

A stout woman in her thirties, she was sitting at her desk, flipping through a sheaf of notes in a buff manila folder. She had a prudish aspect, probably due to her dress, which reached all the way to the floor, covering her legs, decided Rattigan.

Hearing the door close with a snick, she looked up from her notes at him.

"Please lie down, Mr. Rattigan," she said, gesturing toward a divan on the other side of her fifteenth-floor office.

The divan stood beneath a picture window that had raised, cockeyed white miniblinds that revealed a panoramic view of smog-hazed Los Angeles, a city of predominantly runty buildings.

Rattigan made for the window. He stood beside it, looking out. Directly below him, eucalyptuses and jacarandas sprouted from the sidewalks that skirted the boulevard. Jacaranda petals littered the nearest sidewalk like miniature lavender bugles as tiny citizens scurried to and fro trampling them. On the opposite sidewalk a middle-aged man was looking up in Rattigan's direction.

Rattigan pulled away from the window out of the man's view. Was the guy looking at him? So what if he was? decided Rattigan. People could look wherever they wanted. It was Rattigan's nerves getting to him. They were acting up, making him jumpy.

In the distance Rattigan could see the Pacific Ocean evanescing into the horizon. His eyelids twitched. They never used to, but now they did—quite a lot. Because he was scared. For the first time in the thirty-five years of his life he was scared stiff.

He had never known stark fear. He was a paid assassin. Nothing was supposed to scare him. His assignments never scared him. His victims never scared him. It was all part and parcel of the job. He could look a guy holding a gun on him in the eye and not feel fear. He could whack that same guy out, watch the guy's head explode, and not be scared. But this . . . this was a horse of a different color . . . this scared the bejesus out of him.

"I don't feel like lying down," he said, pacing around the carpeted floor.

"I think it would be best," said Hemholz and got to her feet.

"Why?"

"You need to relax."

"I can't relax until I know I'm imagining this."

"Imagining what?"

He strode to the window and peered through the pane at the various-sized buildings that comprised a ragged skyline down below. The skyscraper he was in towered above the other buildings on this block.

"That somebody's going to kill me soon," he answered.

"It would be best if you sit down before we start. Then you can tell me what's troubling you."

He felt her walking toward him. He wheeled around apprehensively, face working.

A laptop in one hand, her purse in the other, she stopped in her tracks, catching the wild look in his eyes.

"All right," he muttered, seeing it was her, not somebody else.

He sat on the edge of the divan, body taut in attack mode.

"It's best for you to lie back," she said, sitting on a chair beside the divan.

Grudgingly, he lay back on the divan, stomach muscles knotted.

"Relax," she said.

He fetched a raucous sigh and let his body go limp. "That doesn't solve my problem."

"I didn't say it did. Now that you're calm you can tell me what's eating you."

Rattigan gathered his thoughts. "Do you believe in precognition, Doctor?"

"What is your definition of *precognition*?" she asked, setting her purse on the floor beside her.

She had a husky voice, Rattigan noticed for the first time. Was she flirting with him?

She smoothed her dress on her thighs then laid her laptop on them. She flipped open the laptop, booted it up, and proceeded to type.

"It's when you can see the future," he answered. "When you can see what's gonna happen to you."

"I can't say that I do."

Rattigan turned his head toward her. "You don't believe in it?"

She returned his gaze. "It's all in your mind. You may think you can see into the future, but it's only your imagination at work."

"It's not my imagination. I know this is gonna happen to me. It's as real as a memory in my mind."

"Everything in your imagination seems real."

Rattigan shook his head. "It's not in my imagination. I believe in second sight. I can see this like it has already happened and I'm seeing it in my mind's eye before it happens."

"What exactly is it you see?"

Rattigan paused. "I see somebody killing me. Which proves it can't be a dream."

"Because?"

"Because you can't dream your own death."

"Who told you that?"

"I don't know. I think I read it somewhere."

"Why can't you dream your own death?"

"Because you can dream only what you've experienced. Since you've never died, you can't dream about your own death. Like when you dream you're falling—you always wake up before you hit the ground and die. You're the doctor. Don't you know this?"

"Can't say that I do. As far as I know, you can dream anything."

Rattigan shrugged it off. "Anyway, it's not a dream. It's a premonition. I can see somebody killing me."

Rattigan broke into a cold sweat.

Hemholz typed on her laptop. "Why would somebody want to kill you?"

Rattigan couldn't tell her everything. He couldn't very well tell her he accepted contracts to kill people for a living. What would prevent her from snitching to the cops if he told her the truth?

*Well, you see, Doc, I'm a paid assassin. A mechanic. A hired gun. A made guy in New York named Joe contracted me to take out a punk in Connecticut named Nicky the Tick. They call him the Tick because he's a bloodsucker. He takes a cut out of every deal Joe makes—without Joe's permission. Joe found out about it. I whacked Nicky, all right. Ever since then, I've been having this premonition of a guy popping me in the head.* No, that wouldn't do, Rattigan decided. He would have to clean it up for her.

"I have a cutthroat job," he said. "I make a lot of enemies in my line of work."

"What's this killer look like? Have you ever seen him before?"

"No. Sometimes he wears a black leather mask like he just walked out of one of those S/M bondage grindhouse flicks."

"Why does he wear a mask, do you think?"

"I don't know. Maybe he doesn't want me to see his face."

"I thought you said you have seen his face."

"Yeah, I've seen it," said Rattigan, fidgeting.

"Then why the mask?"

"You're the analyst. You tell me."

"Maybe it's something from your childhood. Did your father ever wear a mask?"

"Yeah, he used to dress up like the Lone Ranger on weekends and whip me with a riding crop." Rattigan paused for effect, letting his mockery sink in. "My father has nothing to do with this. Let's get back to the subject."

"I'm trying to find out what's causing these dreams."

"It's *not* a dream. It's more vivid than that. I can see it as clearly as I can see a memory in my mind."

"It sounds like a dream to me. Something your imagination would cook up."

"But it's not a dream, I'm telling you," said Rattigan, cut up.

"Take it easy. I'm just trying to uncover the root of your problem."

"It's gonna happen," was all Rattigan said, scratching one of the green tattoos that wreathed his upper arms like barbed wire.

"Why does this man want to kill you?"

"He doesn't explain. He just zaps me in the head with a silenced pistol."

It probably had something to do with Rattigan's whacking Nicky, decided Rattigan, but he couldn't tell Hemholz that.

Seeing that he was hacked off Hemholz changed the subject. "What do you dream about when you sleep?"

"I can't sleep anymore. I feel like I'm wired all the time. If I could sleep, maybe I would feel better."

"Then why don't you sleep?"

"I'm afraid the guy'll shoot me in my sleep."

"Maybe I should prescribe you a sleeping aid."

"You mean, like pills?"

Hemholz nodded.

"I wouldn't take 'em," said Rattigan.

"Why not? A good night's rest would do you a world of good. Without sleep, you'll turn into a nervous wreck."

"I'm a already a nervous wreck."

"See what I mean?"

"I'd rather be a nervous wreck than a corpse with a bullet in my head. I'm not falling asleep for nothing. I fall asleep, I'll never wake up."

"Only in your mind, Mr. Rattigan. It's all in your mind. There's no such thing as precognition."

"I see him clear as day shooting me in the head while I'm lying in bed."

"Do you wake up afterwards?"

"Of course not. I'm dead."

"It's a dream. The thing with dreams is they're trying to tell you something. There is truth in dreams, but it's symbolic."

"Don't give me that Freudian psychobabble. I wasn't born yesterday."

"Pooh-pooh it if you want, but there's much truth in psychoanalysis."

"So, you're saying I'm cracking up?"

"I'm not saying that. What I'm saying is that you're heading for a nervous breakdown if you don't get any sleep. Everybody needs sleep. You can't function like a sane man without it. Sleep isn't a luxury. It's a necessity for all living creatures, including humans."

Rattigan thought about it. "If I could find someplace safe where I could rack out, maybe I could fall asleep."

"Isn't your bedroom safe?"

"No. Not if the killer breaks in while I'm sleeping." He paused a beat then smirked. "Maybe I should get myself busted. Then I could sleep in the joint with iron bars protecting me."

"The first thing you need to realize, to get your head straight, is that nobody is trying to kill you. You're suffering from paranoia. Maybe thanks to your sleeplessness."

"That's not it."

"Do you do drugs?"

"What's that got to do with it?"

"Answer the question."

"No, I don't."

"No cocaine or speed?"

"No."

Hemholz screwed up her face. "Then how are you managing to stay awake all the time?"

Rattigan shrugged. "Nerves, I guess."

"How long have you been awake?"

Massaging the stubble on his cheek Rattigan rolled his eyes, trying to recall. "At least three days."

"No wonder you feel lousy."

"Better lousy than dead."

"You're not gonna say that when you suffer a nervous breakdown."

Rattigan shut his eyes and hiked his eyebrows.

"What's your occupation?" Hemholz asked.

"I'm a termination expert." It was sort of a stretch, but that was all he was going to tell her about his job, decided Rattigan.

"I never heard of it," said Hemholz, frowning with puzzlement. "It sounds ominous."

"I fire people for employers who don't want to do it themselves."

"That's a new one on me."

"Some employees are resentful when they get the axe. Their bosses don't want them taking it out on them, so they hire a middleman like me to do the honors."

"I see. Let's get back to the reason you came here."

"I already told you. Haven't you been listening?"

"Tell me again. Do you mind if I smoke?"

Rattigan waved her off. "No. They're *your* lungs."

Hemholz withdrew a cardboard pack of Marlboros from her purse and tapped out a cigarette, which she fumbled. As it was falling she scissored her legs together to prevent it from dropping to the floor. The cigarette bounced off her laptop and into her lap.

"Butterfingers," said Rattigan.

Hemholz dredged a lighter out of her purse, inserted the cigarette into her lipsticked mouth, lit the cigarette's tip, put away the lighter, and inhaled tobacco smoke. A tangle of smoke veiled her face.

There was something he had missed, decided Rattigan. Something important. Something he should have picked up on, but hadn't. He needed to go over the chain of events in his mind again and see what he had missed. Something was nagging at him, at the corner of his mind—

"Let's begin at the beginning," said Hemholz. "When did you start seeing this person killing you in your dreams?"

"It's not a dream. I flew to JFK in New York to see an employer named Joe. My job takes me all over the country, you see. He hired me to fire one of his employees named Nicky. I rode the New Haven Railroad to Greenwich, Connecticut, where Nicky lived—"

"Lived? Did he pass away?"

*Yeah, he passed away, all right—with a neat little bullet hole in his head courtesy of moi.* "No. He still lives there as far as I know, unless he moved. He might have moved because he probably can't afford to live in Greenwich anymore, now that he's unemployed."

"So how does all this fit in with your premonitions of death?" said Hemholz, exhaling a cone of diaphanous grey smoke.

"Right after coming back to LA, I started seeing these images of somebody killing me."

"A man or a woman?"

"A man."

"Do you recognize him?"

Rattigan could smell the cigarette smoke. It tickled his nostrils and the back of his throat.

"No," he said.

"It's not Nicky?"

"No. I never saw the guy before. Like I said, sometimes he wears a black leather mask."

"But you have seen his face?"

"Yeah."

"Some stranger is trying to kill you? Correct?"

"He's not *trying* to kill me. He *does* kill me. He shoots me in the head with a silenced pistol while I'm in bed."

Rattigan heard a knock somewhere in the office. He jackknifed up on the divan, eyes bulging. It sounded like the crack of a gunshot. "What was that?"

"What?"

"I heard a gunshot. Didn't you hear it?"

"No."

Rattigan scoped out the room, casting around for something that might have fallen to the floor. He didn't spot anything out of place.

"To sum up," said Hemholz, "your paranoia started after you fired Nicky."

"I started seeing my own murder afterwards, yeah."

"Lie back and relax," said Hemholz, gesturing toward the divan.

Still tense, Rattigan reclined, slow to unwind. "I might fall asleep."

"What's wrong with that? It would be the best thing for you."

Rattigan shook his head vigorously. "He shoots me when I'm lying in bed. If I fall asleep, I'm dead."

"Does this figment of your imagination shoot you while you're sleeping?"

"I'm not asleep when he does it," said Rattigan, recalling the terrifying image, seeing it again in his mind's eye, "because I see it happening."

"Think about it. Why would somebody want to kill you? Just because you fired them? Like you said, that's your job."

"Some guys take it personally when I terminate them."

"I can see why they might be upset, but not to the point of murdering you."

"I hate to tell you this, Doc, but it's a jungle out there. People clip each other over a cigarette down in the streets."

Hemholz glanced at her cigarette involuntarily as it smoked between her forefinger and middle finger.

"I want to try an experiment with you," she said. "Close your eyes."

"I'm not closing my eyes. I might fall asleep. Then he'll kill me."

"You said you're not asleep when he kills you."

"That's true, but I *am* lying down." Rattigan made to sit up. "I shouldn't even be lying down."

"Take it easy. There's nobody in this room except me and you. He can't kill you if you fall asleep in here. You need sleep. Look at your eyes. They're so bloodshot they look like maraschino cherries. Lie back down."

"I don't care if they look like vampire eyes. As long as they're open, I can see him coming. He's not gonna get the drop on me if I keep my eyes peeled."

Rattigan cut his eyes around the office. Satisfied that nobody else was in the room, he lay back on the divan.

Hemholz leaned over and tapped cigarette ash into a cut-glass ashtray on a nearby round oaken coffee table. "I'm the doctor here. I know what's best for you."

"You don't understand."

"I thought you came here for me to cure you."

"I came here to find out if you think I'm losing my mind. Because if I'm not bonkers now, I'm gonna be soon if I can't get this shooter out of my head."

"I agree. You'll lose your mind if you don't get any sleep."

Played out, Rattigan couldn't fight it any longer. Sleep was closing in on him. Eyelids heavy, he shut his eyes, no matter how hard he fought the urge to close them.

"That's better," said Hemholz.

Rattigan was remembering something he had seen in his precognitive vision. He saw himself lying on his back. He had assumed he was lying on a bed, but he could see the image more clearly now in his mind's eye. It wasn't a bed he was lying on. It was some kind of sofa. A divan.

He snapped open his eyes.

A black-haired man with a crew cut was gazing at him. The man was wearing a dress.

The dress, realized Rattigan. That was what he should have picked up on earlier but hadn't. If Hemholz was really a woman she would have *opened* her legs when she caught the cigarette in her lap with her dress, not *closed* them like the male impersonating her had done.

On the floor beside the crew-cut man a discarded blonde wig lay like a dead octopus. It was Hemholz or whoever he was staring at him, realized Rattigan. The drag queen was training a silenced Glock 17 on Rattigan's face.

"That wig was making my head itch," said the guy in his real voice, a few octaves lower than the voice he had been using to impersonate Hemholz.

Agog, Rattigan made a move to strike the Glock out of Hemholz's hand. But he wasn't fast enough.

157

Hemholz fired twice into Rattigan's head, making Rattigan's premonition come true.

Hemholz strode over to the closet where the knock had come from earlier and tore open the door. The real Dr. Hemholz, a bloody bullet hole in her head, fell out with a thud onto the carpet, her mouth agape. She flicked her eyes toward his face. He shot her in the temple. Her head must have struck the door when she had shifted in the closet, causing that knocking sound, he decided.

He had entered the office before the secretary had arrived. He had blown away Hemholz in her office. Now all he had to do was ice the secretary, leave, and collect his paycheck from Nicky's wife in Greenwich.

It was true, he decided, putting away his pistol. Rattigan really must have had second sight.

# The Sand Stalker

There was a homicidal maniac on the loose.

The killer was breaking into houses, bungalows, condos, and apartments all along the coast and slicing the throats of his victims in their sleep. So far, his victims numbered three.

It was giving Vince the willies reading about the murders in the papers for the last month. He lived in a guestroom in a bungalow on the Malibu coast a block away from the last murder. He could not afford to rent an apartment in this tony neighborhood, but he had found out about this particular guestroom's availability while surfing the Internet. The room was surprisingly cheap, considering the area.

He wanted to live in Malibu because that was where he worked. He waited tables in a pricy seafood bistro not far from where he lived. He didn't have to spend a dime to commute. He could walk a couple miles to work if he wanted to or he could drive his car. In any case, it beat getting stuck in traffic commuting every day.

He thought himself incredibly lucky to close the deal on the crib before anyone else did.

That was what he thought *before* the murders, anyway. Now he wasn't so sure. Not with this homicidal maniac running amok.

Whoever this psycho killer was, he attacked at night and wielded a knife. Not much else was known about him. The cops couldn't find any witnesses, and they had no description of the suspect to go on.

It made sleeping difficult, decided Vince. The slightest sound at night would startle him awake in bed. The coast wasn't exactly the quietest place to live courtesy of the smashing surf, which was what made the killer so hard to detect. Whenever he broke into a residence, the pounding waves masked his actions, drowning out the sounds of his B&E. None of the victims knew what hit them. The psycho killer cut their throats before they even woke up.

Vince hadn't even reached thirty yet. He was too young to die. A young, good-looking guy like himself. It wasn't fair for him to die that young. Christ, why was he thinking such negative thoughts? he wondered.

Because somebody was following him, he knew. Somebody was stalking him. Who else could it be but the murderer? He hadn't actually seen the guy yet, but he had come close. The guy always ducked out of sight at the last moment—like he could anticipate when Vince was going to look at him and duck out of sight before Vince could turn toward him and catch a glimpse of him. It was downright eerie.

Vince didn't plan on remaining a waiter. It was his night job. During the day he drove to Hollywood and auditioned for parts in movies. Waiting tables paid the rent. Vince knew he had the looks and the drive to make it in Hollywood. Not to mention the talent. It was just a matter of time before he got his break.

Vince decided to walk to work tonight to the Blue Porpoise bistro. It was a balmy night in the seventies. He wore his jacket because even though it was mild now at dusk, the temperature dropped fast when it got dark. He liked inhaling the odor of the briny air sweeping onshore as he strode along the shoulder of the Pacific Coast Highway, cars tearing by him.

The ocean shimmered like an undulating sheet of aluminum under the setting sun. Sometimes he wondered why he risked walking in the dark with this murderer at large, but, as he understood it, the killer murdered his victims only in their houses, not outdoors.

Vince reached the turquoise salt-eroded clapboard Blue Porpoise, which catered to an upscale clientele despite its weather-beaten mien. The seafood entrees cost an arm and a leg, but they tasted scrumptious, he had to admit. If he could afford to eat here, he would.

But he couldn't, so he didn't.

Customers were sitting outdoors constellated on the patio that jutted out over the ocean on dark brown wooden pilings as the waves broke on the beach below, slopped across the sand, then melted away into silence before the next round of waves strummed onshore and broke with a sonorous clatter.

He started as he saw Ludmilla sitting on the patio. She always had that effect on him—like she had on other guys as well. Maybe it was the extreme whiteness of her made-up face or the radiant blondness of her hair juxtaposed with her slash of vermilion mouth that made her stand out and turn heads. Her face had the avaricious aspect of a predatory bird that was forever seeking prey. Her hair piled on her head like a nest carried out the avian analogy.

Vince could feel her acquisitive eyes appraising him with satisfaction.

She was sitting with her date, Vince saw. The guy was obviously well-heeled. Vince had seen her with him here many times. He had the supercilious and aggressive demeanor of a guy who had money and could do whatever he wanted with his perfectly coiffed dark hair and gleaming brown eyes. His name was Randy.

It was hate at first sight as far as Vince was concerned. Randy envied Vince's good looks, Vince could tell, and Vince envied Randy's wealth, but mostly Vince despised Randy's arrogance. For his part, Randy didn't like the way Ludmilla's eyes locked on Vince like he was a delicious feast to savor every time she saw him.

"Look who's here," said Randy with a sneer, deigning to recognize Vince. "The famous actor, what's his name."

Ludmilla shot Randy a look with her cornflower blue eyes. "Do you have to be so rude all the time?"

161

"That's not rude. It would be rude if I ignored him." He turned to Vince. "Right, Olivier?"

"I take that as a compliment," said Vince, walking up to them tensely, knowing it was anything but.

"It wasn't."

Vince never knew how to act with them. Their presence disconcerted him. After all, he was an employee and they were customers. It wasn't like he could stand there and trade insults with them. If he did, it would mean his job. He was attracted to Ludmilla, and both she and Randy knew it. And she made no effort to conceal her interest in Vince, which galled Randy no end.

"Will you be waiting on us?" Ludmilla asked Vince with a smile.

"Aren't you being waited on already?" said Vince.

"Yeah," said Randy. "Now go away like a good little boy," he added, shooing Vince away with a wave of his hand like he was brushing dust off his lap.

Vince had dreams about killing Randy.

"I don't appreciate your tone, Randy," said Ludmilla.

"I don't want him to lose his job," said Randy.

"Yeah, right."

"How's your acting coming along?" Randy asked Vince.

"OK."

"Don't quit your day job, is all I gotta say. Or, in your case, night job," said Randy, surveying the Blue Porpoise.

"It's a rough business."

"Dog-eat-dog, I hear."

"I'm sure you're an excellent actor," Ludmilla told Vince, leaning toward him to reveal more cleavage in her low-cut dress spray-painted on her zaftig figure.

Annoyance registered on Randy's face. He didn't appreciate her flirtatious gesture.

"I am," said Vince.

Nodding, Ludmilla smiled and changed the subject. "What do you think about this maniac that's going around killing people in their homes?"

"We need to keep our houses locked."

Randy looked surprised. "*You* own a house? I didn't know that."

He couldn't pass up a chance to denigrate Vince, Vince knew. "It's not my house. I live in the guestroom," said Vince.

Randy nodded smugly. "Figures."

"No place is safe these days," said Ludmilla. "It's such a shame."

"I heard he kills them in their sleep," said Vince.

Randy's smartphone rang. He made a show of fishing it out of his trouser pocket. Vince watched him with annoyance. Vince couldn't afford a smartphone, the latest iPhone model no less, Vince noticed. He had to make do with an ordinary cell phone that he used for casting calls. Even that put a strain on his wallet with the cell's monthly service charge.

Randy said a few words into the smartphone.

"Who was that?" asked Ludmilla.

"My broker," answered Randy, scrutinizing his smartphone's screen, flicking through his e-mails now with swipes of his fingers like a magician casting a spell.

"That reminds me."

Ludmilla dug her smartphone out of her blue leather purse that had an ostentatious Gucci logo on it and commenced scrolling through her e-mails.

Vince felt like an outcast without a smartphone to check. He thought about pulling out his cell phone, but it didn't receive text messages or e-mails. What was the point?

Randy put away his smartphone.

"Are you still here?" he said, leaning back in his chair, head tilted back, and staring down his nose at Vince.

"I'm not on the clock yet," said Vince.

"Give it a rest," Ludmilla told Randy, sighing as she deposited her smartphone in her purse with a flick of her wrist.

"You actor guys are all alike," Randy told Vince. "You come here from Podunk and stay a year or two trying to get into the movies. Then you go home and end up painting houses for a living."

"If you can dream it, you can do it," said Vince, realizing it sounded like a cliché the moment the words left his mouth.

Randy sniggered.

"I have to clock in now," said Vince, nettled but doing his best not to show it. He didn't want to give Randy the pleasure of seeing him angry.

"Do you have to go so soon?" said Ludmilla, offering him an inviting look with her blue eyes, aware that she aroused him.

"I better get to work," he said, breaking away from her.

He wouldn't mind hanging with Ludmilla if only Randy wasn't around.

Vince headed into the restaurant, clocked in, and shrugged off his jacket. The boss, a florid-faced fiftysomething five-nine man who wore a dark suit and exhaled breath redolent of garlic and some onionlike odor Vince couldn't pinpoint, assigned him to a station inside the restaurant out of sight of Ludmilla and Randy. Vince didn't see the pair again for the rest of the night.

A little after midnight, worn out from filling orders, Vince donned his jacket and walked down PCH's shoulder through the darkness toward his crib. There were less cars on the road this time of night than there had been at dusk, making his walk peaceful. It was so quiet he thought he heard footfalls behind him.

Who would be out walking this time of night? he wondered. He whipped his head around to see who was following him.

He thought he caught a glimpse of a shadow ducking into a narrow pathway that led down to the beach. The light was so bad it was impossible for him to be sure. A paucity of sodium-vapor lamps stood sentry along the roadside. What little peach glow they gave off provided scant light to see by.

It was probably no one, he decided. Nobody went out walking after midnight in these parts. Certainly not with that psycho killer on the prowl. Cars, yes. Foot traffic, no. There weren't any nightclubs around here, just residences.

Vince continued striding at a brisk pace, stimulating his circulation in the chilly night air. Five minutes later he saw someone approaching him on foot. Puzzled, becoming edgy, he watched the guy. This was a first. He never ran into pedestrians on his way home.

The guy staggered a bit, like he was blitzed. With scraggly white long hair and an equally scraggly white beard that flopped down his chest like a mop, the middle-aged guy was wearing a white placard that hung from his neck, reached down to his knees, and said The End Is Near.

A doomsday prophet, decided Vince, who kept walking toward the guy, hoping the guy would ignore him. Vince knew the guy wanted money. These derelicts always carried caps in their hands. Vince was dog-tired. He just wanted to go home.

"The end is near," said the guy, gesticulating wildly. "Are you ready to make peace with the world?"

As Vince neared him, he could see the guy had a crazed look to his saucer eyes that stared out from under bushy white eyebrows. Santa the doomsday soothsayer, decided Vince, except the guy wasn't fat like Santa. If anything, he was emaciated. Santa Slim the Soothsayer, thought Vince with a fleeting chuckle. Vince didn't like the looks of Santa's bugged-out eyes.

All the more reason to avoid him, decided Vince, ramping up his pace.

Santa gawked in terror as they approached each other.

Vince could not figure it out. Why would the guy be scared of him? If anything, it should be the other way around. What was Santa's problem?

"Beware the mirror!" cried Santa as he stared at Vince, mouth hanging ajar exposing broken teeth. "The mirror kills."

Vince had no idea what Santa was jabbering about. The guy obviously had a few marbles loose. Vince had no desire to talk to him. *Just keep walking*, Vince told himself, trying to look cool even as sweat trickled out of his armpits and chilled his flanks like sliding ice cubes. Was the lunatic dangerous?

Santa came to a full stop and gazed at Vince's face in horror.

What was wrong with the nutbag? wondered Vince with a shiver and kept walking. He like to twisted his ankle on a rotten apple core discarded on the roadside. Annoyed at his misstep, he kept on going.

"The end is near," said Santa. "Beware the mirror."

*Whatever you say, buddy*, thought Vince and strode right by him without sparing a glance in the loon's direction.

Tempted to look back and see if the guy was following him, Vince figured it might encourage the loon to do just that and decided against it. Instead, Vince pricked up his ears and listened for the sound of footsteps bird-dogging him.

Vince didn't hear any. He heaved a sigh of relief. Santa must not be shadowing him.

Just another homeless crackpot, decided Vince. *Beware the mirror? What the hell? If I looked like Caliban like you do, I'd beware the mirror, too, buddy. I'd die of fright looking at my reflection.*

When Vince reached his house, still keyed up from his encounter with the whitebeard cuckoo, he decided to a take a stroll to the ocean to relax. Listening to the surf never failed to soothe him. It was one reason he liked living near the ocean.

He thought he heard someone behind him. He wheeled around in the sand, casting about for a stalker.

All he saw in the distance were the fitful glowing cones of car headlights threading the darkness and passing down the road beyond his house. He saw no human figures.

No Santa. Santa wasn't stalking him. Nobody was that he could see.

His nerves were on edge, decided Vince. Taking this walk to calm down was a good idea.

He resumed slogging through the sand as an all but full moon beamed above him at about a forty-five-degree angle casting a glimmering rhinestone path on the black oil slick of sea. The surf was flat, sounding like crumpling paper as it broke instead of roaring like it did when good-size combers stormed onshore.

Out of the corner of his eye, Vince caught sight of movement. He whirled his head around. This time he did indeed see someone walking along the beach to his right. He could not make out a face, only a silhouette of somebody toiling through the sand toward the ocean.

"Hey!" Vince yelled.

Vince could feel rather than see the stranger peering at him through the darkness.

"Are you following me?" said Vince.

The stranger said nothing, remained stock-still as if afraid of being detected. As he stood, the shiny cresting of an incoming wave cast a reflection of moonlight in the stranger's direction, partially illuminating his face.

The guy looked familiar, decided Vince. *Christ!* he thought as he realized the reason. It looked like *his* face! Or was the moonlight playing tricks on him?

Was this the guy who had been stalking him? Or was it the murderer? Or were they one in the same? Disregarding his own safety, Vince broke into a jog, making a beeline for the menacing shadow that now stood completely in the dark as the reflected moon ray vanished off his face. Vince had to find out who this guy was, had to unmask this stalker or whoever he was—even if he *was* the murderer. The guy was driving him nuts, and Vince had to find out what the guy's game was.

The stranger turned tail and ran.

Despite the sand that slowed him down to a degree, the guy managed to sprint to the residences that skirted the roadside and vanish into the shadows thrown by the buildings in the percolating moonlight.

Breathing heavily, Vince dragged his feet to a halt in the sand. He would never catch the guy in this darkness. The guy sure could move whoever he was, decided Vince. The sand seemed to have little effect on his rapid gait. The question was, had the guy been following him? And if so, why? Vince was no closer than ever to finding the answers.

That the guy looked like him was flat-out spooky, decided Vince with a frisson of apprehension running down his spine.

He returned to his crib.

Before he entered, he stood on the patio in the wash of its lamplight, removed his black jogging shoes, and knocked the soles against the edge of the cement floor to dislodge the sand from the treads so he wouldn't track it into his room. His room was attached to the owner's house, but he could enter the room without entering the main house and disturbing the owner and his family.

He slipped his shoes back on, entered his room, and was out like a light as soon as he hit the sack.

#

The next night Vince saw neither Ludmilla nor Randy at work. They didn't come to the restaurant every night, though they were regular customers and showed up there several nights a week.

It was fine with Vince that they didn't show up. He liked Ludmilla and would like to spend a night off with her, but she always had the scurvy Randy in tow, knocking Vince's plans into a cocked hat.

On his way home Vince didn't see the bearded loon either, thankfully.

Recalling his terrifying walk on the beach last night, he decided he would dispense with the activity tonight. He went directly to bed.

He walked onto the beach toward the ocean. Through the darkness he could discern two figures standing with their backs toward him as they gazed out over the water. One was a male, the other a female with platinum blonde hair piled on top of her head.

They were peering at a sailboat with black sails that was drifting in the calm sea parallel with the shore. In the obscurity of the night with only a sliver of moon overhead, Vince had to squint to make out the sailboat thanks to its black sails.

The man turned around to face him as Vince traipsed through the sand toward him. The woman turned around as well. The man doubled over with laughter at the sight of Vince. Vince froze.

What was the guy laughing at? he wondered. The guy couldn't even stand up straight he was guffawing so hard.

Vince bristled. He hated the guy for laughing at him. Vince could not make out the joker's face in the darkness, but it seemed familiar.

The woman's face was another story, decided Vince with a shock. It wasn't a human face. She had the face of a giant bird with a yellow beak like a toucan's protruding from it. *Christ!* thought Vince. Were they wearing Halloween costumes? But it wasn't Halloween yet. And what was that black sailboat doing out there on the ocean in the middle of the night?

Something flared on the sailboat, igniting the jib, which went up in flames. What was going on in that boat? wondered Vince. The boat continued to bob along the ocean as blazes swept upward and engulfed its sails, crackling and snapping as they consumed the canvas.

The joker continued laughing, his laughs sounding like the cackling of the flames. He couldn't care less if the boat was on fire. He didn't even bother to turn around and look at the vessel. He was too busy guffawing at Vince.

Vince wanted to pulverize the clown's face that was contorted with laughter. What the hell was so funny? wondered Vince.

He strode toward the clown, determined to take a swing at the guy, who just stood there laughing his fool head off.

Meanwhile, Bird Head was giving Vince a severe case of the creeps as she swiveled her head to and fro. To make matters worse, the closer he got to her, the less her head looked like a Halloween mask. It really did look like a giant bird's head with platinum blonde hair crowning it like a skein of cotton candy.

Aching to bust the guy in the chops, Vince balled his fists in white heat as he approached the laughing hyena. Vince balked, his body stiff. He all but passed out when he discerned the hyena's face. *It was Vince's.*

Snapping his eyes open, in a cold sweat, Vince jackknifed awake in his bed, terrified.

He cut his eyes around his room, making sure of his surroundings. He was in his bedroom, all right. Not on the beach. It had been a doozy of a nightmare, he decided. But it seemed so real. He could feel the sand in his shoes even though he was in his bare feet as he lay in bed. He scoped out his feet to make sure he wasn't wearing shoes. He wasn't. No sand on his feet either.

He got out of bed. He strode to the front door and opened it. He had to make sure Clown and Bird Head weren't standing outside on the beach.

In the cold, oyster grey light of dawn he peered toward the immense solitude of the ocean. No sign of the duo. No sign of anyone for that matter, except for a lone jogger panting along the shoreline in a navy blue tracksuit, ruddy face twisted in pain, mouth hanging open. A flock of gulls burst off of the sand and into the sky at one fell swoop filling the air like chaff as he jogged past them.

Satisfied that nobody else populated the beach, Vince was about to close the door when he noticed footsteps in the sand leading from his stoop toward the ocean. He recognized his shoeprints. Did that mean it wasn't a dream he had had last night? he wondered. Had he really walked out there in the dark and seen the jokester and Bird Head?

There was one way to find out.

He shut the front door behind him, opened the closet at the foot of his bed, removed his only pair of shoes, and inspected their black soles. Not a trace of sand on them. If he had walked on the beach last night, sand would remain on them. That meant somebody else with his footprints had walked through the sand from his porch to the sea last night!

His brain overheated, Vince shook his head in confusion. He could not make heads nor tails of it.

Dropping his shoes in a daze he made for his bathroom. He gazed at his face in the mirror. He didn't look happy. But he never looked happy when he woke up. That meant nothing. He thought he saw movement behind him over his shoulder. The shape of a head, perhaps? He couldn't be sure. He pivoted around on his heel to see what it was.

Nothing. Nobody was behind him. Just a wall.

He clutched his head in dismay. Was he losing his mind? His brain felt like it was on fire, swarming with a hodgepodge of thoughts racing through it.

He had to pull himself together and puzzle this out. The footprints on the sand might have been left over from the other night when he walked to the ocean. He shook his head no. That didn't track. Any footprints from the other night would have vanished by now courtesy of beachgoers walking over them during the next day, wiping them out.

Those footprints he had seen this morning were fresh. If it wasn't him that had made them, it must have been somebody with the same size and style of shoe that he had. That had to be it. He felt somewhat relieved at his deductive reasoning. But that didn't explain the guy that had stalked him the other night on the beach.

To hell with it, decided Vince.

He was starting to feel better already, now that he was fully awake.

#

That night, as was his wont, Vince walked to work.

As he crossed the parking lot to the Blue Porpoise's entrance, he spotted Ludmilla and Randy sitting at a table on the patio. Vince angled toward them. It was another mild night for sitting outside.

"Wassup?" Ludmilla asked him.

"Not much," answered Vince.

"Well, look who's here," said Randy in his usual obnoxious tone with a smile belying it.

"Nice night," said Vince, refusing to allow Randy to goad him.

"Did you hear the news?"

"What news?"

"They busted the maniac killer last night."

"They did?" said Ludmilla, eyes wide. "I didn't hear that."

"Yeah."

"Who was it?" said Vince.

"Some ex-con from Colorado or something."

"What a relief," said Ludmilla. "Now I don't have to worry about walking outside at night."

Vince felt relieved, too. He wouldn't have to fret about the killer tailing him. Vince suspected it was the killer that had been stalking him on the beach the other night.

"Are they sure it was him?" he asked.

"Yeah," answered Randy. "They found the murder weapon in his dive with his fingerprints all over it. They nailed him cold."

"Good for them," said Ludmilla.

"How's the biz?" Randy asked Vince.

"Fine," said Vince evasively.

"Getting a lot of callbacks on your auditions?"

"Yep," lied Vince, stiffening his spine.

Randy snickered.

Vince was dying to wipe that snicker off Randy's mouth with a right hook to the kisser.

It was none of Randy's business, decided Vince, whether he was getting any callbacks or not. Things were slow. That was all. They would pick up.

Vince turned to leave.

"You can audition for me, sweetie," said Ludmilla, all grins.

Vince paused, reading her meaning. Ludmilla had the hots for him. If only she would ditch her pet dog Randy.

Sighing inaudibly, Vince waved good-bye to them and disappeared into the Blue Porpoise to clock in, feeling Ludmilla's eyes on him all the way.

#

At the end of his shift, Vince walked back along PCH to his crib—and had the misfortune of meeting up with the doomsday prophet with The End Is Near sign on his chest.

Santa was the last person Vince wanted to see.

The minute he clapped eyes on Vince, Santa launched into his speech, eyes bulging from their sockets. "Beware the mirror!"

172

Santa fell to thrashing his arms over his head and shaking all over like he was suffering a paroxysm.

Vince wondered if the guy would turn violent. You could never tell with these whack jobs, Vince decided. And here he was alone in the dark with this crackpot.

As Vince made to pass him, Santa lunged toward him and grabbed a hold of Vince's shoulders, grinding his teeth.

"You're your own worst enemy," said Santa, eyes bright like sheet ice under the noonday sun, breath reeking of jungle juice.

"Get away from me," said Vince, shaking himself free and shoving Santa away from him.

Santa stumbled backward onto the road, mouth agape.

A stray car sped by, swerving out of the way, its horn blasting as it all but struck him.

Vince broke into a run. He didn't want anything to do with the lunatic. The guy had already proven he could turn violent.

Vince reached his digs, gasping for breath. He had had enough excitement for one night. Maybe he shouldn't walk home anymore if that escapee from a bughouse was going to be patrolling the street every night.

Vince unlocked the door to his crib, strode through the room, and entered the bathroom. Why did that madman keep telling him to beware the mirror?

Vince peered into the looking glass. He was a handsome guy, he had to admit. What a crock that guy was telling him. Why did he even bother wasting any time thinking about the kook's words?

Gazing at his reflection Vince glimpsed a flurry of movement over his shoulder. He wheeled around. Had the lunatic followed him into his crib? he wondered, heartbeat accelerating.

Slewing around he was just in time to catch sight of somebody bolting out of his room through the front doorway.

Vince cursed and charged after the guy, who was sprinting through the sand toward the ocean. Vince could tell by the way the guy fled full-tilt that it wasn't Santa. No way the jittery boozehound could hightail it like that.

Bryan Cassiday

Vince gave chase. He had to find out who it was. It must be the guy who had been stalking him all along. Then that meant the murderer hadn't been the one stalking him, because Randy said the cops had busted that guy.

If the murderer was in jail, who the hell was he chasing? Vince wondered. The guy was fast. No question of that. He was making straight for the ocean.

Try as he might, pumping his legs for all he was worth, Vince could not gain on him. Running on sand was twice as strenuous as running on dirt. Vince didn't care. No matter how fast the stalker ran, Vince was going to dog him and catch him. It was now or never. Vince had to nab this guy and lay down the law to him. No more stalking. It was driving Vince batty.

Vince felt relieved when he saw the guy slowing down. The son of a bitch was human after all. He turned around and confronted Vince.

Taken aback, Vince beheld the guy's face. *It was Vince's.*

Was he dreaming this? Vince wondered. This was just like the nightmare he had last night, the one where he chased himself and Bird Head. Maybe this was a new nightmare.

Like the guy in Vince's dream, the stalker standing near the ocean's edge erupted into laughter at the sight of Vince.

Vince belted after him, stumbled in the sand thanks to his haste, and fell flat on his face.

The stalker laughed even louder at Vince's plight.

Furious, blowing sand off his lips, Vince bounded to his feet and took off after the stalker.

The stalker sprang into the black water that was boiling with surf in the moonlight. He commenced swimming out to sea.

Vince gave chase. He was going to nail this scumbag if it was the last thing he ever did.

Legs thrusting, Vince barreled into the cold water as foot-high waves slammed around him, crashing like cymbals. Shivering in the cold he whipped into the water until he couldn't run anymore. Then he dove forward and broke into a swim, chasing the stalker, who was swimming straight out to sea.

174

#

"Where's what's his name?" said Randy, lounging at a table on the Blue Porpoise patio the next night, drink in hand.

"I don't see him," said Ludmilla, casting around the restaurant.

She caught the eye of a nearby twentyish waiter, who approached her.

"Where's Vince tonight?" she said.

"Didn't you hear?"

"Hear what?"

"He drowned last night in the ocean. His body washed up ashore this morning on the rocks on the beach behind his house."

# Crisis

"Promise me you won't bury me until at least seven days after I die," said forty-year-old Stuart, who was sitting in a Wendy's in LA across from his wife Rowena.

"Isn't that kind of an odd request?" said Rowena, looking startled. "Especially over lunch."

Five years Stuart's junior, she had blonde hair whose wavy tresses cascaded down her shoulders in rebellious coils.

"Odd?" said Gilbert, Stuart's middle-aged friend, a real-estate salesman who was wearing jeans and a fluorescent green aloha shirt that wasn't tucked in. "I'd call it more like bizarre."

They were sitting on a patio under a polished blue October sky, an onshore breeze caressing them.

"You wouldn't call it odd if you knew the reason," said Stuart.

"Shoot."

"Why do you want to talk about death on such a beautiful day?" said Rowena.

"I've never told this to anyone, but I'm going to tell you two," said Stuart, casting a glance at both Gilbert and Rowena. "You're my witnesses."

"To what?" said Gilbert.

Stuart leaned closer to them over the white-painted round steel tabletop and lowered his voice so the chattering diners nearby would not overhear him.

"To my confession."

"How exciting," said Gilbert, cracking a smile.

Stuart ignored Gilbert's flippancy. "I have catalepsy."

"I think I've heard of that," said Rowena.

"It's a state of paralysis that mimics death. Not even a doctor can distinguish it from death. I had a cataleptic fit once when I was younger."

"You never told me before."

"It's not something to brag about. When I had my fit, doctors assumed I was dead. I snapped out of it only after the undertaker laid me in my coffin as he was preparing me for burial."

"My God!"

"Ever since then, I've had this fear of being buried alive."

"I don't blame you," said Gilbert, cringing at the thought of premature burial.

"Now you can understand why I don't want to be buried until at least seven days after my death."

"But what about the smell?"

"I don't care about that," said Stuart.

"But what about us? We're the ones that'll suffer. What if we put your body on ice to prevent a stench?"

"Or what about refrigeration? That will prevent decomposition," said Rowena, nodding.

"Aren't you forgetting something?" said Stuart with annoyance.

"What?" said Gilbert.

"I'll freeze to death."

"But you're already dead."

"But am I? That's the point of not burying me for a week. To make sure I'm really dead before you have the funeral."

"The point is, your body will decompose and start to reek, if it's not buried soon after you die."

"Can't we talk about something else?" said Rowena, feeling nauseous as she leered at her hamburger.

"Haven't you been listening?" said Stuart. "I don't want you to mistake my catalepsy for death. That's why I want you to delay my burial."

"That's all well and good for you," said Gilbert, "but it's unsanitary to leave a corpse hanging around without treating it in some manner to avoid decomposition and the spreading of disease. Think about poor Rowena, living with a dead body rotting in her house."

"I'm not joking," said Stuart, agitated.

"Neither am I."

"I am deathly afraid of being buried alive," said Stuart, face drained of blood.

"You're exaggerating, dear," said Rowena. "I'm sure the doctors these days can distinguish death from a cataleptic fit. They have so much technology at their disposal. How could they muff a diagnosis?"

"They muffed it the last time it happened."

"We'll get a competent specialist to examine you after you die," said Gilbert. "You worry too much, Stuart."

Stuart downed a couple of French fries, thinking about it, expression intense. "Just do as I ask."

"All right," said Rowena. "If it'll set your mind at ease." She reached forward and patted the back of his hand that lay palm down on the tabletop.

"It will. You must *do* it, though. Not just *say* you'll do it."

"I will."

"The odds of this happening are a million to one," said Gilbert. "This catalepsy thing really doesn't happen very often. You have a better chance of becoming president of the United States."

"Just do as I say," said Stuart, voice level, eyes intense.

"We are receiving reports of sporadic rioting in the streets of LA," said a newscaster over a transistor radio that a shabby homeless man wearing a grey hoodie was playing at a nearby table as he laid his face on his crossed arms on the tabletop.

"Let's just change the subject so we can finish our lunch," said Rowena.

"I'll drink to that," said Gilbert. "If only this place served beer."

"You wouldn't say that if you were the one who had catalepsy," said Stuart.

"That I wanted a beer?" said Gilbert, puzzled. "Dude, I'd drink even more beer if I knew I had catalepsy," he added, with a broad grin.

Stuart hated it when Gilbert called him "dude."

Rowena picked up on the scowl that crossed Stuart's face and decided to play peacemaker. "Let's just calm down and eat our lunch. It's such a beautiful autumn day," she said, taking in the sky behind her pink-framed sunglasses that had heart-shaped lenses.

"You need to stop obsessing on death, dude," said Gilbert. "It'll bum you out for sure. We're all gonna die. Why dwell on it?"

"We shouldn't think about things we have no control over," said Rowena.

"Why don't you think about getting a job?" Gilbert asked Stuart.

"Is that supposed to cheer me up?" said Stuart.

"You're becoming a bit of a hanger-on."

"I have a job. I'm a writer."

"You can't possibly pay the bills with the pin money you make. Rowena is the breadwinner. She's the one paying the mortgage, and everything else for that matter."

"Is that how you think of me, too, Rowena? Some kind of 'hanger-on'?"

"Of course not," she said, but she didn't sound sincere to Stuart. "I know you're trying."

"If I wanted money, I wouldn't choose to be a writer," said Stuart.

"Then do something else," said Gilbert. "Nobody's forcing you to be a writer."

"Writing is my only interest, regardless of how poorly it pays."

"You're no better than a pauper," said Gilbert, and whipped his head away from Stuart with a trace of disgust on his face.

Pressing his hands on the tabletop, stiffening the muscles in his thighs, Stuart prepared to leave. "I don't have to sit here listening to you dressing me down."

"Chill out, dear," said Rowena. "Gilbert is only trying to get you to stop thinking about catalepsy."

"Not really," muttered Gilbert.

Rowena glanced askance at him.

"He needs to start carrying his own weight," Gilbert went on.

"Are you jealous of me?" said Stuart.

"*Jealous?*" Gilbert all but spat out the word. Then he laughed. "Why in the world would I be jealous of you of all people? A loafer. Christ, why would I be jealous?"

"Boys . . . ," chided Rowena.

"Don't 'boys' us in that patronizing tone."

"Why are you all bent out of shape?"

"Yeah, Gilbert. I'm the one with the catalepsy, not you," said Stuart.

"Screw your catalepsy. Is catalepsy your explanation for everything? Is it the explanation for your loafing sloth?"

"I feel like another lemonade," said Rowena eagerly. "Does anyone else want one? I love the fresh lemonade they make here."

Nobody said anything.

"Pockets of rioting mobs have been spotted in several parts of Los Angeles," said the newscaster on the homeless man's transistor radio. "Police are baffled as to the cause of the disturbances."

"Is catalepsy your explanation for your being a moocher and a sponge?" said Gilbert, unwilling to drop his conversation with Stuart.

"I invited you here as a witness to my request to not bury me right away," said Stuart, choking back his anger at Gilbert. "I didn't invite you here as a hostile witness."

"I'm taking Rowena's side in this argument."

"Rowena can speak for herself."

Gilbert glanced at Rowena, who remained mute. "She can, but she won't." He confronted Stuart. "I'm getting the impression you live off women."

"Would one of you please get me another lemonade?" said Rowena.

"I'm getting the impression you're macking on Rowena," said Stuart.

Face taut with anger, the tendons in his neck rigid, Gilbert balled his fists and made to stand up. "Somebody needs to teach you a lesson."

"What kind of a friend are you, anyway?"

"People are looking at us," said Rowena in a low voice, full of rebuke.

Indeed, the homeless man had turned his head on his folded arms so he could view the commotion at their table.

"I don't want to get into it with you, Gilbert," said Stuart. "Just don't bury me until at least seven days after I die. That's all I ask. You're turning this into some kind of referendum on my character."

"That's assuming you have one."

"I'm not gonna sit here any longer and listen to these attacks." Stuart got up, sliding his chair back angrily as he stood.

Gilbert rose also, spoiling for a fight.

"Why is everything about you?" said Gilbert. "Do you ever think about anyone but yourself?"

"That's not fair, Gilbert," said Rowena.

"It's true, I tell you. All he cares about is his own death. Why do you think he invited us here in the first place? Because he's obsessed with himself, that's why. Who else but a narcissus would be obsessed with his own death?"

"Obviously it was a mistake to invite you," said Stuart. "I should've just invited Rowena. She understands me. You don't."

"I understand you're a selfish prick who's full of himself."

"You're the one who started these attacks on me. I'm just defending myself."

"That's right. Blame your shortcomings on me. Never take responsibility for anything."

Stuart stalked off down the cement steps of the patio onto the sidewalk, cars whooshing by on the street. For the first time he had seen Gilbert for what he really was—a conniver who was scheming on Rowena. It wasn't a pretty sight, Stuart had to admit. Unbidden, thoughts about how Rowena really felt about him revolved in his mind. Did she think of him as a moocher, as did Gilbert? wondered Stuart. Was hanging around Gilbert and listening to Gilbert's snarky drivel about him poisoning her mind against him?

Stuart kept walking, stepping up his pace, glad to be alone out in the open air. But the thought kept pressing on him, niggling at the back of his mind, chilling his spine—what if he had a cataleptic fit and they buried him alive? Could he trust Gilbert, the real Gilbert, the envious Gilbert, who he had never known existed till now, to refrain from burying him for seven days after his death? Would Gilbert convince Rowena to bury Stuart right after Stuart died, burying him alive? Stuart could not bear to think about it. Surely, Rowena would heed his wishes . . . he hoped.

#

The next thing he knew, he found himself in an alley, lying supine on his back, staring at the infinite blue sky.

A crow the size of a cat cawed, kited down from a telephone wire overhead, and alighted on the pavement beside Stuart's motionless head. Stuart could glimpse the bird out of the corner of his eyes, which he could not move.

The crow hopped over to his head and stared down at him, its head twitching, wondering if Stuart was food.

Stuart wanted to swipe at the bird with his hand and shoo the creature away. But he could not move his hand. Even worse, he could not move anything. He lay paralyzed, yet aware of everything around him. He could hear a jet flying overhead. He could see the crow's sheeny black head as the bird bounded around on its talons near his face, trying to decide whether to start pecking at him with its black beak and eat him.

*Get the hell away from me!* Stuart screamed in his mind at the crow, face a frozen mask. He was terrified the scavenger would start pecking his eyes out, thinking him dead.

The crow did not leave. It kept jumping around Stuart's head, flapping its wings, suspecting he was a corpse.

A splash of white in the sky, a seagull bawled and swooped down, startling the crow. Fluttering its wings the crow flew away, calling in what might have been interpreted as distress. Dust kicked up by the wings flew into Stuart's eyes, but still he could not blink. He kept staring into the sky.

He felt relieved the crow had departed, leaving his eyes intact.

A scruffy homeless man traipsed into view. He shuffled toward the five-foot-deep, cylindrical blue plastic recycling bin the better part of fifteen feet from Stuart, lifted open the lid, dipped his head into the bin, and scrounged around through the contents, heedless (for now) of Stuart.

*Help me! For Christ's sake, help me!* Stuart cried at him mutely, mouth locked shut.

The homeless man pulled his head out of the bin and let go of the lid, which slammed down with a loud thwack against the bin. He ambled past Stuart, not even favoring him with a glance.

*Can't you see me, you fool?*

The man kept walking down the alley, casting around for another blue recycling bin or even a dark green trash bin.

Stuart wanted to scream at the guy for being such a fool, but no words emanated from his mouth. *Does he think I'm part of the scenery? Why doesn't the fool open his eyes? Call for help, you moron! I can't move!*

The scraggly man wandered away.

Stuart heard two women chattering in Spanish. As they approached, he could make them out as they angled down the alley toward him. Squat Hispanic women with olive complexions and curly brunette hair that topped their heads like crowns, they wore black dresses with bright splotches of yellow and red on them. The roly-poly woman looked about forty, the younger one in her twenties. Perhaps they were mother and daughter, decided Stuart.

183

Bryan Cassiday

They were toting plastic shopping bags with boxes of merchandise for babies, it looked like.

*Help me! Call the police! Call 911! I can't move!*

The older woman glanced at him with what looked like disgust to Stuart, but she didn't break stride. Following the tubby woman's gaze, the girl caught sight of Stuart and stared at him, slowing her gait.

*Help me!* he cried at the wide-eyed girl with his voice that wasn't a voice.

The mother grabbed the girl's arm and jerked her forward. "*Borracho.*"

*Drunk? No, I'm not drunk. Can't you see I need help?*

Distraught, he watched them abandon him in the alley without so much as a glance back at him.

Minutes later, a beige four-by-four drove by his leg, missing him by less than a foot, its wheels crackling against the dirt and sand on the pavement.

If he could only reach the smartphone in his trouser pocket, he could call for help. But he could not do anything, not in his present condition.

A bearded man and a reedy man wearing spectacles approached him. He had never realized alleys had so much pedestrian traffic. More bums? Stuart wondered. These two appeared to be pushing thirty.

The first newcomer had a dark beard that tapered to a point. Stuart harbored a wild urge to yank the beard and jerk the guy's face down into his own face so the guy could peer into Stuart's eyes and see he was neither drunk nor dead.

*Help me!*

"Who is it, Ron?" the Beard asked his cohort.

"Some bum, I guess," answered Ron, leveling a stare at Stuart.

"He doesn't look like a bum. He's wearing nice threads, not rags with stains all over them."

"What's wrong with him?" said Ron, scratching his chin. "The way his eyes are staring out of his head gives me the willies." He shivered to choreograph his words.

184

"He looks like he's dead," said the Beard, screwing up his face.

*No, I'm not dead! I need help! Call a doctor!*

The Beard squatted down on his haunches beside Stuart and commenced rooting through Stuart's trouser pockets. The Beard fished out Stuart's leather wallet, flipped through it, and plucked the paper bills from it.

*That's my money! Put it back, you crook!*

"What are you doing?" asked Ron.

"What's it look like? There's over a hundred dollars here," said the Beard, brandishing the cash in front of Ron's face.

"What if he wakes up?"

"He's not gonna wake up."

"How can you be sure?"

The Beard leaned his head down and pressed his ear against Stuart's rib cage, listening for a heartbeat. "His heart's not pumping. He's stone cold dead."

The Beard raised his head and continued ransacking Stuart's wallet, removing all of the credit cards and shoving them into his trouser pockets.

"Who is he?" said Ron.

"Who cares? He's just some dead guy."

"Look at his driver's license."

"Do I give a shit?"

*Robbers! I'm not dead! Help me!*

"His eyes," said Ron.

"What about his eyes?" said the Beard.

"It looks like he's trying to say something."

*Help me! Call 911! Hurry!*

"You're seeing things," said the Beard. "Dead men tell no tales."

"I don't know."

The Beard tossed Stuart's empty wallet onto the pavement as he rose, groaning with the effort. "My knees are killing me."

"What's going on?" said Ron, looking up.

A mob of people was shambling down the mouth of the alley toward them.

"Maybe a movie just let out or something," said the Beard. "What difference does it make?"

"What if they catch us rolling this guy?"

"How can they? I already jacked his paper," said the Beard, spotted Stuart's open discarded wallet lying nearby, and kicked it onto the cement driveway that led to the garage of the nearest apartment house. "See? There's no evidence."

"Like nobody's gonna see that? You ought to toss it somewhere."

"You toss it."

The crowd kept galumphing toward them, taking up the entire width of the alley as they maneuvered down it in a solid row of flesh.

"Hadn't we ought to do something with this guy?" said Ron, scoping out Stuart.

"Why?" said the Beard. "He's dead meat. It's not on us to do anything."

*Can't you see I'm still alive?*

"There's something about his eyes," said Ron.

"Forget his eyes. Let's take his watch." The Beard stooped down and slid Stuart's watch off his wrist. "Not exactly a Rolex," he said, inspecting it with disdain.

The vanguard of the grumbling throng was now about six feet from him and Ron.

"What's wrong with those guys?" said Ron, eying the clamoring mob with apprehension.

"Maybe they want a piece of the action," said the Beard.

"They don't look right," said Ron with increasing dread, inspecting them more closely.

"And they stink. Are they a bunch of unwashed bums? Why are there so many of them? I don't get it."

The foremost member of the mob, a female with long, frowsy bleached hair, lunged at the Beard, snagged his arm, and, with a sudden jerk, yanked it out of its socket. The Beard wailed in pain

186

as blood spurted out of his mutilated shoulder and arced into the teeming mob that reacted in a frenzy of wild gesticulations of their arms.

An eightysomething member of the horde collared Ron around his throat and took a bite out of Ron's neck. Arterial blood geysered into the air and splashed the bloodthirsty mob.

"They're not human!" cried the Beard, trying to stanch the flow of blood from his shoulder, eyes gaping in terror.

Indeed, the "bums" had white-filmed eyes that stared blankly out of their heads, and their faces looked like papier-mâché masks, as they swarmed around the Beard and Ron, tore them apart, and devoured their flesh.

Stuart could not believe what was happening around him. He was lying in the middle of an abattoir, powerless to move, powerless to flee. He could not get his head around the blood-soaked debacle that surrounded him. This could not be happening. It must be a nightmare. Maybe he had been dreaming ever since he found himself lying paralyzed in this alley.

Except everything looked real. Impossible to comprehend, but real.

He didn't know what was going on. All he knew was he had to get out of here before these cannibals, or whatever they were, polished off Ron and the Beard and turned on him as he lay helplessly on the pavement.

But how could he flee when he could not even move?

A member of the mob with grizzled close-cropped hair and a stocky build skittered toward Stuart and gazed down through glazed eyes at him.

Scared out of his wits, Stuart wanted to scream, but his vocal cords betrayed him, and no sound emerged from his throat. It probably was just as well, he decided. What good would screaming have done, anyway? Like this cannibal was going to hightail it when he heard Stuart scream? No way. These bogeymen didn't look like they'd take flight from anything or anyone.

With mounting anxiety, he waited for them to start scarfing him down like they had done with the Beard and Ron.

Another member of the horde streeled toward Stuart and stood beside him. The male wore a fluorescent green aloha shirt that hung loose over his waistband.

*Christ!* thought Stuart. It looked like Gilbert. His face looked like it was suffering from decomposition, but still it resembled Gilbert's. And that tasteless aloha shirt had to be Gilbert's. It had to be Gilbert, and yet it wasn't Gilbert. It was Gilbert transformed into something else, some kind of aberration that consumed living human flesh. A travesty of humanity, a two-legged monster hatched in the bowels of a madman's dream.

And then a thirtysomething blonde shuffled up beside Gilbert's mutation and gazed down at Stuart.

*Rowena!* Stuart wanted to cry, sickened at the sight of the monster she had become. Even with her face deformed by necrotic flesh, enough of her beautiful features remained intact that he could recognize her. It had to be her.

She didn't seem to recognize him, however. She simply stood there gazing down at him with sightless milky eyes that had once been the clearest blue.

*Rowena, what have they done to you!* What in the world had happened? Stuart wondered.

The world was going mad as he lay paralyzed in an alley, he decided. Any minute now, his wife and best friend would commence eating him, chomping on his flesh like it was fried chicken. He would have recoiled at the thought if he could have contrived to budge. But nothing had changed. He still could not move.

The three phantasms born of a nightmare seemed to become bored as they stood huddled over Stuart as if in a voiceless powwow, studying his inert body.

Why didn't they start eating him? he wondered. What was holding them back? There was nothing left of either the Beard or Ron to eat. Just jagged fragments of broken, worried bones strewn on the pavement. Stuart could not fend the trio off. He could do nothing. They must have realized his helplessness.

But still they did nothing.

The idea of them sinking their decaying teeth into his flesh made his blood run cold. He would have to lie there as mute witness to the horror of being consumed alive. He wished he could at least pass out so he would not have to watch it. To be eaten alive was bad enough, but to have to watch it in a state of paralysis was ten times worse. The horror of it boggled his mind.

If only he could move!

Grumbling, the rest of the mob maundered down the alley with uncoordinated jerks of their limbs, casting around for fresh human flesh to gobble down.

Stuart wondered if Rowena and Gilbert recognized him in their present state. Was that what was giving them pause? Stuart doubted it. Neither one of them looked like they were in any kind of shape to recognize their own mothers.

And then, incredibly, they moved on, moseying after the departing horde.

Could it be that they thought he was dead and they did not eat dead meat? Stuart wondered. How ironic it was to think that his catalepsy, his body's mimicry of death, had saved his life.

The very same ones he had asked to save him from his fit, should it parrot death and cause him to be buried alive, had themselves fallen victims to death in the form of some fantastic plague.

But what kind of a life was the one he lived now? It was more like a living death. And how long would he have to "live" like this, a mind trapped inside a motionless husk? The horror of it was inconceivable.

Even worse, Stuart realized, now that the plague had claimed both Rowena and Gilbert, was the fact that there was nobody left to tell the undertaker that Stuart wasn't really dead, merely paralyzed; and he would, as he had always feared, end up being buried alive.

Bryan Cassiday

# Cellular

"Promise me you'll kill me before midnight," said Charles Landers, his hatchet face squeezed with tension.

Though he was in his early thirties, he looked all of twenty years older. His normally chestnut hair was now streaked with white, and his brow was etched with deep creases that, indeed, crisscrossed his entire careworn face, which looked more like a rubber mask than it did a face.

His friend Hickey almost didn't recognize him.

"What kind of nonsense are you talking?" said Hickey, eyes gaping, shocked as much at the ghastliness of Landers's appearance as at the bizarreness of Landers's request.

The twenty-five-year-old Hickey could not believe his ears as he and Landers sat in their shirtsleeves and Bermuda shorts on their brightly colored yoga mats on the beach near the Santa Monica Pier. Hickey wondered if Landers was losing his mind. Was the stress of either his job or his personal life, or perhaps both, getting the better of Landers?

The combers rolled in and slammed against the barnacle-swathed wooden piles that supported the weathered pier that had a mustard-painted two-story Mexican restaurant perched on its outermost end and a Ferris wheel and a rollercoaster looming over its opposite end that extended from the strand.

Hickey and Landers sat near enough to the water that they could hear the waves strumming as they marched in and then roaring as they broke on the shore in a flurry of spume. Screaming children were cavorting on the shoreline, their voices carrying over the littoral, while gulls, fluttering white crescents cut out of the clear sky, gyred overhead in the onshore breeze and cried down like it was all part of a game they were playing with the tots.

Only it wasn't a game with Landers, Hickey could see. Landers was dead serious.

"Just promise me you'll kill me before midnight," repeated Landers, hunched over, wrapping his arms around his knees as he sat.

He looked for all the world like a kid that had just finished swimming, emerged from the cold water, and was now freezing to death sitting on his yoga mat on the sand with his teeth chattering and his face turning blue. But he didn't have the smooth face of a kid. He had the wizened face of an old man, an old man that had seen somebody walk over his grave.

"What's this all about, Charlie?" said Hickey with concern for his friend's sanity.

"It's about stopping me."

Hickey jacked his eyebrows with bemusement at Landers's strange reply. "Stopping you from what?"

"Stopping me from doing—" Landers sneaked a glance toward his trouser pocket in horror and held his tongue before he could finish his sentence.

Hickey shook his head in bafflement. "Stopping you from doing what?"

Landers shut his eyes in anguish. "Maybe I should begin at the beginning."

Somebody's stomach growled, Hickey noticed. He could not tell if it was his or Landers's.

"You're not making any sense," said Hickey.

"I got a new smartphone a week ago."

A smile on his face, Hickey sighed with relief. "Welcome to the twenty-first century."

Eyes bulging, Landers lunged forward and snagged Hickey's naked forearm. "You don't understand."

191

Which was true, decided Hickey as he flinched when Landers latched onto him.

"Calm down and tell me what happened," said Hickey, trying, with little success, to pry Landers's clenched fingers off his arm.

*Christ!* thought Hickey. They gripped him so tight they felt like they were stricken with rigor mortis as they cut off the circulation in his arm.

Landers let go of Hickey's arm and seemed to relax a bit. "I'm trying to."

"I'm listening."

Landers stared out at the water that stretched like an endless sheet of graphite to the distant horizon.

Hickey wondered if he should call 911 for paramedics. But what would he tell them? That Landers was acting like a psycho? What would they give him? Thorazine? Hickey decided not to make the call. He had no desire to get Landers into trouble. If Hickey could coax Landers into getting off his chest whatever was bothering him, that might be enough in itself to calm him down and set him to rights.

"I've killed three people—that I know of," said Landers as if in a daze.

"Stop talking like a lunatic."

"It's true."

"I doubt it, Charlie. I know you like my own brother. You wouldn't hurt a fly."

"It wasn't my idea."

"Pull yourself together. You obviously had a nightmare. That's all."

"I wish."

"So who did you supposedly kill?" said Hickey, not believing any of it for a second.

"Barbara, Janine, and Maria."

Landers's quick response took Hickey by surprise. Come to think of it, Hickey had seen neither Barbara nor Janine in at least three days. He didn't know who Maria was. But that didn't mean all three of them were dead. That was preposterous.

"You must have dreamed you killed them," said Hickey, shrugging it off.

"I murdered them, I tell you."

"Why?" said Hickey. He didn't believe a word of what Landers was telling him, but humoring Landers might settle the poor guy's nerves.

"I don't know."

"That makes a lot of sense. You killed them and you have no idea why? Listen to yourself, Charlie."

"It wasn't my idea."

"This is making less and less sense as you talk about it," said Hickey, scratching his head. "Which only goes to prove it's a nightmare. It didn't really happen. That's why it makes no sense. Dreams and nightmares never make any sense. Just because they seem real doesn't make them real."

"I didn't want to kill the three of them, but I did."

Hickey fetched a sigh. "OK. Let's hear your nightmare."

"Like I told you, I recently bought a smartphone. I thought it would help me get jobs."

"Nothing could help *you* get a job."

Landers gave Hickey a stare that was difficult to comprehend. Hickey interpreted it as a kind of anguished fear.

"I was kidding," said Hickey. "Can't you take a joke?"

What was wrong with Landers? wondered Hickey. A week ago Landers would have shot back with a dig of his own aimed at Hickey. Now Landers looked traumatized by a good-natured rib. His whole personality had become warped.

They were both independent truckers, Hickey knew. They were both always trying to scrounge up work. It was the nature of the job. And part and parcel of that was the ribbing they gave each other when they were between jobs, which was often nowadays on account of the Great Recession, or whatever the talking heads on TV wanted to call it.

In short, Hickey and Landers were close. They even had similar tats on their biceps. They both had coiled snakes preparing to strike. Hickey had a cobra, and Landers a rattler.

193

Something was really eating Landers, Hickey realized and started to become worried for his friend. At first blush, on seeing Landers's miserable physical appearance, Hickey had thought Landers was suffering from a hangover. After all, Landers liked hoisting a brew as much as the next man. Now, however, Hickey figured Landers had something seriously wrong with him, but, for the life of him, Hickey didn't know what it could be. All Landers's rambling so far wasn't making a great deal of sense.

"It all started when I got that phone," said Landers, and snuck a furtive glance at his trouser pocket.

"What started?"

"My killing spree."

Hickey sighed. "Are you on that again?"

"I can't get off it. That's the problem." Shutting his eyes in anguish, Landers ran his hand through his marbled close-cropped hair.

"If you tell me what this is all about, maybe I can help you."

"I doubt it, but I need to tell someone," said Landers, staring at Hickey with hollow eyes.

"Is it money? Do you need a loan? I can help you with that."

Landers shook his head. "No, no. It's not that. It's my phone."

"What?"

Landers blew out his cheeks, expelling air. "The day after I got my new cell, I woke up in my apartment to the sound of someone talking to me. I couldn't understand who was talking to me, since my daughter Ann was at school and my wife Barbara was at work. And, in any case, it was a male voice that was talking to me."

"A dream," said Hickey, nodding knowingly.

"No. It was a male voice telling me to wake up. 'Wake up!' it was saying over and over again. 'Wake up! Wake up!' I looked to see who it was, and all I saw was my cell lying on the bureau near my bed. The voice was emanating from the cell."

"It was somebody calling you, of course."

"How could it be somebody calling me? I hadn't answered it."

"Then it was your answering machine recording the message."

"I don't have an answering machine. I have voicemail."

"I'm sure there's a logical explanation for it."

"Like what?"

"Some of these smartphones can talk. You've heard of Siri."

"But they're not supposed to talk unless you ask it a question. I was asleep when it started talking."

"Maybe it's defective."

"There's more."

"I figured."

"The voice started ordering me around. It told me to dress, shave, and eat breakfast as soon as I got out of bed."

Not buying it Hickey shrugged. "It wasn't a voice. It was your own mind telling you to do your daily routine."

"I heard a voice, I tell you. It was quite distinct. And it wasn't friendly. It sounded downright hostile."

Hickey pooh-poohed Landers's response. "You probably felt guilty for oversleeping, so your mind was berating you. It's all psychological. You were mad at yourself for oversleeping. Dreams and nightmares can signify a guilty conscience acting out."

Landers shook his head vehemently, no. "I went over to the phone to turn it off, to shut the nagging voice off somehow. I couldn't do it. It kept talking to me, issuing orders. It commanded me to drink a glass of orange juice, eat four bowls of cereal, and drink a cup of green tea because I had a big day ahead of me so I needed a big breakfast. It was very specific about what I should eat and drink."

"It was your guilty conscience."

"Then why did it tell me to kill my next-door neighbor Janine?"

At that moment, a Day-Glo pink Frisbee soared toward Hickey and Landers and wedged itself in the sand at their feet. Clad in an olive drab bathing suit, a teenage boy with shoulder-length sun-streaked blond hair came running after the plastic disc,

195

laughing. He wrenched it out of the sand, glanced for a moment at the haggard-looking Landers, then tossed the Frisbee at his friend who was standing some thirty feet away. Smiling and waving his hands, the teenager sprang in his bare feet through the sand back toward his friend.

The teenager had not brightened Landers's mood in the least. Landers continued looking glum.

"You're pulling my leg," said Hickey. "You don't think I'm gonna swallow that hogwash that your cell told you to kill somebody."

"The fact of the matter is, it did," said Landers, a morose expression fixed on his face.

"Why did it tell you to kill her?" said Hickey, humoring Landers.

"It gave me no reason. It just told me to do it."

"That's ridiculous," said Hickey.

He could not help himself. Even if Landers's sanity was at risk, Hickey had to tell the truth. If the truth shook Landers up, so much the better was Hickey's thinking. What Landers was saying was preposterous. A cell phone commanding him to murder someone! The idea!

"It told me to kill her," said Landers evenly.

"Why didn't you say no? You don't have to take orders from a phone."

"That's the problem!" Landers burst. "I couldn't say no. Somehow it was controlling me. I had to do what it told me."

"No way. You expect me to believe this cock-and-bull story? No way." Flabbergasted, Hickey flourished his arms at his sides.

"I don't care what you believe. I'm telling you the truth about what happened."

"Stark raving nonsense! I never should have humored you by going along with your fish story. You're selling me a bill of goods."

Bummed out by Hickey's words, brooding, Landers fell silent.

Hickey wondered if he had gone too far, if his rebuke would prevent Landers from talking anymore. Indeed, Landers appeared lost in a funk now. Hickey wondered if his remark had caused Landers to lose his already-tentative grasp on sanity. Hickey immediately regretted his words.

"I didn't mean what I said, Charlie," he said. "Just tell me the rest of it and get it off your chest. You'll feel better."

"I knocked on Janine's door," said Landers matter-of-factly. "She opened the door. I went in and strangled her to death. It was easy. I'm much bigger than her. She put up a fight, but she never had a chance. I hid her body under her bed. I don't know if anyone has found her yet. She lives alone, you know. It might be a while before anyone finds her."

Dumbfounded, Hickey stared mutely at Landers.

At last Hickey said, "You need professional help, man."

"Are you talking about a shrink? What's he gonna do? Tell my phone to stop ordering me around?"

"Your phone can't order you to kill a person."

"You're right. It's ordered me to kill three of them—and another one at midnight." Landers lunged at Hickey, clutching Hickey by the shoulders. "Which is why you have to kill me before midnight!"

With difficulty Hickey dislodged himself from Landers's frenzied grasp. "Get ahold of yourself."

Landers dropped his arms and slumped back onto his yoga mat. "I can't stop myself on my own from doing what it tells me. I'm terrified I'll kill my daughter Ann tonight."

"You're not gonna kill anyone." Hickey paused, thinking. "Maybe you have issues with your cell phone and you're giving it human attributes."

"Psychobabble," scoffed Landers.

"You're humanizing it and demonizing it at the same time," said Hickey, puzzled now that he thought about it.

"I killed Maria, our babysitter, the day after I killed Janine," Landers droned on as if in a trance. "Maria had come to my apartment to pick up her paycheck. I invited her inside. I was alone. She gladly entered, eager to get her money. I told her to have a seat. She sat on the sofa, while I pretended to retrieve my

197

checkbook from the kitchen. Actually I went to my bedroom, scoffed up a belt that lay on my bureau, and returned to her. I strangled her with the leather belt as she sat on the sofa, her back to me."

"You're talking bullshit!" exploded Hickey, becoming increasingly angry with Landers for spouting such nonsense.

"I hauled her corpse into the bedroom," Landers went on, voice flat. "She didn't weigh very much. Just over a hundred pounds, I'd say. She was a petite girl in her early twenties. I tossed her on my bed and wrapped her in an old blanket. I couldn't have Barbara finding her. I wondered how to dispose of Maria's body—"

"Stop!" cut in Hickey, fed up with listening to Landers's insane recital.

"I decided I had to remove her from the apartment," said Landers, ignoring Hickey's outburst. "I threw her over my shoulder and hauled her down to the garage, where they keep the Dumpsters. The garage is kept locked to prevent the homeless from entering and pawing through the garbage. I figured if I tossed her body into the Dumpster, her body wouldn't be found for a while, and when it was, there wouldn't be any way to connect her murder to me."

"I don't want to listen to any more of your nightmare." Hickey kneaded his forehead in despair. "I'm starting to feel as lousy as you."

"Don't you want to hear how I strangled Barbara?"

"Why the hell would I?"

"My cell told me I had to murder her," said Landers, despite Hickey's retort.

"Think what you're saying. Why would it tell you to murder your own wife?"

"It never gave me any explanations. It just gave me orders. It said, 'Kill Barbara. Kill Barbara.'"

"You sound like one of those wackos that hear voices in their heads."

"The voice is coming from my phone, not inside my head."

198

"Turn the stupid phone off."

"I can't turn it off. I don't know how."

"Then trade it in for another model."

"It won't let me."

"You sound like you're scared of a little cell phone."

"You would be too, if it was ordering you to kill."

"What can it possibly do to you if you refuse to obey it?"

"I can't refuse to obey it. I don't have that option," said the hapless Landers. "Why do you think I'm asking you to kill me before I can kill Ann tonight?"

"I'm not gonna kill you, Charlie, no matter how messed up your mind is. Count me out."

Landers's face clouded and became gloomier than ever. "Then how can I save Ann from being murdered?"

"You've got to come to grips with the fact that you haven't killed anyone, that these murders are all in your wacked-out mind. You must be having some kind of mental breakdown."

Landers covered his closed eyelids with his hand. "I wish it was that easy." He brought his hand down his face and opened his bloodshot eyes that seemed to have lost their focus.

Hickey thought about it. For whatever reason, Landers's phone seemed to be at the root of his troubles.

"It *is* that easy," said Hickey. "Where's your phone?"

Fidgeting, Landers glanced at his Bermudas' pocket. "In my pocket."

"Take out the phone."

"Why? I don't want to look at it. Just looking at it gives me goose bumps."

"Just take it out."

Gingerly, Landers's hand delved into his pocket and fished out the smartphone.

"Why?" he said, holding the handset, terrified that it would begin talking.

"Throw it away."

Landers became motionless, as if paralyzed, staring at the phone. "I can't."

"Do it!"

"I can't, I tell you."

Hickey leaned forward, snagged the phone, and flung it the better part of twenty feet toward the onrushing, bubbling surf of the ebb tide. The phone fell short of the damp sand near the water's edge and buried itself in dry sand near one of the wooden legs of a faded robin's-egg blue lifeguard tower.

"There," said Hickey, getting up and brushing sand off his legs. "Now it can't tell you what to do anymore. It's that simple. Let's get out of here."

Landers gazed after the phone in horror, uncertain what it meant to be free of the handset's presence. Could it be that simple? he wondered. Throw the phone away and all your problems disappear? Landers didn't believe it for a second. After all, he had throttled three women and was going to do the same to his daughter tonight. But did he have to commit the murder tonight, now that he was free of the phone? Or *was* he free of the phone? Just because it wasn't on his person, did that make him free of it? He didn't think so. He knew that he still had to strangle Ann at midnight. Nothing had changed in that regard.

All his life he had wanted to be a somebody. That's all he wanted. Just to be a somebody. Not a truck driver. A *somebody*. And now he had ended up being a serial killer.

Snapping out of his reverie he bolted to his feet and snatched Hickey's arm. "That solves nothing. You've got to promise me you'll kill me before midnight."

With growing exasperation Hickey broke free of Landers. "Your phone can't tell you what to do. You can't hear it any more. It's gone."

Hickey leaned over, picked up his yoga mat, and shook the sand off it. He rolled the mat up, snugged it under his arm, and plodded through the sand toward the asphalt parking lot. Across the Coast Highway that skirted the lot, a rucked palisade loomed over him like a lowering thundercloud.

Landers pelted after him. "You can't leave me alone. If you leave me, I'll kill her."

"I don't believe you killed anyone. You're having nightmares, is all."

Hickey caught sight of three policemen dressed in black uniforms strutting across the parking lot He. wondered what was up. They were probably rousting some bum loitering on the beach. But they seemed to be heading toward him and Landers.

As soon as Landers picked up on them, he shut his mouth.

The trio of unsmiling cops met Landers and Hickey on the sand, blocking their way.

"Charles Landers?" said the tall one that had a harelip under his black mustache, gazing at Landers with a no-nonsense mien.

"What do you want?" said Landers.

"We're arresting you for the murder of your wife, sir." The cop produced a pair of handcuffs from his waist.

"How did you find me?"

"The GPS on your cell phone."

Then what Landers had been telling him had been true, decided Hickey in stunned silence. The man *had* murdered his wife. And was planning on murdering his daughter.

Landers gazed in the direction of his smartphone discarded in the sand, the device that had ordered him to kill three women and then had led the police here to bust him.

The blond teen Frisbee thrower was loping past the smartphone to retrieve his nearby Frisbee when he heard a voice coming from the sand saying, "Wake up! Wake up!"

Stooping down, he glommed onto the smartphone. "Look what I found," he hollered toward his buddy and held up the handset like it was a trophy.

"Wake up! Wake up!" repeated the device.

Bryan Cassiday

# Boxed

I caught sight of a twentysomething blonde ducking into the elevator and I ran for all I was worth to catch up to her. I had no desire to meet the same fate that my wife had just met at the hands of a ghoul: to be torn to pieces and eaten in the hotel lobby where I now stood, wondering how to escape the onslaught of the ghouls.

Maybe I could find refuge in the elevator. It was a cinch there was no safe place on the street outside the lobby of the hotel, where packs of zombies were staggering amok and killing everybody in sight amidst screams of their victims being ripped apart and devoured.

Ghouls were shattering the plate-glass picture windows of nearby shops and breaking into the stores to kill and consume the customers that were cowering in fear inside. Shards of broken glass, overturned metal wastebaskets, and offal littered the sidewalks, where the bloodthirsty, rioting ghouls roamed at will, ransacking Santa Marita and chomping on anybody unfortunate enough to get in their way.

Pillars of smoke billowed across the California town, borne by the summer breeze, and daubed the sky purple, blotting out the sun.

In the streets, derelict cars with blood-smeared windshields were the order of the day. The heat from the fresh blood steamed the cars' windows, obfuscating them, preventing anyone from peering inside to glimpse the carnage sprawled on the car seats. Fine with me. I had no desire to peek inside those slaughterhouses.

I wanted none of it.

I dashed for the hotel elevator and reached it as its door was sliding shut under the annunciator light. I jabbed my arm inside the doorway, causing the closing door to reverse direction and open up.

Half a dozen people stood in the elevator, cringing at the sight of me, terrified that I was one of the flesh-eating ghouls.

I couldn't blame them.

"I'm not one of them," I said.

But I knew from what my wife had told me that my troubles were just beginning.

It was a hard decision for me to make to duck into the elevator after what she had told me as she had died in my hands.

Besides the blonde, five other passengers in the elevator sized me up suspiciously. They weren't entirely convinced I wasn't a cannibal.

"How do we know you're not one of them?" said a middle-aged man in a dark business suit.

He had deep-set blue eyes that stared out at me from behind his black-framed spectacles. His receding hairline revealed an expanse of bald head. He wore shiny black oxfords that were polished to such a brilliant sheen that I could make out the image of my face reflected in their uppers.

"Because I can talk," I said. "Those infected cannibals can't talk."

The elevator door slid shut behind me. The elevator commenced to hum as it rose.

"I guess we're stuck with you now," said the man.

"You don't sound too happy about it."

"What's to be happy about? We're surrounded by those creatures. They're all over the streets killing everybody."

Another middle-aged man, who still had most of his hair and was also dressed in a conservative business suit, stood beside the first guy and eyed me warily. He had thick bushy black hair, no lips to speak of, and looked a couple years younger than his buddy.

"Bob and I were going to have lunch together when those infected people went berserk and started attacking everyone." He nodded at the balding guy who had spoken to me. "I'm Jack, by the way."

"I'm Vince," I said.

"I'm Sarah," said the blonde I had seen ducking into the elevator.

She picked at her tight pink blouse just above her jeans' waistband. I didn't know why. Probably a nervous habit. I looked at her blouse. She turned her head away.

Following suit a seventyish woman with grizzled hair decided to introduce herself. "I'm Rebecca."

She was wearing an aqua pantsuit that hung loose on her bony frame.

"I'm Don," said the teenager that stood beside her.

Clad in an Abercrombie & Fitch T and jeans, he was listening to white plastic earbuds that were connected by white wires to his iPhone.

"I'm Franco," said the deliveryman that stood directly across from me.

He was pushing forty and was wearing a grey uniform with a torn sleeve on it. He had close-cropped dark hair and a surly cast to his mouth that sported a thin mustache above it.

I eyeballed him. "What happened to your sleeve?"

"It got torn." His brown eyes glared back at me with annoyance. "What's it to you?"

"I've got bad news for you."

"For me? I never saw you before in my life."

"Not just you. Everybody." I surveyed the inquisitive faces around me.

"What? That there's some plague going around turning everybody into zombies?" said Bob. "Is that your bad news? I wouldn't exactly call that a scoop, buddy."

The elevator jerked to a halt.

"What the hell?" said Don, feeling the elevator grind to a full stop.

"What's going on?" said Franco.

"If this elevator doesn't start moving pretty soon, my news is gonna be even worse," I said.

"Stop talking in riddles, will you?" said Rebecca.

She held her short arms in front of her like they were frozen stiff. They seemed to have limited movement. Perhaps she had rheumatism. She wore her hair piled on top of her head, which made her look taller than she actually was. She couldn't have been more than five four. Her hair added at least three more inches to her height.

"My wife told me this before she died," I said.

My voice felt tight as I recalled her gruesome death at the hands of a ghoul. I didn't know if I could continue. I could still see the creature taking a huge bite out of her throat. The resultant arterial spray from her carotid splattered the hotel's lobby ceiling. I closed my eyes and ran my hand down my brow, trying to blot out the memory.

"Spit it out," said Bob. "What did she tell you? Or do we care?"

He had the expressive face of a salesman trying to read your mind. One minute he could be smiling at you like he was your best friend, the next he could be glowering at you with a sneering mouth and sizing you up as a loser if you didn't fall for his sales pitch and buy his product. His face was all about manipulation.

Bob annoyed me. I didn't want to buy whatever he was selling. His domineering, brassy personality turned me off.

"Are you a salesman?" I said.

"How'd you guess? I sell cars."

"I don't want to buy a car."

"You probably couldn't afford one, not the kind of cars I sell." He snickered then cut his eyes toward Jack and smiled. "We sell sports cars." Bob returned his gaze to me, his face sneering now. "You know what they say. If you gotta ask, you can't afford it."

"Whatever you're selling I don't want it," I said.

"What's your racket?"

His question threw me, though it was natural enough considering I had just asked him his line of work. I just wasn't expecting it.

"I'm a voice-over artist," I said.

That sounded harmless enough. I couldn't exactly tell him that I had escaped from a sanitarium to find my wife when the plague broke out. They would think I was a lunatic if I told them the truth. I wasn't a lunatic. I simply had a breakdown. I was bipolar and could not rouse myself out of a depressive state I had got into.

It was a long story and I didn't want to get into it. Especially in this crisis we found ourselves in. Under the gun, individuals weren't likely to converse reasonably with each other. Nobody in this elevator would want to hear that they were cooped up with an escapee from an asylum. They wouldn't give me time to explain myself. It was best not to tell them the truth, for now anyway.

Bob just looked at me when I told him what I did. He wasn't impressed. He wasn't anything. He looked neutral. He certainly didn't want to shake my hand or offer me his business card. He looked blank.

I guess he couldn't figure out a sales pitch to hit me with. Maybe he had never sold a sports car to a voice-over artist before.

"Will you tell us what the bad news is, already?" said Sarah.

"My wife told me." I had to pause again as I thought about her grisly death.

"Told you what?"

"Yeah. Get on with it," said Franco.

I took a couple of deep breaths and pulled myself together.

"Get a grip," said Bob.

I did not want to listen any longer to Bob telling me what to do, so I told them. "She told me she saw somebody get bitten by a zombie before they entered this elevator."

"You're saying one of us is infected with the plague?" said Franco, eyes wide.

I nodded. "I told you I had bad news."

"Then that means whoever it is will turn into a ghoul and try to eat us."

"The question is, who is it?" I surveyed the passengers in the elevator. "Which one of you was bitten?"

Nobody said anything.

I couldn't say I was surprised. The person who had been bitten would not want to admit it, lest the other passengers turn on him and kill him.

"Come on!" said Bob. "Whoever it is, fess up. I don't know about the rest of you, but I want to know who it is right this moment."

He searched everybody's face, expecting somebody to answer. Nobody said anything.

It was Don who said at last, "Was it a man or a woman? At least we could narrow down the suspects if we knew that."

Apparently Don was listening to everything we said, even though he had earbuds stuck in his ears and had looked distracted, like he wasn't paying attention to us.

"I don't know," I said. "My wife . . . died." My voice caught. "My wife died before she could tell me," I managed to say.

Don sighed. "Then we're back to square one."

"It could be anybody in here," said Franco, keyed up, eying his neighbors suspiciously and shifting edgily on his feet.

"There's one easy way to find out," said Jack.

"What's that?" said Franco.

"We examine everybody for bites."

"Nobody's examining me for nothing," said Rebecca. "You can keep your dirty paws to yourselves."

She hunched her body together, like she was drawing into a shell.

Bob leered at Sarah. "What about you? Were you the one who was bitten?"

Sarah cringed. "Nobody's touching me either."

"We're gonna have to start touching each other sooner or later to find that bite mark."

"Says who?"

"Nobody's touching anyone," I said.

I was trying to calm everybody down. It felt like we were about to break out into a brawl.

"Then how are we gonna find out who's infected?" said Bob.

"Bob's right," said Jack. "We have to find out who's infected before they turn."

"How do we know it isn't you?" said Sarah. "Maybe you're the one who got bitten."

"I can guarantee you it wasn't me," said Jack smugly.

"I can guarantee *you* it wasn't *me*."

"All right, let's do it this way," I said. "Whoever wasn't bitten, raise their hand."

Everybody raised their hand.

"What did you expect, bright boy?" said Bob. "Did you really think anyone's gonna admit they got bit?"

As difficult as it was for me, I ignored Bob.

"Somebody's lying," I told the others.

"Tell us something we don't know. And who put you in charge anyway?"

"I'm telling you what my wife told me. That's all."

"It sounds to me like you're telling us what to do." Bob squinted at me and hung his mouth open, exposing his teeth in a grimace-sneer, trying to mau-mau me. "How do we know *you* aren't the one who got bit?"

Bob was rubbing me the wrong way with his accusations. "If I was the one, I wouldn't have told all of you that somebody had gotten bitten."

"Why not?" said Franco, not following my logic.

"Because if I *had* gotten bitten I wouldn't want anybody to know about it."

"Makes sense to me," said Jack.

"Hold on a second," said Bob. He turned to me. "Maybe you told us about the zombie bite in order to deflect suspicion from yourself."

"Yeah," said Jack, suddenly switching to Bob's side and challenging me. "Maybe you're trying to hoodwink us into thinking you weren't bitten."

I heaved a sigh. I had thought Jack was on my side.

"But I wouldn't have brought the subject up at all, if I was the one who had been bitten," I said. "You should be thanking me, not accusing me."

Bob continued to stare distrustfully at me. "You want us to think it's not you that got bit. That's why you brought the subject up."

I threw up my hands in frustration. "I wasn't the one who was bitten."

"Nobody's exonerated here," said Bob. "That's all I can say." He swept his eyes over the faces surrounding him.

To his surprise he saw Franco reach behind his back and pull out a gun from his rear waistband. He waved the muzzle at the others.

"Whoa!" said Bob. "Where'd you get that? I thought you said you're a deliveryman."

"I am," said Franco.

"Deliverymen don't carry guns. Cops carry guns."

"And robbers," said Jack.

"I have the most dangerous route in the city," said Franco. "I've got a permit to carry a concealed weapon."

Franco stood about five five. Maybe he carried a gun to compensate for his shortness or maybe, like he said, he really did have the most dangerous route in the city. In the end it made no difference. The fact was, he had a pistol and he was aiming it at the rest of us, swinging it back and forth, describing an arc to include all of us.

"Take it easy," I said. "What do you expect to do with that thing?"

"If I kill all of you, I won't have to worry about getting infected," said Franco.

He may have been short, but he was stocky and muscular. He was built like a bull. He looked like he worked out in the gym. He wouldn't be easy to overpower. Whoever tried to disarm him would be in for a fight. Also, the corner of his mouth was twitching. Not a good sign. It indicated he was nervous and might discharge the gun accidentally.

"What's the point of killing all of us?" said Don, who stepped back as far away from Franco as he could get.

"I don't know who got bit. All I know is, it wasn't me. If I kill all of you, I'll be safe."

"Do you have enough bullets to kill all of us?"

"I count only six of you. This Sig has a fifteen-round clip. You don't need a computer to dope out the answer."

"You're not gonna be able to kill all of us," said Bob. "You think we're all gonna stand here and let you gun us down like we're a bunch of sheep?"

"I wasn't bitten," Jack told Franco. "You don't have to shoot me."

"Me either," said Don.

"Shut up!" said Franco. "How do I know you aren't lying? I can't believe any of you. The safest course for me is to shoot all of you."

He brandished the automatic at us again.

"You'll never be able to kill all of us," said Bob. "If we rush you at once, one of us is bound to get through and beat the living shit out of you."

"You think?"

"I know. You can't pull that trigger fast enough to kill all of us if we rush you." Bob scoped out the elevator. "Look how cramped this elevator is. Each of us is only a few steps away from you. You'll be lucky to kill even one of us if we all charge you at once."

"And the rest of us will gouge your eyeballs out before we stomp you to death," said Jack.

Grimacing, Sarah held her hands to ears. "Shut up. Will you just shut up?"

Franco seemed to be having second thoughts. He lowered his pistol somewhat.

"Just put it away," I said.

"I don't want to put it away," said Franco. "I don't trust any of you."

"Don't point it at us for Christ's sake," said Don, holding his hand up in front of his chest like he was trying to block a bullet.

"Nobody better try to take this away from me or I'll shoot you. I know how to use this." Franco wagged the gun at us for emphasis.

"That gun isn't gonna solve anything," I said.

"It's causing more problems than it's solving," said Rebecca.

"It'll solve everything once we find out who got infected," said Franco, holding the pistol up in front of his face.

"It's not gonna help us find out who got infected," I said.

"Oh yeah? What if I aim it at each of you and one at a time ask you if you got bit? If you don't tell the truth, I'll shoot you."

"It won't work."

"The infected person will lie," said Bob.

"Not if I threaten to shoot him if he lies."

Bob shook his head. "If he tells you he's infected, you'll shoot him anyway. What's he got to lose by lying?"

"His life."

"He loses it either way."

"Does anybody know how long it takes for somebody to turn into one of those creatures after being bitten?" asked Rebecca.

Everybody searched everybody else's face, drawing blanks.

"How long did it take your wife to turn into one after she got bit?" Bob asked me.

"She died in my arms soon after the zombie bit her," I said.

I wanted to erase the memory of her death from my mind, but my fellow passengers wouldn't let me. They kept bringing up her death. I didn't want to think about death anymore.

"That doesn't help us any," said Jack.

211

"What we need to know is how long it takes for somebody who gets bit but doesn't die to turn into a ghoul," said Bob.

"What difference does it make?" said Franco, holding his gun lower now, its muzzle pointed at the floor.

"It would let us know how much longer we'll be safe in this elevator."

Jack nodded. "Maybe we'll be out of this elevator before the bitten person turns. Then we'll all be safe."

"If the frigging elevator would start moving again," said Bob.

He swept his eyes around the elevator as if looking at it might get it to start ascending again. His eyes lingered on the ceiling.

My eyes followed the direction of his gaze. "Maybe there's a way out of here."

"That looks like a trapdoor in the ceiling," said Bob.

"So we crawl out on the roof," said Franco. "Then what?"

"He has a point," said Jack. "What are we supposed to do when we climb into the elevator shaft?"

"Maybe we can climb up the cable that holds the elevator," I said.

"I'm sick of listening to you," said Franco. "Ever since you got in this elevator, everything's been going south."

"Yeah," said Bob, turning on me. "You got us into this mess."

I noticed glares from most of the other passengers focusing on me.

"Don't kill the messenger," I said. "I told you I had bad news for you when I first stepped into this car, but don't blame it on me."

They wanted to blame their predicament on somebody, it was easy to see.

"He didn't do anything," said Rebecca, referring to me.

"Let's concentrate on finding a way out of here," I said. "If we can get out of this elevator, it won't matter when one of us turns. We'll all be free to go wherever we want."

"I still think you're the problem," Franco told me. "You're like a damn albatross around our necks. I ought to shoot you on principle."

He trained his automatic on my chest.

I froze. I didn't know what to do. I didn't want to make any sudden moves that might cause him to squeeze the trigger. He was already worked up, and the slightest move on my part might set him off.

"What good is it gonna do if you shoot him?" said Rebecca.

"I tell you he's bad luck," said Franco.

"Oh phooey."

I suddenly became aware that it was getting hot in here. Stifling, actually. I broke out into a sweat. I wasn't the only one who was suffering from the heat.

Jack yanked uncomfortably on his shirt collar. "What happened to the AC?"

"The power for the entire building must be out," said Bob, face sweaty.

"Wonderful," said Franco. "What next?"

At least he wasn't leveling his gun at me anymore. I was thankful for that. The heat must have distracted him.

"Let's see if we can open that trapdoor," said Bob, checking out the ceiling. "If nothing else, it'll at least let some fresh air in here."

He wiped sweat off his brow with the back of his hand.

"How are we gonna reach it?" said Don, head tilted up toward the trapdoor.

"Somebody give me a boost," said Bob.

"Don's lighter than you," I said. "Why don't we boost him up there?"

Bob leveled a glare at me. He could not stand anyone disagreeing with him.

I started when I heard a thump on the ceiling. Everybody else in the elevator had the same reaction. I riveted my eyes on the ceiling.

"What was that?" said Jack, voicing what was on everybody's mind.

"There's only one way to find out," I said, not looking forward to the prospect.

"I'm not so sure we should open that trapdoor," said Sarah, eying the ceiling with dread.

"Why not?" said Bob.

"We have no idea what's up there."

"Ignorance is bliss, huh?" said Jack.

"For all we know, the building may be falling apart. If you open that trapdoor, a block of cement might fall in here."

"Why would the building be falling apart?"

"There's no power. Why not?"

Jack shook his head. "I don't see the connection."

Sarah fished her cell phone out of her purse. "Why didn't I think of this earlier?" She punched out 911.

"Good idea," said Don.

Sarah shook her head. "I can't get through."

"Let me try."

He tried to put through a call on his iPhone. He shrugged. No dice.

"The cell phones must be jammed because everybody's trying to use them at once," said Bob.

Rebecca shushed them. "Listen," she whispered.

Everybody fell silent.

I could hear scraping and sliding on the top of the elevator. It sounded like something heavy was dragging across the roof of the car and scraping the metal. I caught myself grinding my teeth in apprehension. And then I heard another sound—like fingernails scraping across a blackboard. It was enough to set my nerves on end.

Sarah shivered. "I hate that sound."

"Maybe there are firemen up there coming to rescue us," said Rebecca.

"Why don't they cut their fingernails?"

Rebecca shot Sarah a baleful look.

"Why aren't they knocking on the trapdoor to signal us?" I said. "That's what I want to know."

"Yeah," said Bob. "Why aren't they talking to us, if they're firemen?"

214

"Maybe they don't know we're in here," said Rebecca.

"Then why are they on our roof?"

"We need to let them know we're here so they can save us."

"And what if they're ghouls?" said Bob. "If we say something, they're gonna know we're in here and they're gonna try to get at us."

"Whoever it is up there must know we're in here," said Jack. Listening to the scuffling above him, he ran his eyes along the ceiling. "They must be able to hear us talking."

"Not necessarily," said Rebecca. "These elevator cars have good insulation to deaden sound."

Jack gave her a look. "How would you know? Are you some kind of building inspector or something?"

Rebecca bridled, but said nothing.

"That's what I thought," said Jack.

The scuffing on the roof became louder.

We craned our necks toward the ceiling.

"One way or another, we're gonna have to see who's up there," I said.

"Why?" said Don, remaining unconvinced that they had to open the trapdoor.

"If for no other reason than to find out if we can get this elevator to start moving again."

"How are we gonna do that if we open the trapdoor?" said Bob.

"Do what?" I said.

"Get the elevator moving?" said Bob in exasperation.

"I don't know without having looked. Maybe there's something up there blocking our movement."

"If there are ghouls up there and we open the trapdoor, they're gonna come down in here and get us," said Franco.

"What's your solution?" I said.

"I still think I should kill all of you."

Needless to say, I did not like his answer. "Then what?"

"What do you mean?"

215

Bryan Cassiday

"Even if you do manage to kill all of us, and you won't, but even if you do, how does that get you out of this stuck elevator?"

Franco's shoulders slumped. "I didn't think of that."

"We have to attempt to escape." I peered at the trapdoor. "The way I see it, *that's* the only way out of here."

Franco slewed on his heel and faced the elevator door. He wedged the fingers of both his hands into the crack between the metal door and its frame and tried to prize the door open. Screwing up his face he yanked on the door without budging it.

"That's not a good idea," said Jack, watching Franco.

"Says who?" said Franco and continued to struggle to open the door to no avail.

"If you open it, then what? We're between floors. We're not gonna be able to step onto a floor if you pry that door open."

"And there's another reason to keep it closed," said Bob.

Ignoring them Franco continued working on the door trying to slide it open.

"Like what?" said Rebecca.

"If the power comes back on, this elevator won't go anywhere if its door is open," said Bob. "Elevators can't move with their doors open. It's a safety feature."

Franco stopped wrestling with the door. Bob's words had sunk in.

"We have to get out of here somehow before one of us turns into a ghoul!" Franco cried in an access of frustration.

"Maybe not," said Sarah. "Maybe the best thing for us to do is to sit tight."

"No," said Bob. "That won't do. One of us is gonna turn. We'll be trapped in here with him."

Don looked apprehensively at Franco. "That guy waving a gun around is making me hinky."

"Maybe that's because you were the one who was bitten," said Franco, face grim.

"I'm tired of all this yakking! Let's get out of here!" Don stepped under the trapdoor. "Somebody give me a boost."

216

Jack strode over to him, bent his knees, and knitted his hands at knee level.

"No," said Bob. "That won't work. Let him get on your shoulders," he told Jack.

Jack shrugged and crouched farther down on his haunches. Don climbed onto Jack's shoulders.

"You need to lose weight," grumbled Jack as he struggled to straighten up.

Seated on Jack's shoulders, Don could reach the trapdoor now. He pressed against it with the heels of his palms, trying to dislodge it. The metal trapdoor wasn't budging. It looked like it had been painted over, and the paint had sealed it shut.

"I can't open it," said Don.

"Give it a good shove," said Bob, watching Don.

I could hear movement on top of the elevator car, just over the lamp in the ceiling.

"I don't know if this is a good idea," said Sarah, eyes widening at the ominous sound above.

"I'm getting out of here," said Don. "Hold steady," he told Jack beneath him.

Don withdrew his hands a foot from the trapdoor and stabbed them upward, slamming the heels of his palms into the steel. The impetus of his simultaneous blows cracked the paint around the trapdoor's edges and rocked the door loose from its frame. The trapdoor clanged against its frame, and Don shoved it onto the roof.

"Look!" cried Franco.

"What?" said Sarah.

"It's him!"

Franco trained his pistol on Don and shot him in the chest.

The elevator car's cramped enclosure increased the intensity of the deafening blast, which reverberated through the car. I grabbed my ears to block out the explosion, but it was too late. My ears were already ringing, and I was having trouble hearing.

Don groaned and toppled off of Jack's shoulders.

"What the hell are you doing?" Bob asked Franco.

"He's the one that got bit," answered Franco.

"How do you know that?"

"When he shoved open the trapdoor, his shirt raised up. I saw the bite mark on his belly," said Franco, shifting his weight back and forth on his feet in agitation.

Don was writhing in pain on the floor.

Bob leaned over him and lifted up Don's shirt, which was hanging loose over Don's jeans.

I saw a ragged black-and-blue bite mark on Don's abdomen. Franco had been right.

"Shoot him in the head," said Bob. "If you don't kill his brain, he'll turn and attack us."

Jittering, Franco aimed his gun at Don's head and blasted the skull apart.

Don stopped squirming on the floor. Skull spalls, dollops of brain matter, and blood littered the floor behind Don's bullet-shattered head. Don did not bleed long. He died quickly.

Franco calmed down. "I guess we're OK now, huh?"

"Except we're still stuck here in this elevator," said Bob.

Rebecca gazed at Don's body. "I always figured it was him."

"Why?" said Sarah. "I had no idea it was him."

"Just a sixth sense, I guess."

I heard a scraping sound at the trapdoor's frame and looked up.

A fortyish ghoul's face was peering down at us through the opening. Red buboes sprouted from the creature's face, and strips of purulent flesh dangled from its cheek. Its milky green eyes gazed down at us with a dead stare. It opened its mouth and emitted a weird groaning noise that sent goose bumps up my spine.

"Shoot it!" said Bob.

Franco drew a bead on the putrescent face. He squeezed off two rounds into the ghoul's head. The first round grazed an ear. The second hit home. It drilled through the ghoul's cheekbone and out the back of the creature's head.

The creature slumped motionlessly in the doorframe. One of its arms flipped into the elevator and dangled above us.

"We need to pull that thing out of there so we can get out," said Bob, eyeballing the dead ghoul wedged in the doorway.

"Who wants to ride piggyback this time?" said Jack, wincing at the pain in his back muscles as he stretched them, not looking forward to boosting yet someone else through the trapdoor. "How about somebody light this time?" He peered at Sarah.

"What do you want me to do up there?" said Sarah, looking in disgust at the ghoul's necrotic head that lolled through the trapdoor's opening.

"Let's get that ghoul out of the way," I said. "Nobody's getting out of here with that thing stuck in the ceiling."

I snagged the creature's limp arm.

"Do we really want that thing in here with us?" said Rebecca. "I sure don't."

"It's infected," said Bob. "We don't want it anywhere near us."

"It's probably contagious," said Jack.

"OK," I said, letting go of the hand with more than a trace of revulsion. "Then one of us will have to shove it out of the doorway, off the roof, and down into the elevator shaft."

"And you think *I* can do that?" said Sarah, dumfounded.

"You're the lightest one here," said Bob. "It makes sense for you to climb up there and do it. You're the only one Jack can hold up."

"Just don't get any of the brains on you," I said. "They're infectious."

Sarah pulled a face.

"You've been elected, so get going," said Franco.

"You call this an election?" she said.

"Stop bitching and go." Franco trained his pistol on her.

Grudgingly, Sarah climbed onto Jack's shoulders as he stooped down for her to mount him.

Jack straightened up with Sarah astride his shoulders.

She could not disguise her repulsion at the idea of touching the ghoul. The creature's arm was dangling beside her. She had to

Bryan Cassiday

force herself to touch it and try to stuff it through the aperture and onto the roof.

"Put down the gun," I told Franco.

"I'm just keeping her honest," he said, his pistol still leveled at Sarah.

Then, without warning, he shot her.

The elevator reverberated with the blast of the gun. Again I was deafened. I flinched from the pain in my ears.

"What's got into you, man?" cried Bob, grimacing.

Sarah screamed and toppled off Jack's shoulders. Bleeding from the chest she crumped against the floor and sprawled out beside Don's prostrate body.

"She's the one that got bit," said Franco. "When she stretched out, I saw the bite on her stomach."

"That's impossible. Don was the one who got bit."

"I swear I saw a bite mark on her! Lift up her blouse!"

Sarah was moaning on the floor in pain.

I bent over her and lifted up her blood-soaked blouse. Blood was streaming down her stomach. But Franco was right. I could discern a nasty-looking bite mark in her stomach's flesh about an inch above her hip.

Bob saw the bite too. "Finish her off with a shot to the head."

Franco clenched his teeth and blasted Sarah's head as she was pleading for her life.

I had just watched Franco kill two of us, but it was obvious he was having difficulty with the act of committing murder. He could pretend he was a tough guy all he wanted. The facts said otherwise. Murdering his fellow man did not sit well with him.

"This is insane!" said Jack. "How can there be two people that were bitten?"

"Why not?" I said.

"You said your wife saw only one of us get bitten."

"That doesn't mean nobody else here was bitten."

"So what are you saying?" said Bob. "That all of us were bitten?"

220

He swiveled his head around, scoping everybody out with mistrust.

"It's possible," I said.

"This is getting worse by the minute," said Franco. "I was right the first time. I should've shot the lot of you."

He brandished the gun at us.

"Wait a minute," said Bob, eyes locked apprehensively on Franco's gun. "You don't know that all of us were bitten."

"I don't know anything for sure," said Franco, face sweaty.

"We need to get out of here," I said.

"Is that your way of saying more of us were bitten?"

"I'm saying I don't know, but it's possible."

"That means I can't put this gun away."

"I'm telling you, you can't kill all of us," said Bob. "One or more of us is bound to get to you before you can shoot everybody."

I figured I could read Franco's mind. He was calculating his chances. He had already killed two of us. That made two less that could rush him. His odds had improved. The question was, had they improved enough for him to risk opening fire with the intent of killing all of us before one of us could get to him?

"There's only one way I can be safe in here," said Franco.

He opened fire. He took out Bob first, fearing him the most. Bob reeled and dropped with a wound to his head.

Realizing Franco's plan, Jack and I rushed Franco. Petrified with fear, Rebecca stood motionless and watched us.

Franco cut me down with a shot to my chest as I lunged at him. I could have kept charging him, even though he had wounded me, but I decided to play dead. I plunged to the floor. Anyway, I could not put up much of a fight in my present condition. He could easily have overpowered me and finished me off. In any case, I wasn't exactly playing dead. I really did feel like I was dying.

Jack reached Franco and snatched Franco's hand.

Franco threw a fist into Jack's jaw with his free hand, wrested his gun hand out of Jack's clutches, and fired a round into Jack's face. Jack's knees crumpled. He hit the elevator floor hard and slammed into it with his face.

Franco turned his attention toward Rebecca as she cringed in a corner of the elevator. He had saved her for last because he decided she posed the least threat to him on account of her advanced age.

Then we all felt it. Those of us who were still alive.

The elevator jerked upward. It ascended in fits and starts.

"Finally!" said Rebecca. "The power's back on."

I lay motionless on the floor, trying to remain under Franco's radar.

Franco pressed all the buttons of the floors on the control panel beside him. One after another, each white button lit up.

The elevator came to a halt at the next floor.

Drowsy and in pain, I was experiencing difficulty keeping my eyes open. I peered through the slits in my almost-shut eyelids at the door sliding open.

A shiny axe in hand, a fireman was standing in his heavy yellow asbestos uniform in the hallway. He stared in horror at the massacre on the elevator floor before him. Sprawled bodies with bullet wounds. Blood everywhere. Blood scrawled on the elevator walls from bullet-shredded arteries continued to drip and stream down the walls.

Nonplussed, he picked up on the gun in Franco's hand, which jarred him into action.

"You bastard," the fireman said.

He wielded his axe before Franco had a chance to explain. The axe slammed into Franco's chest, crashing through his rib cage and cleaving his heart. Franco died so quickly he never got the chance to scream.

I still had enough life left in me that I could make out Rebecca bending down and pulling up her pant leg at the cuff. As she exposed her shin I could see her scratch a deep, puckered bite mark on the side of her calf. And I could see as she stood up that her eyes had a milky glaze to them and I knew the infection had metastasized and turned her into a ghoul. And she was shambling

222

straight toward the fireman as he stared in consternation at Franco's corpse and had no inkling of his peril.

And I knew. At least four of us had been bitten before we had entered the elevator.

I hadn't been the only one.

# Mallory's Last Stand

Mallory killed what looked like a man on the sidewalk.

The tall sixtysomething guy had a bald head and wore black plastic thick-bowed glasses that framed his eyes like a raccoon's mask. His head had the shape and whiteness of one of those Styrofoam peanuts used in packing crates. He was glaring at Mallory with dead unseeing eyes, his complexion scabrous like papier-mâché.

Six feet tall and then some, Mallory raised his hatchet over his head and buried it deep into the crown of the guy's head, cleft the skull in half, and sank the blade into the guy's necrotic brain. The revenant dropped dead on the cement sidewalk at Mallory's feet.

It used to be a nice neighborhood, decided Mallory wistfully. Until the dead started coming back to life and taking over. Not quite, though. They hadn't quite taken over everywhere. There were still pockets of resistance, strongholds that continued to fight the flesh-eating plague-infected creatures that had once been human.

He surveyed his neighborhood. A quiet little beachside town in Southern California with lofty palm trees lining the sidewalks with rows of pale-toned stucco apartment houses nestled behind the screens of arching palms on either side of the street under the bright afternoon sun on a November day. A beautiful and safe neighborhood where he could walk with his wife Tanya, a CPA, and their two young girls Trudi and Babs, aged twelve and eleven respectively, and enjoy the view as well as the onshore sea breeze without a care in the world.

Their only concern had been Trudi. She was struggling with her studies in school—to the point where she was close to flunking out. Nobody could figure out why she was doing so poorly. She was an intelligent child, decided Mallory. Everyone who knew her had said something to that effect after meeting her. And yet she was flunking school.

It made no sense—until the family psychiatrist Dr. Hammer diagnosed her as dyslexic. As soon as they treated her disability, Trudi's grades improved dramatically, to nobody's surprise, least of all Mallory's. In no time, she rose to the top of her class.

Mallory, the cop, didn't realize how easy he had it back then. Mallory the cop and Tanya the CPA. Nobody could figure out how they could get along, let alone get married. His family life was like a dream come true for Mallory—back then.

Now he hardly ever saw his family courtesy of his job policing the neighborhood. When he did get a chance to be with them, there seemed to be an insurmountable wall erected between them. He felt like he was living in his own little world and could not communicate with them. He could not explain to them the nightmare that the demands of his job were putting him through.

What the hell had happened? wondered Mallory. The quiet little beach town had turned into a slaughterhouse in a matter of weeks with infected flesh eaters feeding on what few humans remained alive in the neighborhood. It was like this everywhere, though, Mallory knew. It wasn't just here. The creatures were taking over the world.

Nowadays, he had to walk around town gripping a weapon at all times. He used to tote a Mossberg tactical shotgun around with him, but its ear-shattering reports attracted the flesh eaters. As a result, he ditched the Mossberg for a hatchet. An old-fashioned weapon, but it got the job done nonetheless—in all but complete silence, save for the cracking of the skulls when the hatchet cleft them.

In his forties, Mallory leered down at the defunct creature. He was tired of killing the things. He had killed hundreds of them. What was getting to him was that they looked just like humans. It seemed too easy to kill them. Killing anything resembling a fellow human being shouldn't be that easy, he decided. It was screwing up his mind.

But these flesh-eating creatures existed, and they had to be destroyed. It was them or us, he knew. Still, it was playing havoc with his mind.

Knowing he was turning into a mental basket case, he took to seeing Dr. Hammer. Mallory was heading for an appointment with Hammer right now, as a matter of fact.

The sidewalks were deserted save for corpses here and there that had been picked clean by marauding flesh eaters and were now teeming with writhing bugs, Mallory noticed. Everybody was too scared to walk. But driving was out of the question, as well, because derelict cars choked the streets.

His wife and two daughters were waiting for him at home, but they would just have to wait a little longer. Mallory didn't want to return to them with his mind as scrambled as it was now. If he didn't have to kill that peanut-headed bald revenant, maybe he would have made it through the day with his mind intact. Maybe . . . but then again, he probably would have ended up killing another flesh eater later in the day.

Rounding the corner he caught sight of the nondescript two-story building that housed Dr. Hammer's office. Mallory detected movement across the street. A thirtyish grimacing weedy male zombie and a bottle-blonde one that looked over six feet tall were shambling down the sidewalk with their milky eyes staring into the distance as they crashed into a green Dumpster that sat catercorner in front of them on the sidewalk, blocking their path. They displayed no concern for their bodies, bumping into whatever happened to be in their way.

The creatures were making that weird growling gurgling sound in their throats that reminded Mallory of water coming to a boil and made his flesh crawl every time he heard it.

226

Mallory ducked into the office building's lobby seconds before the creatures laid eyes on him. He would do anything to avoid having to kill two more of the things. In the funk he was wallowing in at the moment he could not handle killing even one more. He closed the lobby door behind him. The creatures had no idea how to turn a doorknob, so he didn't have to lock it. In any case, they hadn't seen him.

Dr. Hammer's office was on the second floor. Mallory could not use the elevator thanks to the power outage. He used the stairwell at the other end of the hall to reach the second story.

Mallory glanced at his wristwatch. He regretted he was some fifteen minutes late for his appointment, but he had not expected to run into as many zombies as he had. The point was, he was here.

He rapped on Hammer's door.

"Mallory?" said Hammer.

"Yeah."

Hammer opened the door and faced Mallory.

"You can't be too careful these days," said Hammer, poking his head into the corridor past Mallory, and casting around the hallway circumspectly.

"I hear ya."

Satisfied that none of the flesh eaters were present, Hammer retreated back into his office, ushering Mallory inside with him, and locked the door behind them.

"I didn't think you were gonna show up today," said Hammer.

"I got delayed."

For the first time, Hammer picked up on the hatchet in Mallory's hand, the hatchet that had gobbets of oozing brains sliding down its tempered ice-smooth carbon-steel blade onto the office's carpet.

"Could you put that thing away while you're in here," said Hammer in disgust.

Mallory raised the hatchet in his hand, examining it in a daze. "I don't like being unarmed."

"We're safe in here. I locked the door. Put that away. It's making a mess."

227

"I'd rather not."

"If you don't put it away, I'll have to reschedule your appointment," said Hammer, asserting himself.

"I need to talk to you."

Mallory searched Hammer's face. Mallory hated to admit it but Hammer reminded him of the flesh eater he had just killed on the sidewalk. Like that ghouls, Hammer was bald and wore spectacles, but, in Hammer's case, the spectacles had horn-rimmed bows, not black ones. Another difference was the full white mustache that sprouted under Hammer's pinched aquiline nose. And then there was the shape of Hammer's head, which was blockier than that of the flesh eater whose brains Mallory had dashed in.

Seeing the similarity between the flesh eater and Hammer, Mallory realized at the same time that he could kill Hammer just as easily as he had killed the creature. That Mallory felt no moral compunction about killing Hammer sent a shiver down Mallory's spine. It was all part and parcel of his neurosis, which was taking him to the teetering edge of insanity.

"Put the hatchet away and we'll talk," said Hammer, as additional nubbins of brains slid off the hatchet's blade onto his thick-piled angora carpet.

As much as he hated to part with the hatchet, Mallory knew if he didn't undergo therapy with Hammer soon, he might be heading for a mental breakdown the likes of which he would never be able to recuperate from.

"Where do you want me to put it?" said Mallory.

Hammer cast around his office, swiveling his head to and fro like a featherless owl.

"In the bathroom," he said, flustered as if he wanted to drop the subject.

Mallory retreated to the bathroom and stood the hatchet on its head in the bathtub so the brains would slide off the blade into the porcelain tub and not onto the linoleum floor.

"It's obvious you're feeling paranoid," said Hammer, watching Mallory return from the bathroom.

"What do you mean?" said Mallory, taking up station in front of Hammer's desk.

Hammer, who was standing behind his desk, ambled over to a brown leather divan set up for his patients. Wearing an orchid bowtie and a scarlet cardigan sweater with its two bottom buttons fastened, he had intense brown eyes that seemed to be digging for something as he eyed Mallory.

"Your refusal to part with the hatchet indicates you're constantly scared of being attacked," said Hammer.

"That's true. There are flesh eaters all over the place. Does that mean I'm crazy?"

"Lie down on the divan," said Hammer, gesturing amiably toward it.

Mallory lay down, body rigid, hands clenching and unclenching.

"Relax," said Hammer. "That's why I want you to lie down. Take it easy."

Mallory found it difficult to unwind. His body felt coiled like a rattlesnake's ready to strike.

"What's wrong with me?" he said.

"You're way too tense, for one thing," said Hammer, taking a seat beside the divan, a yellow legal pad affixed to a clipboard in one hand, a ballpoint pen in the other.

"Why?"

"That's what I want to know. Once we determine the cause, I can prescribe a cure."

It took Mallory a few minutes, but he felt like he was calming down to a degree as he lay on the comfortably uptilted divan, head slightly raised.

"I wish I knew," he said.

"Let's begin at the beginning. Why are you seeing me in the first place?"

"I'm getting sick of killing all these zombies."

"Why? That's your job. Your job as a policeman entails protecting and serving society. By killing these creatures you are fulfilling your job's purpose."

Bryan Cassiday

"But it's getting too easy, don't you see?"

"In what sense?" said Hammer, puzzled, canting his pen against his undershot jaw.

"In the sense that they remind me of human beings."

"Go on."

"It's getting to me. I think I could kill living human beings now as easily as I'm killing these creatures."

"But you haven't gone around on a killing spree, have you, in regards to fellow humans?"

"No." Mallory paused. "Not yet, anyway," he added with a worried expression creasing his careworn face.

"The very fact that you are aware of this feeling inside you indicates you are well adjusted and are not suffering from a psychosis."

"I hate to tell you this, Doc, but I don't feel well. I'm getting inured to all the killing I'm doing. Emotionally I'm feeling like a robot. That can't be good."

Hammer nodded. "I see. And I agree. You need to get in touch with your feelings. You seem to be alienated from your emotions."

"Except for one."

"Which is?" said Hammer, hanging on Mallory's words.

"Fear. Those flesh eaters scare the hell out of me."

Hammer relaxed in his chair. "Welcome to the club." He paused a beat. "But fear isn't the only emotion. It is, however, at the bottom of most neuroses. It works as a blockade to your other emotions. You need to get in touch with them—like love and happiness."

Mallory heaved a sigh. "Easier said than done."

"As I said before, you're out of touch with your emotions."

"I think that's it. But what's the cure?"

"You need to realize that your job is important to society, that you are important to society as a policeman, a protector of society."

"That all?"

230

"You need to realize you can't do it all yourself. You're just one man fighting your battle against these flesh-eating enemies of ours."

"I'm not pretending I'm Superman, if that's what you're worried about."

"I'm just pointing out that you need to be aware of your limitations."

"I'm not following you," said Mallory, cocking his head toward Hammer.

"You can't allow yourself to become obsessed with your job of killing flesh eaters. There's more to life than that. What about your family?"

"What about them?"

"You need to spend more time with them. Just being near them will put you more in touch with your feelings."

"I'd like to, but who's gonna kill the zombies?"

"You're not the only cop in the world."

"This is bullshit," said Mallory, raising himself to a sitting position on the divan.

"Take it easy," said Hammer in a soothing voice.

"All this chitchat isn't curing me."

"I can't help you until I know exactly what you're suffering from."

"I already told you," huffed Mallory. "How many times do I have to repeat it? Is this how you get off? By listening to other people's problems?"

Hammer ignored Mallory's outburst. "Do you have any physical symptoms?"

Mallory didn't want to go into it. "No," he hedged.

"I can tell you're lying. You have to be honest with me in these sessions or they're a waste of time."

"I don't like talking about it, that's all."

"That's why you're talking to me, your doctor, and not to one of your buddies."

"What buddies?"

"Don't you have any buddies on the force?"

Bryan Cassiday

"I *had* two of them. Flesh eaters tore them both apart."

"I'm sorry to hear that."

"I don't want to talk about it."

"Where were we? Oh yeah, what are the physical symptoms you're feeling?"

Mallory could feel cold sweat trickling out of his armpits and down his flanks. "OK, I'll tell you. I'm throwing up almost every day."

"Anything else? Let me remind you, you can be perfectly frank with me. We have patient/doctor confidentiality here."

Mallory gave Hammer a look. "I'm having trouble with the wife."

"What do you mean? Arguments? Fights?"

"No, no. You know . . . you know . . ."

"No, I don't know."

The words finally came gushing out of Mallory's mouth, like he was vomiting molten bile. "In bed," he muttered.

Hammer nodded compassionately. "It's all the same thing, then, isn't it?"

"What do you mean?"

"You're out of touch with your feelings. Hence, your vomiting and your problems getting intimate with your wife. It all boils down to your blocked feelings, which you are unable to get in touch with."

"It's because I'm spending my whole life killing those fucking zombies. That's what's turning me into a robot."

"I'm convinced spending more time with your family is the answer. Do you ever hug your wife anymore?"

Mallory thought about it. "I can't say that I do. Like I said, I'm all messed up. I don't even think about that touchy-feely stuff."

Hammer nodded. "Next time you see her, hug her. It's the little things like that which can make a big difference in your emotional life."

"I don't want to become weak, Doc."

"Hugging your wife is not a sign of weakness."

232

"But it might weaken my resolve when it comes to killing the flesh eaters."

"I don't see the connection."

Mallory stretched out his hands and clasped his knees. "It's all a part of life. Is that what you're saying? Feeling and killing."

Hammer scribbled on his legal pad. "You're not killing fellow human beings. You're killing monsters. It's not the same thing. Killing a monster isn't murder."

"But they look just like us. That's the problem."

"Just because they look like us doesn't mean they *are* us."

"They used to be us before they turned."

Hammer shook his head, pen poised above his legal pad like a humming bird hovering above a flower. "We're just playing word games now. Clear your mind so you can relax."

"How can I relax when those monsters are walking the streets stalking us?"

"You're obsessed with them. That's the problem," said Hammer and jotted something on his pad. "Think about something else. Your wife. Your family." He glanced at his wristwatch. "All right. Your session's up. Too bad you were late."

"I feel like I just got here," said Mallory, getting to his feet.

Hammer escorted him to the door. "Remember to spend more time with your family."

Mallory entered the hallway and feeling naked stopped in his tracks.

"What's wrong?" said Hammer, watching him.

"I forgot my hatchet."

Mallory brushed by Hammer, who was standing in the doorway, cut through the office, ducked into the bathroom, retrieved his hatchet, and emerged in the hall, feeling complete now.

"Be sure to be on time for your next visit," said Hammer, about to close the door when he espied a middle-aged woman who had the face of a Neanderthal bundled up in an overcoat ambling toward him. "Hello, Mrs. Chavez. You're just in time for your visit."

"Why are you wearing such a heavy coat?" Mallory asked the woman. Mallory had only a light jacket on.

"It's freezing out there," said Mrs. Chavez, tawny face scrunched up like she was constipated.

"Come in," Hammer told her.

Indeed when Mallory exited the office building, he shivered. It felt like it had dropped at least ten degrees since he had arrived at Hammer's. Ominous dark clouds were scudding overhead from the west and darkening the once-bright blue sky. The wind was picking up, increasing the windchill factor.

Lightning flashed, rending the sky with its jagged thrust that branched into a network of phosphorescent tree limbs.

It looked like it was going to rain, decided Mallory forlornly as he gazed at the bleak, bloated clouds that herded above him like buffalo. Then it sounded like stampeding buffalo as a thundercloud exploded.

Hunching his shoulders Mallory winced. He wasn't dressed for rain. He had to get back to his house on the double.

It was so dark now it looked like dusk even though it was early afternoon. Mallory had not expected rain today. He never knew what to expect from the weather anymore since weather forecasters had no way to impart their predictions without the ability to communicate over the airwaves. No power, no TV, no radio, no Internet.

Mallory had no time to think about it. He sniffed the air. It smelled like rain. He sensed a palpable dampness in the air. Gusts of wind knifed through his jacket, chilling him.

Eager to beat the rain, he broke into a trot heading for his place.

The threat of rain did not deter the flesh eaters. Every so often Mallory would see one or two of them shambling down the sidewalks foraging.

About a block away from his bungalow, he felt it start to rain. He cursed. He hated getting wet, especially when it was so cold. Not only that, the temperature was still dropping.

As he came into view of his bungalow, the howling wind seemed fraught with a putrescent odor that unnerved him. It smelled like some behemoth creature from the ocean's depths had crawled out of the sea and died. A palm frond loosened above him by the harrying wind toppled onto the sidewalk six odd feet in front of him with a clatter. He started. The rain set to coming down faster now, soaking his clothes and all but blinding him. Regardless of the torrential rain, he broke into a run, even as he shivered with cold.

In front of his house, he fancied he saw something scurrying across the sidewalk through the downpour. *Christ!* he thought. It looked like a rat on steroids—almost as big as a South American capybara. One of the many rats that roamed free, spreading the plague that had turned the population into flesh eaters. What was a rat doing in front of his house? Had it been inside his home? he wondered anxiously.

Shivering both with cold and mounting dread, he belted through deep, raindrop-stippled puddles across the street to his front door, splashing sheets of water to his sides. He stood at the door and shook himself like a bedraggled dog trying to get dry, but it did no good. He was soaked to the bone.

He tried the doorknob. As he had expected, it was locked. He always told his family to keep the door locked.

With red, swollen fingers he pulled the house key out of his trouser pocket. He could barely grip the key with his freezing, bloated fingers that felt like phalanges of ice. He dropped the key. Cursing, he somehow managed to pick it up with his next-to-useless fingers and tried to insert it into the lock.

He had to get inside. He had to get out of this pouring rain and be with his wife Tanya and his kids Trudi and Babs. Like Dr. Hammer had told him, Mallory needed to get in touch with his feelings by spending more time with his family. He also needed to tell them about the rat that had been scampering in front of their house. If rats were in the neighborhood, they had to make sure to keep them out of the house.

A blinding sheet of lightning flashed nearby. Mallory squinted his eyes. Seconds later, a thunderclap roared and reverberated. A Dumpster in the neighboring alley rocked. Mallory flinched and ducked at the sonorousness and proximity of the fulmination. It seemed to have occurred right next to him. The acrid redolence of hot sulfur assailed his nostrils. The odor seemed to be emanating from the alley, from the Dumpster, he supposed. The lightning bolt must have struck the steel bin.

Fumbling with the key Mallory at last contrived to open the door. Dripping wet he barged into the lobby.

"Tanya!" he cried.

She was nowhere in sight.

Of course, it was difficult to see much of anything thanks to the dearth of light. The storm had darkened everything, throwing the living room and the rest of the house into darkness. Where were the candles? he wondered. Tanya and the girls usually lit the candles when it became dark.

A shudder of fear ran down his spine as he heard the scampering of claws in the dim-lit corridor to his right. He recognized the sound of a small animal scurrying across the floor. He pegged it for a rodent, probably a . . . he didn't want to think about it. But he had seen a rat outside the house in the rain. What if that rat had just bugged out of Mallory's house, and its buddies were inside here, as indicated by the scuttering of tiny feet in the hall?

Face dripping with rain, Mallory clenched the sopping wet hatchet tighter in his hand. He had no compunction about killing rats.

He felt sick, thinking of what might have happened to his family. He retched on the damp rug beneath him. The sickness was coming back. He had no time to be sick. He had to find Tanya and the girls.

Hopefully, they were hiding somewhere in the house, if they even knew rats were running amok in the house. What if they didn't know? he wondered in consternation.

The front door swung open with a whump as it slammed into the wall beside it, blown open by a gust of wind ginned up by the raging storm. He realized he had forgotten to shut the door behind him. Bursts of rain billowed into the lobby from outside.

Mallory darted to the door and shut it.

Then he heard it. The sound of footsteps. If his ears weren't deceiving him, the footfalls were coming from the living room. Tanya, he decided.

Indeed, a dark figure was making its way toward him. He could not discern who it was in the gloom. It must be Tanya, he decided. Who else could it be? It was too tall to be one of the girls.

He made a beeline toward the figure.

A jarring bang sounded behind him. He jumped and wheeled around. It was the door again. Somehow it had blown open. He thought he had closed it. He pivoted around to face Tanya.

Standing a couple yards away from her, he could make out details on her face. Not everything. It was still too dark. But he saw enough of her features to realize she didn't look well. She looked livid. She was dragging her feet as if too weak to lift them.

"Tanya," he said, relieved at the sight of her, even if she seemed unwell. "I'm so glad you're all right. There are rats in here. Be careful."

She said nothing.

She must be overcome with emotion at the sight of him, he decided. He knew how she felt. The frightful turbulence of the storm was wreaking havoc on everybody's nerves. She kept schlepping toward him. Scarcely twenty-eight years old, she was hobbling like a ninety-year-old.

He fancied he could hear the sound of boiling water issuing from her lips.

Lightning flashed in the bay window, illuminating the room and highlighting Tanya's face.

Mallory gasped.

237

Her face looked like a misshapen mask, her features withered and contorted, with bits of skull visible through the decadent flesh. Unblinking, her sightless glazed eyes stared back at him.

Realizing what had happened to her, Mallory raised the dripping hatchet above his head and slammed it down into Tanya's skull, splitting the bone and penetrating the brain, the bone cracking like a calving glacier.

Sickened by what he had done, hatchet in hand, he stared down at her body as it sprawled before him. Tears welled in his eyes. He could not move. He could not believe what he had done. But he had had to do it. Vomit caught in his throat, crammed there like a clump of molten lava. As he had suspected, it was easy to kill her, just as easy as killing hundreds of zombies, but sickening at the same time. Sickening because he knew her. Sickening because he was looking her in the eye when he killed her. Sickening because she was his wife. *Sickening because it was too damn easy to kill her. It shouldn't have been that easy. What the hell was he turning into?*

He wondered where Trudi and Babs were. He had to save them, to get them out of this charnel house.

Rousing himself from his stupor, he headed down the hallway toward their bedroom.

Lightning flashed outside, accompanied by the rumble of thunder a few seconds later. The center of the storm must be directly over his house, decided Mallory. The thunder's peal jerked him fully awake, stirring him into action.

Eyes wide, hatchet at the ready, he bolted to his daughters' bedroom door, which hung ajar. Mallory shoved it open and barreled into the room. He swung his gaze around the room, seeking his daughters.

Clad in grey hoodies, their hoods up, they were sitting on one of their beds, their heads turned away from him as they gazed out the window, taking in the fury that the storm was unleashing outside as the limbs of a wind-tossed eucalyptus tree thrashed the windowpane.

"Trudi! Babs! We have to leave! There are rats in here!" he cried so they could hear his voice above the storm's din.

They didn't respond. They kept staring out the window.

The thunderous racket of the storm must be drowning out his words, decided Mallory. He sprang to the bedside.

He snagged Trudi's arm. "Come on, honey. It's not safe to stay here."

Trudi peered down at Mallory's clutching hand, bowed down, and made to bite it. He jerked it away.

A flash of lightning shimmered in the room, and in the glare Mallory could distinguish Trudi's and Babs's faces framed in their hoodies.

Appalled, he gnashed his teeth as the realization dawned on him that he had to kill them.

Wielding his hatchet he split their heads in two before they could attack him.

Nauseated at what he had done, vomit slobbering out of the side of his mouth, he stumbled out of their bedroom into the corridor and out of the corner of his eye glimpsed a rat that was scurrying away from him toward the open front door. Maddened by the sight of the creature, he tore off after it, brain-splattered hatchet in hand.

The rat scampered out the door onto the sidewalk into the storm.

Mallory seethed with rage.

He belted after the rat in white-hot fury, disappearing into the downpour, screaming his lungs out like a maniac as the rain drowned out his bellows and the last vestiges of his sorrow.

# A Way Out

The cabbie looked like a fiend with his adrenaline-bright eyes that gleamed in the rain-slicked darkness of LA's streets. He had an olive complexion and thick black hair that bristled an inch high from his scalp. From his neck a bolo tie hung down the front of his guayabera shirt.

"Where to, boss?" he said, grinning and gazing up at Raleigh's face.

Raleigh hated it when people called him boss. He wasn't anyone's boss, except his own. It sounded like they were being sarcastic. But then again, maybe that wasn't their intent. Maybe they said it as a sign of respect. Coming from this guy with a fiend's face and a wolflike grin, though, it didn't sound like respect.

"To hell," said Raleigh, ducking into the backseat of the cab.

"Say again, boss," said the hack, craning his neck around to peer at Raleigh through brown eyes that had bags under them.

The cab reeked of strawberry, decided Raleigh, which made sense after he spotted an oversized cardboard strawberry air freshener dangling from twine fastened to the rearview mirror. The closeness of the cab combined with the heavy humidity intensified the odor. A tad below the dangling strawberry Raleigh made out the hack's name on the dashboard. Diego.

"To hell, Diego."

Frowning, Diego shut his eyes in confusion. "I don't get it."

"If you can drive me to hell, that proves I'm not in hell now. Otherwise . . . ," Raleigh trailed off.

"Otherwise what, boss?"

"Otherwise, I'm already there. Which is what it feels like," said Raleigh, gazing into the distance like a lost soul.

Diego shook his head and faced forward, not wanting to look any longer than he had to at the oddball he had just had the misfortune of picking up, but thinking all the same this could be a candidate for his moonlighting business.

"You tell me how to get there, boss, and I'm your man."

"Just drive."

Diego threw the cab in gear and pulled away from the curb, plowing up a sheet of water from the puddle he was parked in.

It wasn't raining anymore, decided Raleigh, taking in the wet streets that gleamed with nacreous oil and the reflections of peach sodium-vapor streetlights overhead that shimmered in puddles like necklaces of fire as car tires sliced through the water. It had been coming down in sheets just shy of an hour ago.

"What's this all about, boss?" said Diego, digging deeper, assessing his fare. "I'm not any good at riddles."

"It's about time I got out of here."

"There you go again with the riddles."

Raleigh had just finished killing a man, which wasn't in itself significant, decided Raleigh. Killing was, after all, how he made a living. But maybe his job as a hired gun was getting to him. He usually didn't feel this way afterward. It wasn't a feeling of remorse. It was more like world-weariness that was weighing on him.

He wasn't getting any job satisfaction, nor any sense of fulfillment from his hits. He killed people purely for monetary reasons. He made beaucoup bucks in his profession. But there was something missing from his life. Maybe it was about time for him to find out what he was missing. If not now, when?

"It looks like you got a problem," said Diego.

"Mmm," said Raleigh, eyes half shut as he pondered, not really listening.

241

"Are you looking for a way out? Is that what you're trying to say?"

At that moment the taxi slammed through a sprawling, deep puddle in the road, kicking up a loud splash as the car slowed down and pulled to the right on impact with the standing water. Raleigh wasn't sure he had heard Diego correctly and gazed into the rearview mirror, where he saw Diego's eyes staring intently at him.

"You got a problem?" said Diego, negotiating his way out of the puddle.

"Everybody's got problems. I already heard that part. What did you say after that?"

"You mean, do you want a way out?"

"In what sense?" said Raleigh, puzzled.

"You got problems, right?"

"Like everybody else. So?"

"Do you want a way out?"

Who was this cabbie? wondered Raleigh. Raleigh was trying to escape the scene of his last contracted hit when he had hired the hack. Now the guy was acting like he knew all about him. Which was impossible. Raleigh had never seen the guy before, and nobody knew what Raleigh did for a living, except for his clients. Raleigh made sure it stayed that way.

Diego must be working some kind of angle, decided Raleigh. That was all. Everybody had an angle. Just trying to make ends meet you had to have an angle. But what was Diego's?

"A way out of what?" said Raleigh.

"Your problem."

Could Diego possibly know who he was? wondered Raleigh, alarm sirens sounding in his mind. No. Raleigh decided to play along.

"OK," he said. "Yeah."

Diego nodded in satisfaction. "I can help you start a new life."

A new life, decided Raleigh. Maybe that was what he needed. A makeover. A change in careers. A reinvention of himself.

242

"How?" said Raleigh, not giving Diego any credibility, but playing along just for kicks if for no other reason.

"It'll cost you."

Raleigh snickered. "You think?"

"But you look like a guy that could afford it."

"How can you tell?"

"You have that look. Like you're your own man."

Diego had Raleigh's attention. Raleigh wasn't looking forward to another contract killing. He must be burnt out. He felt like he was pushing himself too hard. You could only push yourself so hard before you became just another heart-attack statistic. The job of assassin incurred more than its share of risks, all of which reduced life expectancy.

"What's the catch?" said Raleigh.

"No catch. If you got the money, Charley'll give you a new life. Your old self will vanish off the grid. Then you'll get a new ID."

"Charley?"

"Charley can make it happen."

"It's not that I don't trust you—"

"I'm not shitting you," cut in Diego.

"I dunno."

"Unless you still want to go to hell?"

Raleigh couldn't figure out where this Diego guy was coming from. It sounded like a bunch of bunkum. Still, Raleigh wanted to find out what the upshot was.

"OK," said Raleigh, stone-faced.

Diego nodded. "Most people don't like their lives, their jobs, the whole nine yards."

"So you and Charley make out like bandits?"

Diego puffed out his cheeks. "Not everyone can afford our services. Joe Six-Pack doesn't have a million bucks handy."

"That the going price of admission?"

Diego stopped at a red light, turned around, and cocked a long eyebrow at Raleigh. "In your ballpark, I'd say."

"I'm still listening," said Raleigh, unfazed.

Bryan Cassiday

Buying a new life wouldn't come cheap, he figured. Not
many people could pull it off. The question was, was this deal
legitimate? A million dollars to be able to start life over again as
somebody else. Could that be true? For him such a life would be a
godsend. As a hit man he had cops and vindictive relatives of
well-fixed victims out for his blood. To drop off the earth and
become somebody else was just what the doctor ordered.

Such agencies that disappeared their clients did exist on the
black market, he knew. In his line of work dealing with the
criminal element, he had heard of them. If you had enough Ben
Franklins you could get whatever you wanted.

"You'll be able to buy a second chance in life," said Diego.
"How many people can say that?"

"Where's this Charley guy?"

"Where's the money first?"

"I want to talk to Charley before I commit to this."

"Charley doesn't talk to anyone till the customer ponies up."

A scam? wondered Raleigh. There was no way he could vet
it.

"What's this operation called?" he said.

"It doesn't have a name. For obvious reasons, we don't want
to be found out. We don't want anyone to know we exist. Being
nameless helps keep us under the radar."

A siren bawled behind them. Wincing, heart in his mouth,
Raleigh started in his seat and wheeled his head around to peer out
the back window. A squad car was screaming toward them, its
light bar flashing red.

Raleigh cursed.

"It can't be us they're after," said Diego, consulting the
driver's side-view mirror watching the patrol car bearing down on
them. "I'm under the speed limit."

Eyes glued to the black-and-white looming behind him,
Raleigh wasn't so sure. "Somebody may've seen me enter your
cab."

"So?"

"They may've seen what I did before I entered."

244

Raleigh hadn't seen any witnesses. He wouldn't have gone in for the hit if he had. Still, he could have overlooked somebody.

"What did you do?" said Diego.

"My job."

"Which is?"

A cop's electronically enhanced voice boomed from the squad car that had pulled up directly behind the cab. "Pull over to the curb on the right."

Raleigh's heart skipped a beat.

Diego slowed his cab to a halt and parked alongside the curb like the cop told him, all the time his eyes riveted on the image of the squad car in his side-view mirror.

"This ain't looking good, boss."

Raleigh felt for the concealed pistol wedged inside his waistband. He was packing a Belgian FN 5.7 semiautomatic, his weapon of choice. He used it thanks to its accuracy and its high-velocity $5.7 \times 28$ mm SS190 rounds that could pierce all but the strongest body armor. On account of their wealth and the danger of their professions, which were frequently illegal, many of his more difficult targets wore bulletproof vests, which the 5.7 rendered useless. Raleigh had, truth be known, whacked out cartel bosses as well as arms dealers who had thought they were invincible courtesy of their body armor.

The FN 5.7 was an assassin's dream.

Cops wore vests, too, Raleigh knew as he watched them through the cab's rear window climb out of their car and, splitting up, swagger toward both sides of the cab, hands hovering at the ready over their holsters on their waists, as they gripped Maglites in their other hands and played their high-intensity beams on the cab.

The shorter cop who had a shaved head and a scar over his right eyebrow headed for the driver's-side door as his partner, a lanky redhead with an awkward gait like he had a game leg, made for the passenger side.

"What'd I do, Officer?" said Diego, squinting in the blinding beam of the flashlight that Scarface was directing at Diego's face.

245

"I wasn't speeding." Diego made a move to raise his hand and shield his eyes from the flashlight's beam.

"Hands down," said Scarface, body tensing. "Don't move your hands, sir."

Diego couldn't lower his hand fast enough.

Meanwhile, standing outside the cab, Red was training a blue-eyed glare and his Maglite on Raleigh in the backseat, who froze in the wash of the beam, hand on the butt of his 5.7 shielded from view by his Windbreaker.

"Step out of the car, sir," Red told Raleigh.

"What'd I do, Officer? Jaywalk?"

Red wasn't laughing. If anything, his glare hardened into ice.

"Slide over here and step out of the car, sir," he said.

Somebody must have witnessed him whacking out his last victim before he got into the cab, decided Raleigh.

As he scooched across the backseat he whipped out his 5.7 and double-tapped Red in the face, taking out the window and one of Red's eyes and dropping him instantly as the glass shattered into greenish shards that tinkled on the pavement. Raleigh was already wheeling around to shoot Scarface, who was yanking out his Glock to blast him as Red crumpled to the asphalt beside the cab.

Raleigh blew out his rear side window with the first shot from his 5.7 that caught Scarface in the chest. Scarface retaliated with a shot from his Glock that went wide of its mark and ended up embedded in the front seat back, his aim thrown off by the wound in his chest, which was spurting pressurized blood through his bullet-pierced body armor.

Scarface fell to coughing up bright red blood from his wounded lung. Raleigh finished him off with a shot to his cheek that blew out his occipital bone as it exited his skull.

"Jesus Christ!" cried Diego, taking in the bloodbath. "What'd you do that for?"

"They were coming for me," said Raleigh.

Things had changed irrevocably now, he knew. He had never killed a cop before. He had no choice. A witness must have ratted him out to them. Raleigh couldn't allow them to bust him, even if they didn't convict him. Nobody would hire him again if he got busted. They only hired him because he had no record and was untraceable. A rap sheet made him a liability to his clients.

Cops would be all over him from here on in, Raleigh knew. The fat was in the fire. Willy-nilly he would have to take Charley's deal. He had to disappear off the grid, become somebody else.

In a muddle, panic-stricken, Diego peeled off, leaving the two dead cops behind. Should he call the cops? he wondered. His fare had a gun, though, and showed no reluctance to use it. Diego didn't want to get involved in this mess.

"I'll take Charley's deal," said Raleigh.

"What?" said Diego, unable to concentrate.

"You said I could start a new life. Are you telling me that was a crock you fed me?" said Raleigh through his teeth.

"No, no. It's legit. But you have to have the cash."

"Drive me to the Greyhound bus station."

"I thought you wanted me to take you to Charley."

"The money's at the bus station."

"We need to get out of this cab ASAP. People are gonna be staring at us with these broken windows we got. There may be blood on the car, too."

"As soon as we get the dough."

The bus station wasn't far away. Diego pulled over in front of it and disgorged Raleigh on the sidewalk.

"Come inside with me," said Raleigh.

"Why? I'll stay here and keep the motor running."

"I don't want you taking off."

"I'm not going anywhere. Why would I bug out from a million bucks?" Diego picked up on a grey-haired sourpuss of a woman standing ten-odd feet from him on the sidewalk leveling a dirty look at one of the shattered windows in his cab. "I was in an accident," he told her.

"Come with me," said Raleigh in a flat voice that brooked no argument.

Shrugging, Diego followed Raleigh into the bus terminal, where Raleigh approached the bank of metal lockers and singled out one in the right corner. He strode over to it, fished a key out of his trouser pocket, inserted the key into the lock, and swung open the locker door. He withdrew two stuffed navy blue gym bags and shut the door, locking it.

He and Diego returned to the cab and clambered into it.

"Take me to Charley," said Raleigh.

Diego put the car in gear, signaled with his arm out his window, and pulled into traffic.

"I'm gonna have to disappear, too, after this mess," said Diego.

"That's right," Raleigh muttered.

"What?" said Diego, craning his neck around to eye Raleigh.

Raleigh said nothing, the gym bags on either side of him on the backseat.

Shaking his head in bafflement Diego faced forward. He had been right pegging this guy as a prospective client for Charley. Diego would feel much better when the guy was out of his cab and in Charley's hands. Charley could have the guy and keep him for all Diego cared. Guy was bad news.

Now if only the cops didn't pull him over for driving with busted windows, decided Diego.

Palms sweating, Raleigh was thinking the same thing about the cops as he kept his eyes peeled for them. He didn't see any at the moment. He was sure a witness to the spur-of-the-moment shootout had notified the cops by now. It would be a piece of good luck for him if nobody had seen the shootout. He never counted on luck, though. He couldn't trust it. He could trust his planning skills and his reflexes' dexterity, but never his luck. Luck was a flirt that rarely came across. Unlike his assigned hits, this shooting had been unpremeditated. As such, blowback was all but guaranteed.

He had to ditch this cab pronto. Driving around in a cab with broken windows was begging for attention and tempting fate.

"How much longer?" he asked.

"We're almost there."

Five minutes later Diego drove into a multilevel parking garage and parked his cab.

He and Raleigh piled out of the cab. Diego was going to lock it then realized it was pointless seeing the broken windows.

He angled toward a rusted white van at least ten years old parked nearby, Raleigh in tow.

"Where's Charley?" said Raleigh, gym bags in his hands.

"We're taking this van to see him," said Diego, unlocking the van and climbing into the driver's seat.

"Why the rigmarole?" said Raleigh, sliding onto the passenger seat beside him.

"Charley thinks cabs might draw attention to his hideout. If he sees a cab or any official vehicles coming he'll split."

Raleigh wondered what he was getting himself into as Diego drove the van out of the parking structure. On the other hand, what was the point of worrying? It wasn't like Raleigh had a raft of options left. Not after he had become a cop killer.

Diego took the 405 north, exited it, and entered the westbound 118. A half hour after he had left the parking garage, he exited the 118 on an off ramp that led through mountainous, boulder- and scrub-strewn terrain in Simi Hills.

It was difficult for Raleigh to see in the darkness, especially when they drove onto an unlit, deserted dirt road that snaked up the mountain.

"What is this Charley guy?" he said, scoping out the uninhabited surroundings, what he could make out of them in the periphery of the headlight beams, anyway. "A doomsday prepper?"

"He lives on what used to be called the Spahn Ranch."

The name sounded familiar for some reason, but Raleigh could not place it. He was too busy calculating his next move to think about it. All things considered, this might be a good place to hide thanks to its remoteness, but it wasn't much of a life to look forward to. A new life as a hermit in a mountain wasn't his idea of a dream life.

What was his idea of a dream life? Raleigh wondered. Sailing on a lake, free of any cares, fishing rod in hand. That sounded nice. With a trophy wife to come home to. Now *that* he could go for. A happy life. No more dodging bullets and worrying about cops. But not a life as a mountain goat.

"Is this where I get my new life?" he said, not envying the prospect.

"It starts here. You don't end up living here, though. This is where Charley conducts business."

Raleigh's smartphone riffed. He dug it out of his pocket and answered it.

"You still alive?" said the voice in surprise and hung up.

It was his latest client, Raleigh realized. The double-dealing bastard that had sicced the two cops on him, tying up loose ends by selling Raleigh out. A risky maneuver, considering that Raleigh might have ratted him out after being busted. But Raleigh wasn't supposed to live, obviously. His client must have figured, rightly, that Raleigh would go down shooting rather than allow himself to be arrested.

"You all right?" said Diego, facing Raleigh.

"Are we almost there?" said Raleigh, putting away his cell.

"That's Charley's place up ahead."

At the end of the headlight beams, Raleigh could discern a ranch house that looked the worse for wear with peeling, sun-bleached beige paint. A couple of windows with closed grimy white curtains in the house were lit. Diego was driving slowly in the darkness better to make out the muddy road.

"Pull over," said Raleigh.

"Why?"

Raleigh screwed a silencer on his 5.7 and shot Diego point-blank in the temple. "You're not going with me."

Diego had been living on borrowed time ever since he had seen Raleigh blow away the two cops. Diego had outlived his usefulness. Raleigh never left witnesses alive.

The van veered to the right, decelerating as Diego's foot slipped off the gas pedal, and rolled over the camber onto the side

250

of the road where it juddered to a halt as its front bumper struck a weed-choked dirt bank.

Raleigh sprang into action. He hauled Diego's body out of sight into the back of the van, hopped into the driver's seat, and drove the van behind a manzanita that screened it from the ranch house and the road. He secreted the van there and got out.

Gym bags in his hands, he walked along the deserted road's shoulder toward the house. He reached the front door. He couldn't hear any noise in the house.

Heartbeat accelerating, he knocked three times on the weathered door, not knowing what to expect. Nobody answered. He knocked three more times.

A brunette in her twenties opened the door. She was wearing faded jeans and a yellow blouse that hung out of her pants. There was something about her that didn't ring true, decided Raleigh. Strung out on dope? Her green eyes had a dreamy expression.

"Hello," said Raleigh with a smile. "I'm looking for Charley."

"Who are you?" she said.

"Diego sent me. Charley's expecting me."

"Oh. Where *is* Diego?" she said, craning her neck and peering past Raleigh's shoulders into the gloom of the night.

"He dropped me off and drove away. Didn't he tell you I was coming?"

She nodded. "OK. Come in. I'm Leslie."

Backing up, she opened the door wider for Raleigh to enter.

She seemed like she wasn't there, decided Raleigh. It was hard to put a finger on. He felt like waving a hand in front of her eyes to see if she blinked. There in body, but not in mind.

"Thanks. I'm Raleigh."

"Charles Manson doesn't get many visitors."

*Charles Manson?* wondered Raleigh with a shock. The Spahn Ranch. He knew he recognized the name. It was the Manson Family hangout in the sixties. Was this some kind of time warp he had set foot in?

"Charles Manson's in Corcoran State Prison," said Raleigh.

"His father is."

Raleigh didn't believe what he was hearing. "Are you saying this is his son that runs this place?"

"Charley Sr. slept with a lot of women in the Family. He had several sons and daughters, including Charley Jr."

"When do I meet him?" said Raleigh, not at all sure he wanted to.

Leslie led him down a hallway into a capacious room that had a cathedral ceiling with exposed wooden beams. On the walls were painted in dripping red blood Kill the Pigs and the incorrectly spelled Healter Skelter. From the mezzanine's steel balustrade hung a hangman's noose. It looked like a scene straight out of the book *Helter Skelter* about the Manson Family murders of the pregnant actress Sharon Tate and her socialite friends in her Benedict Canyon mansion on a hot August night in 1969.

Bowled over, mouth dry, Raleigh took in the grisly re-creation of the Tate murder scene, feeling his knees becoming weaker by the moment.

"Who's your interior decorator?" he deadpanned at length.

"We did it ourselves," boasted Leslie.

A short man in a black cowl entered the room from a different door, seemingly gliding in, as the hem of his cowl reached to the floor and covered the motion of his legs. He had scruffy shoulder-length dark hair and a short, ragged beard.

Maybe this wasn't such a good idea, decided Raleigh.

The man approached him.

The five-six guy had the same kind of febrile, speed-freak eyes that Diego had, Raleigh noted. The guy also had a swastika tattooed on his forehead in crimson ink. Raleigh pegged him for Charley.

"I'm Charley. Who are you?" said Charley with a slight Texas twang, lowering his hood.

"Raleigh. Diego said you could give me a new life."

"Do you have the money?"

Nodding, Raleigh raised one of his gym bags for a moment then lowered it.

"Open it," said Charley.

Raleigh dropped the other bag to his feet and unzipped the one in his hand, exposing a higgledy-piggledy pile of bundles of hundred-dollar bills secured by thick red rubber bands.

"Where's Diego?" said Charley.

"He left after he dropped me off here."

Charley looked like he was wearing eyeliner or kohl, which enhanced the freakish wildness of his eyes, decided Raleigh.

"I thought he wanted to go with you," said Charley.

"I guess he changed his mind."

"Just as well. I doubt he could've afforded it."

"How does this work? How do I get a new life?"

"Actually you get a new body."

A throng of figures in scarlet cowls streamed into the room, surrounding Raleigh as they chanted, "Charley," over and over again.

"I'm still listening," said Raleigh, unnerved by the cult corralling him. "Do I join your family? Is that how it works?"

"Not really," said Charley.

Cowls rippling around them, hoods raised, four of the cult members lunged out of the horde toward Raleigh and pinned his arms behind his back before he could whip out his automatic. They bound Raleigh's arms behind his back, secured his legs at the ankles with black plastic zip ties, and frog-marched him toward the noose that dangled from the balustrade.

"What are you doing?" said Raleigh, struggling to free himself. "Let go of me!"

"Your body must die that you can be reborn," said Charley. "We're sacrificing you to Satan."

"Are you nuts? That wasn't the deal."

"You will be reborn as one of Satan's children after we complete the ritual."

"I never said I wanted to die. Let me go!"

"You have to die that you can be reborn."

"You're nuts! I'm out of this! Stop it!" said Raleigh, struggling for all he was worth with his four assailants, heartbeat jackhammering.

253

Bryan Cassiday

"The sacrifice is in progress.  You can't renege on the deal and cancel the ceremony once it has begun."

The four cult members upended Raleigh and strung him up by the feet with the hangman's noose as the surrounding members fell to chanting "Helter-skelter" louder and louder while they queued up behind Raleigh.

Twisting at the end of the rope, blood rushing to his head, Raleigh grimaced, mouth a rictus, while Charley sliced Raleigh's jugular with a carbon-steel dagger that he produced from his cowl, sucked a mouthful of the blood jetting from the wound, and swallowed the hot fluid, followed by his members, who repeated the procedure to the last man until they had drained Raleigh's body completely of its ten pints of blood and his body hung wan and motionless over the blood-spattered hardwood floor.

# About the Author

Bryan Cassiday writes horror books and thrillers. He wrote the Chad Halverson zombie apocalypse series, which includes *Zombie Maelstrom*, *Zombie Necropolis*, *Sanctuary in Steel*, *Kill Ratio*, and *Poxland*. His short stories have appeared in anthologies, such as *Horror Society Stories Volume One*. He lives in Southern California. Visit BryanCassiday.com and Facebook.com/bryancassiday.author.

Made in the USA
Charleston, SC
28 November 2014